BODY HEAT

BODY HEAT

KATHERINE GARBERA

KENSINGTON PUBLISHING CORP.
http://www.kensingtonbooks.com

BRAVA BOOKS are published by

Kensington Publishing Corp.
850 Third Avenue
New York, NY 10022

All Kensington titles, imprints and distributed lines are available at special quantity discounts for bulk purchases for sales promotion, premiums, fund-raising, educational or institutional use.

Special book excerpts or customized printings can also be created to fit specific needs. For details, write or phone the office of the Kensington Special Sales Manager: Kensington Publishing Corp., 850 Third Avenue, New York, NY 10022. Attn. Special Sales Department. Phone: 1-800-221-2647.

Brava and the B logo Reg. U.S. Pat. & TM Off.

ISBN 0-7582-1241-0

First Kensington Trade Paperback Printing: March 2006
10 9 8 7 6 5 4 3 2 1

Printed in the United States of America

For my husband, Matt,
who knows how to keep life interesting.
Thanks for the
love and laughter.

Acknowledgments

Special thanks to my editor, Kate Duffy, for being excited about this project. Also thanks to Lori Foster for introducing me to Kate.

Thanks to Beverly Brandt for listening and being there when I needed someone to chat with. Also to Mary Louise Wells, who always finds time to read something when I'm panicking.

I want to thank Tammy Strickland for patiently answering all my questions about nursing; any mistakes are my own. Also thanks to Pat Kelly for chatting on the phone with me about being a firefighter . . . I hope I got the passion you have for your job right in this book; again any mistakes are my own.

Lastly, thanks to my children, who were so good while I wrote this book. We moved from Florida to Texas, and they were trapped in the house in a new neighborhood with a mother who said don't knock on the door unless it's an emergency.

Chapter 1

Andi O'Roarke knew trouble came in many different sizes. Sometimes trouble came in the form of a cop who caught her speeding when she was late for work. Sometimes it was a wildfire blazing out of control that she just couldn't get ahead of. Or other times it was a group of subordinates bored from sitting too long in the fire station.

Andi leaned back in her chair and propped her booted feet on the edge of her desk. The three men standing before her had been at Station Two for almost five years. Johnson, McMillan, and Powell. She'd fought fires side by side with these men. Cried with them when they had responded to their first child fatality due to parents not using a car seat. And drank them under the table on St. Paddy's Day. So she knew these guys.

And she knew they were up to no good. Mick Palmer, her second in command, arched one eyebrow at her. He sensed the same thing she did. No one who hadn't been a firefighter could understand the kind of boredom that going almost a week without a blaze entailed.

The station house sparkled from top to bottom, every engine had been washed and waxed and they were all bored from too many games of pool.

"What can I do for you boys?" she asked, crossing her arms over her T-shirt clad stomach.

"We got a bone to pick, Cap," Johnson said as they entered her office. On the wall were certificates she'd received over the course of her fifteen-year career and one picture of her family—taken last year at Easter.

"I'm all ears."

They shuffled farther into her office. Johnson stood in the doorway; McMillan and Powell leaned against the credenza. They were all in their twenties and in good shape.

"Well, we want to know why these boys in Hillsborough got a couple of strippers in the firehouse and all we ever get are kindergartners," McMillan said, holding the newspaper out to her.

Andi took the paper from McMillan. Opened it up and read the article. Not that the story was news to her. Word had spread quickly through the entire Florida firefighting community.

A story of a fire chief who'd abused his rank to keep his subordinates quiet about having a couple of strippers act out his sexual fantasies at work. The accompanying photo showed a stripper wearing turnout gear, red spiked heels and, well, nothing up top. Pretending to study the photo, she wondered how many male fire captains were having this exact same discussion.

She folded the paper in half and handed it back to McMillan. There was no way she'd ever jeopardize her career or the careers of her men the way that captain had in Hillsborough.

Andi hadn't been a firefighter for fifteen years for nothing. She was willing to play along. "Okay, if that's what you guys want."

"Really?" Johnson asked. McMillan and Powell both straightened from the credenza. She saw anticipation and excitement on their faces. Some days she really loved her job.

Mick sat up straighter in his chair, and she knew he wasn't

sure where she was going with this. She was as by-the-book as they came.

"Are you sure you guys want to do this?" she asked them, careful to keep her voice neutral.

"Oh, yeah," McMillan said.

"Hell, yeah," Johnson added.

She nodded, then put her booted feet on the floor and leaned forward on her desk. "Just checking. My brothers have always sworn that they'd go blind if they ever saw another man naked."

"What are you talking about, Cap?" asked Powell. "We want strippers."

"I know. Male strippers."

"Cap, that's wrong. Why would we want to see naked men?" McMillan asked.

Johnson turned three shades of red. "Well, damn, Cap, that's just mean. You knew what we were thinking."

"I know that you weren't thinking too well. Why would I want to see naked women?"

"Maybe they forgot you were a woman," said Rodney Coltrane from behind Johnson.

Rodney had been giving her a hard time since they'd met nearly sixteen years ago, while her crew accepted her because of the job she did. Rodney had a burr under his saddle about women in any unit. It didn't help their relationship any that whenever the two of them had come head-to-head in any competition for a job or for fun, Andi had always come out the winner.

"Ah, that's not it, Cap. We were just joshing you, hoping to ruffle your feathers," Powell said.

"Shoulda known it wouldn't work," Johnson added.

"What can I do for you, Rodney?" she asked as her men filed out. Mick lingered in the room, but Andi tilted her head at him until he sighed and left as well.

Mick had been her best friend for too long, and there

were times when he still wanted to fight her battles for her. Despite the fact that she'd never needed him to do so. It had always made her feel good deep inside where she'd never admit she needed it—the fact that Mick sometimes tried to protect her.

There was another man standing by Rodney. Someone that Andi had never met before.

He was tall, at least four inches taller than her five-foot-eight frame. His hair was dark brown, and his eyes were deep dark green. The color of the grass on that first spring morning after winter let go of the landscape. Bright and brilliant. Oh, hell, no. She wasn't attracted to one of Rodney's pals.

"Actually, I was just helping out Tucker here. He's the arson investigator you had to call in."

She didn't respond to that. Their only option was to call in an outside arson investigator. They were a rural firehouse and didn't have a full-time arson specialist on staff. Tucker must be the state guy she'd sent for due to the three warehouse fires they'd had over the last month.

"Tucker Fields, ma'am," he said, holding out his hand. His breath was scented with mint, and his aftershave was a clean, crisp one that made her want to breathe deeper.

"Andrea O'Roarke," she said, taking his hand. His palm was big and callused. He shook her hand the way she suspected he would shake another man's hand. And that gesture showed her a measure of respect that Rodney had never offered.

When she tried to pull her hand free, he held it for an extra second before releasing her. And when she glanced up at him, she noticed his gaze was on her face. Nervously, she licked her suddenly dry lips.

"I don't think anyone could mistake you for anything other than a woman."

"Careful, Tucker. Andi's not like other girls; she bites,"

Rodney said as he turned on his heel and walked out the door.

"My favorite kind," Tucker said, letting her hand slip from his grasp. "But I'm here for business, not pleasure."

"And arson is your business?" she asked, moving away from him. She had an untouchable aura about her. She was open and friendly, but only to a certain extent. Since he'd seen her with her men, Tuck realized he wasn't getting genuine warmth from her now.

He was a stranger, and clearly she didn't know if he was going to be a jerk like Rodney Coltrane or not. He knew she had to have worked hard to be the fire chief at this firehouse. But how many times had she been forced to prove herself to get the job?

Tucker admired the way Andrea regained her composure and took a minute to gather his own. He was used to seeing women in the firehouses he visited; gone were the fire stations of the past that were solely the domain of men.

He just wasn't used to being turned on by them. His job came first usually. She wasn't model beautiful, but there was a clean-cut, athletic grace to her that showed in every movement she made.

"What can I say, I like the heat," he said, wishing for a moment that his legendary charm hadn't deserted him.

But it had. He couldn't help himself. Everything about Andrea O'Roarke got to him. It wasn't anything overt that she was doing, just the entire package she presented. He'd always been drawn to strength. Something she had in spades.

Her eyes were deep and dark, guarding her secrets in that enigmatic way that only women had. Her lips were full— her mouth lush, beckoning him forward. If that ass Rodney hadn't been in the office with them, Tuck would have been tempted to pull her closer and taste her lips when he'd shaken her hand.

She had a mouth made for kissing. He realized she was speaking to him, but didn't hear a damn thing she said. She tipped her head to the side and stopped talking.

"Sorry about that; my mind wasn't here. What were you saying?" he asked. *Get it together, man. Your reputation is on the line.*

"Where do you want to start?" she asked while offering him a chair across from her desk.

"Who was the first on the scene?" he asked, trying to prove his mind was on the suspected arsonist, when in reality, it was on her confident movements as she took her own seat.

"Johnson and Powell responded. But they had to wait for a second unit before they could go inside."

"Why?"

"We have the two-in, two-out rule here."

He nodded. The two-in, two-out rule meant there had to be two guys waiting outside in case the two who went in got into trouble and needed assistance.

"Most firehouses do. So what'd they find?" he asked, taking notes on a small pad. In bigger firehouses they had a special crew that just waited outside as backup.

"Gas cans. The blaze took us a while to put out. The men were tired, but we went over the site carefully."

He'd read the report she'd written and knew that her men had done everything by the book. She was a rule follower, and that worked in her favor. "You know your stuff."

"Of course I do. Don't believe what Rodney says. I got this job the same way everyone else does."

"With hard work?" he asked, but he knew that was what she meant. He'd heard about Andi O'Roarke long before he'd come here. Everyone in the state knew her by reputation. She was a damn fine firefighter despite her sex.

"Damn straight."

He narrowed his eyes, watching her carefully. He was walking the kind of fine line he'd rarely had to with the opposite sex. But the stakes seemed higher with her. "You know, you've got a chip on your shoulder."

She arched one eyebrow at him. "Only for men who ogle me and think a woman can't do this job."

He fought to keep from grinning at her. She was so sassy, it was hard to believe that the men who worked with her forgot she was a woman. "Ogling you doesn't equal a disbelief in your abilities."

"Really?" she asked, as if she didn't believe a man could be attracted to her and still admit she was very competent at her job.

"Really," he said. He leaned back in his chair, pretending to study the papers she'd handed to him. But he felt as if that business was out of the way. He already had the information he needed to start his arson investigation. Now he wanted to start another, more personal inquiry.

"Do you want something to drink?" She fiddled with the papers on her desk. She had long fingers, and her nails were short, functional. She was totally feminine to him, yet not fragile.

"A Coke would be nice."

She walked to the credenza and bent over to open one of the doors. She had the kind of hips that made a man's hands tingle wondering what they'd feel like in his hands.

She straightened and caught him staring. He shrugged. He was attracted to her and wasn't even going to pretend he wasn't. Everything about her turned him on.

Suddenly all the confidence he'd seen seemed to drain away. She held the can out to him and hurried behind her standard-issue desk. There was something different in her body language now. This wasn't the same woman who'd joked with her men about strippers.

He hooked his ankle over his knee. Popping the tab on

the top of the can, he took a long drag, hoping the icy beverage would cool the heat of his body. The heat that was being generated by the woman sitting across from him—eyeing him warily.

He held the Coke can loosely in one hand, trying to look as nonthreatening as possible. But he wanted her, and he knew himself well enough to know that he wasn't going to back away without a fight. Watching her, he waited for everything to click into place.

As an arson investigator he had to be intimately aware of human behavior. The subject had always intrigued him. He'd never met a person whom he hadn't wanted to figure out. Find out why they behaved the way they did. Those were the same techniques he used to find the arsonists he was responsible for catching.

He just had to figure out what the turn-on was. Why they were drawn to fire. And what they hoped to get out of it.

Shamelessly he used the same techniques with women. And nine times out of ten it worked. Of course, that one time when it didn't work, had served to keep him humble. He knew on one level that he wasn't privy to everything about women or about human nature. But he was willing to turn failure into success.

"Why are you staring at me?" she asked, her voice dropping an octave.

"I like the way your mouth looks," he said, his own voice sounding deeper and huskier than normal. Damn, this woman made him hotter than he'd been in a long time. And honestly, she wasn't doing anything other than being herself. He didn't understand this attraction to her, but he didn't question it.

"You are making me uncomfortable," she said, chewing on her lower lip. "And I don't like it."

"Your mouth is making me uncomfortable." She wasn't

helping him get his mind back on business. "And I do like it."

"I can't be responsible for your wayward fantasies," she said, in a way that made him realize this was a woman at home in the business world but not in a one-on-one with a man.

"Yes, you can." She was solely responsible for those fantasies. He'd never had this problem on the job before. But if she nibbled on her lower lip one more time, he was coming across the desk and tasting her mouth for himself.

"Why? If I was a guy sitting here, you wouldn't be having those fantasies, would you?" She sat up straighter in her chair, and that fire he'd seen earlier was back.

It was there in her eyes. She had the kind of passion that most women were afraid of. And he sensed she was afraid of it, too, but when she felt threatened, it came out with her temper.

"No, but neither of us can change the fact that you are a woman. One I can't help but notice."

She opened one of the files on her desk. "Well, stop. Let's talk about the case."

He let her change the subject. Listened to her voice as she read him the initial incident reports. He liked her voice. It was throaty and husky, making it all too easy for him to picture the two of them in bed on a long, lazy afternoon.

"You're doing it again," she said, without looking up. Her hair was pulled back in a ponytail, but a few strands escaped to curl enticingly along the back of her neck, which was long and slim, seemingly fragile.

"Doing what?" he asked. After he finished with her mouth he was going to spend a lot of time nibbling on her neck.

"Staring," she said, glancing up at him.

"I think we're going to have to just go with it. I can't seem to help myself."

She closed the folder and leaned back in her chair again. "I heard you were one of the best."

"I am the best."

"Then prove it. Because all I see is a hound dog who can't keep his tongue in his mouth."

"Touché."

"It's nothing personal. I just don't want the men to suddenly start looking at me . . . the way you do."

"How do I look at you?"

"You know."

"Do I?"

"You're a pain in the ass, right? Someone, sometime, told you it was charming, and you've clung to that."

He laughed for the sheer joy of it. "You're the first woman to mention it."

"Maybe I'm the first woman to see through your façade."

"I have a façade?"

"You know you do," she said, leaning forward and resting her elbows on her desk. "Does it work?"

He shifted, setting the papers and the Coke at his feet, and leaned his arms on the desk so that only a few inches separated them. Her eyes were really several different shades of hazel and brown. They were beautiful up close.

"Have dinner with me and find out for yourself."

She flushed and pushed back away from him. "Uh . . . no, thanks."

Staying where he was, Tuck sorted through the possibilities. She didn't want to go out with him or she was scared to go out with him. His ego and his money were on the latter.

"Chicken?" he asked, playing a hunch.

"I'm not afraid of you."

"Prove it. I'm only asking you for dinner."

Chapter 2

"And then he left," Andi said, taking a deep swig of her beer. She was kicked back on a patio lounge chair at her best friend's house. "So what does that mean, Sara?"

"I have no idea. I don't know why you think I understand men."

"Because you're married. You must have done something to figure out at least one guy."

"Ah, but Mick's not like other guys."

"That's right, I'm better."

"Define better," Sara said.

"Me," he said, bending down to kiss her.

Andi watched her friends, envious and a little jealous of what they had. She'd resigned herself to being single for the rest of her life. Lots of firefighters were. The job was too hard on relationships. And it didn't bother her. But ever since Tucker had invited her to dinner three days ago, it had been all she'd thought of.

"What did it mean, Mick?"

"Hell, I don't know. I wouldn't have asked you out like that."

"Why not?"

"Because Sara would have killed me."

Sara flexed her muscles from where she stood at the grill. "He's scared of me."

Andi realized her friends were going to be little help. Or maybe they didn't realize she was serious about wanting to understand Tucker. She hadn't been able to sleep for the last few days from thinking about him. There was something about that man that wouldn't let her go.

He was in her dreams and in her mind as she ran her five miles each morning, his words echoing in her head, that watching her didn't mean he thought she was incompetent. It had been a long time since any man had looked at her the way he had.

Sure, she dated and had sex with guys, but they were always kind of . . . not as strong as she was. She'd always set the tone for her relationships, and men always backed down when she confronted them. Why hadn't he?

"You okay, Andi?"

She glanced at Mick. He'd set the table and brought over the tray of burgers that Sara had grilled. Mick couldn't cook, something that everyone in the firehouse had learned the hard way.

"Yeah, fine."

"Tell me again about this guy," Sara said.

"Never mind. I'm sure he was just having fun at my expense."

"I don't know about that. How many men ask you out at work?"

She frowned, taking a huge bite of her burger to keep from having to answer. Why the hell had she brought this up? No man at work ever noticed she was a woman unless she accidentally walked into the sleeping area when they were changing, and even then they usually didn't think anything of dropping their trousers and changing in front of her.

She just wasn't a girly girl. She'd always known it. Growing up with her four brothers and a strict father had reinforced that. But unless she missed her guess, Tucker Fields had noticed she was a woman.

Too bad, because she wouldn't mind seeing him drop his pants.

"Are you going to answer the question?"

"What do you think? No one asks me out at work. Unless you count that one Fourth of July picnic when Joe Zenwicki got drunk and told everyone in the park that someday I'd be his bride."

"No one counts that. He asked every woman there to be his bride."

Just as she'd thought. She'd never really been special to any man. Not in a womanly way. The men whose homes she'd saved from burning to the ground thanked her. The men whose kids she taught to stop, drop and roll thanked her. But usually men didn't look at her the way Tucker had. As though she was his favorite flavor of ice cream and he couldn't wait to lick her up.

"What are you going to do about it?"

"I don't know. The man called me a chicken. I can't let that pass."

"No, you can't," Mick said around a bite of pickle. "That kind of word gets out and you'll lose your reputation as a tough-ass."

"Funny, Mick, really funny. I don't think he's going to tell anyone he said I was a chicken."

"Really?"

"Yeah, he didn't seem like the kind of guy who was going to talk about me."

"Maybe you should go out with him, then," Sara said.

But she couldn't. Too much time had passed. How was she going to bring up the subject and not be embarrassed? And that was the problem. She would be embarrassed, especially if he'd changed his mind. What if he hadn't meant to ask her out?

"Men!"

"Uh-oh, I think I should be going. I'll wait for our other

guest up front," Mick said, taking his beer and leaving the table.

"What other guest?"

"We can't play Risk with only three people. Mick invited some new guy over to even things out. He's so paranoid that you and I are going to team up against him."

Mick had probably invited Danny Brown, their newest recruit. He was fresh from training. She glanced around for her T-shirt. She should probably put that on before he got here.

"Tell me more about this guy," Sara said.

Andi wrapped her arms around herself, forgetting her T-shirt for a minute. "What's to tell?"

Sara smiled across the table at her. "Remember when Mick asked me out?"

"Yes, what a nightmare. He was a basket case until you finally said yes."

"Well, maybe this guy is a basket case waiting for you."

She swallowed. There was no way any man would be that crazy for her. She had nothing that Sara did. That was no slam against herself; it was just that she wasn't a woman that men went crazy for. She was a woman whom they called when they needed advice on how to fix things up with their wives or girlfriends.

But still, the man had called her a chicken. Maybe he didn't know what he was letting himself in for. Maybe that rat Rodney had said something to make him think she'd be easy game. But there had been something charming about him.

"I'm going to call him on his dare."

"What if it wasn't really a dare?" Sara said.

But Andi ignored that. She tried to concentrate on her food, but the only thing she hungered for was more knowledge of Tucker Fields.

* * *

Tucker wasn't sure why he'd accepted Mick Palmer's invitation to drinks on Thursday night. But he had. It had been obvious from the time Tucker had spent around the station house that Mick and Andi were friends. And Tuck knew Andi would be there. Considering she'd avoided him for the last few days, he wasn't sure how she'd react to his being in her friend's home.

He couldn't figure her out. He gave her space, but she still didn't respond. Maybe that was the problem; he was being too cautious. She needed a man to storm her defenses and take control.

He raised his hand to knock on the door of the modern ranch house. Tuck hadn't spent a lot of time in Polk County, Florida, but the area was rural and remote. Most residents lived a quiet life reflective of old Florida. Mainly ranchers and citrus growers, they were called Florida Crackers. Small-town folks who still lived by the morals that were slowly fading from the fabric of American life.

Mick opened the door. "Hey, you're just in time to grab a burger."

"Thanks," Tuck said, handing the pack of Coronas to Mick as he followed the other man into his house.

The sound of Jimmy Buffett played on the patio, and he heard two women talking. His body tightened, and his blood flowed heavier through his veins as he recognized Andi's voice.

Jimmy was singing about coastal connections, a warm breeze blew through the open glass sliding door and Tuck felt a kind of settling deep inside where he was always restless. Why he'd find it here in this rural community with these people he really didn't know; he had no clue.

"I hope you brought your game with you."

"Why?"

"Because I have a feeling it's going to be men versus women, and Andi plays to win."

"What about your wife?"

"She can hold her own. But can you?"

Tuck stopped him in the doorway before they stepped through. "What do you mean? Of course I can hold my own against a couple of women."

"Ah, but you have to forget they are women. They can be tricky and ruthless. Don't forget that."

Mick stepped through the doorway, and Tuck followed him. "Look who's here."

Andi glanced up and choked on a bite of her burger. Mick casually reached over and smacked her several times on the back. Both women wore bikini tops and shorts. They had their hair pulled back in ponytails, but that was where the similarities ended. Mick's wife was petite, a curvy little redhead with warm cinnamon brown eyes.

And Andi . . . Well, she was an Amazon goddess with some of her wild brown hair escaping the elastic to curl around her neck.

"Sara, this is Tucker Fields. Tuck, this is my better half, Sara. You know Andi."

The casual introduction belied the fact that both women were glaring at Mick. Tuck had the feeling that he was a surprise addition to what was clearly a ritual event between them. He smiled at Sara, hoping to ease the tension.

"Help yourself to a burger, Tuck, while my husband and I get something in the kitchen."

"What do we need from the kitchen?" Mick asked.

Sara glared at him until he nodded at her. "Oh, I'm going to put your beer on ice and help Sara," he said to Tuck.

The other couple left the patio, and Tuck sat down next to Andi. Time hadn't diminished the attraction he felt for her. He'd been concentrating on his job, wanting to apprehend the arsonist before he focused on her, but it had been hard.

"How's the investigation coming?" she asked her plate.

He made his burger and then just sat back and waited. Eventually she lifted her head and met his gaze. She had the kind of eyes he could drown in.

"Did you hear me?"

"Of course. I was waiting for you to ask me and not your plate."

"Why do you care?"

"Because I know that you are hiding from me," he said.

"That's the second time you've inferred that I'm some kind of coward. It's not true. I'm not afraid of any man."

"I know that. You're an Amazon goddess, and woe to the man who doesn't notice that."

"Stop making fun of me. I knew you were one of those guys."

"What guys? I don't really fit in any one category well."

"The type who think I'm some kind of freak," she said, then flushed and pushed away from the table.

He followed her the short distance to the porch railing. She had braced her hands on the wrought iron that surrounded the cement pad. He stood behind her and then slowly lowered his hands on either side of hers so that his body completely enfolded hers.

He kept a small inch of space between them so they weren't actually touching. He leaned closer to her, barely resisting the temptation that her long, slim neck represented. "I don't think you are a freak."

She turned her head, glancing over her shoulder at him, her eyes wide with confusion and a trace of fear. "Then what do you think?"

"That you are a woman I'll never be able to forget."

He canted his body farther into hers and lowered his head to kiss her.

His mouth moved over hers, not a tentative asking for permission, but a bold taking of what he wanted. Andi was used to men being intimidated by her, both in and out of bed. There was something about her strength that kept them at bay. But not Tuck. He took what he wanted.

That made her feel . . . She didn't know. Couldn't think when his mouth moved over hers like that. She turned in his arms, putting her hands on his slim hips and leaning up into him.

He tasted of minty gum and something else. Something different and deeper. He tasted like adventure and daring, and she realized that she'd let him shock her into forgetting that she backed down for no man.

She slid her hands up his sides and around his neck. She tunneled her fingers through his hair and went up on tiptoe to take control of the kiss. She thrust her tongue deeper into his mouth and massaged the back of his head as she tasted him.

He moaned deep in his throat, the sound making her squirm with excitement. But then slowly he turned the tables on her. His hands swept up and down her back in languid caresses that made her skin so sensitized that she was anticipating each of his touches.

His thumbs slipped under the sides of her bikini top. Not touching her breasts, but so close that her nipples immediately tightened. She shifted in his arms, trying to put some space between them. Trying to readjust the balance of power.

But he held her firmly. Slipping her fingers under the collar of his shirt, she scraped her nails against his neck. Felt the reaction in him as his erection nudged her stomach.

She rubbed her hands over his chest and reached between them to touch him. But he captured her wrists, gently pulling her arms behind her back and anchoring them with one of his hands. The position of her arms forced her breasts forward against his chest.

She pulled her mouth from his, staring up at him. He watched her, and she knew the vulnerability she felt in that moment was clear to him. But instead of triumph or gloating, she saw a tenderness in his eyes that made her want to cry. No one had ever looked at her that way.

"Kiss me again," he said.

She nodded and leaned up toward him. His mouth came down on hers, but the embrace and tone were controlled by her. He let her set the pace and take her time. This time she explored his mouth carefully. Dropping several soft kisses on his lips and nibbling at his lower one. She sucked it into her mouth and teased him with soft touches of her tongue.

Her breasts were cushioned on his chest. They felt full and needy. She tried to rotate her shoulders so that she could rub the tips against his chest, but he held her too securely.

She pulled back. She felt his erection between them. Knew he wanted more. "Why?"

"I want to know your mouth completely before we move on to anything else."

"I don't know if we're going to move on," she said honestly. He overwhelmed her in a way that she'd never experienced with anyone before.

"We will be. Kiss me again."

Mick cleared his throat from the doorway. "I thought we were going to play Risk."

"Hell, kissing this lady is risky."

Mick laughed. "Five-minute warning. Sara and I are making margaritas for the ladies, and then we'll be right out."

Andi fought to control her body's reaction to the interruption. Damn, Mick was the last person she wanted to see her and Tuck together. She wanted more time alone with Tuck. She wished they were anywhere but here. But she knew that if Mick hadn't invited Tuck over, Andi wouldn't have decided to accept Tuck's dinner invitation.

Her body was already telling her that her mind had been right. This man was dangerous.

"I'll show you risky," she said, damning the husky sound of her own voice. She tried to pull her arms free, but he continued to hold them securely. She didn't want to make a scene, and it was important to Andi to bring the situation back to normal as quickly as possible.

"I like danger," Tuck said, looking right at her.

"I'm not dangerous," she assured him.

"Oh, I think you are."

She wasn't going to argue with him. "Let go of my arms."

"Not yet."

"Not now, Tucker. Mick and Sara are going to be here any second."

"We're not finished."

"I kissed you," she said.

"Now it's my turn."

He lowered his head one more time, and Andi forgot to breathe. His lips were firm and commanding, yet all the time careful of her. He slipped one of his hands to the back of her head and angled his mouth over hers. Tipping her head in a way that made her totally open and vulnerable to him.

He had complete control over her. She couldn't do anything but submit to him and to his will. She shivered in his embrace. Wishing her hands were free so she could wrap her arms around him.

She stretched up on her toes, leaning into his body while he set her soul on fire with his mouth on hers. His chest pressed to her aching breasts. His cock was hot and hard next to her stomach. She felt him through the layer of his pants, right against the skin of her stomach that was left bare by her low-riding shorts.

When he lifted his head, his lips were wet and his eyes narrowed. He wanted her. She tipped her head to the side to study him, but there was no time. He let go of her wrists.

Placing his hand at the small of her back, his heat burning into her skin, searing her with his touch, he led her to the table and seated her. He acted so calm when every inch of her felt as if it was on fire.

Calmly he picked up his burger and took a huge bite. Her heart was racing, and her skin was so sensitive that the slight breeze blowing through the night made her every nerve pulse.

She stared at him, realizing that something was changing inside her and that she was powerless to stop it.

Chapter 3

Tuck had never been so glad for a board game before. Mick and Sara were both funny and outgoing. And he knew that Andi felt at home with them. Unlike at the firehouse where she kept her guard up and her humor firmly in check, here she let her hair down.

Twilight had darkened into night, and the Palmers had lit tiki torches to keep the mosquitoes from the small table. Jimmy Buffett had given way to Bob Marley. The Coronas he'd brought were half gone, and the pitcher of margaritas the women were sharing was almost empty.

The attitude was light and fun, laughter and threats filled the air and Tuck felt a part of this circle of friends. He knew that it was an illusion. That he was seeing the inner circle only because it was obvious that Andi and he might hook up. But for the rambler who always moved on, never stayed in one place for very long, it was tempting.

Andi enchanted him. Risk was a game of strategy and cunning. A smart man's or in this case woman's game. Tuck learned a lot about her watching her. She wasn't above manipulating or strategizing with everyone at the table as long as it forwarded her toward her objective—to win.

He'd met other men with her attitude and knew he'd been guilty of it himself a time or two—that determination to win at any cost. But there was something damned attractive about that attitude in her. She just liked winning.

Her game was fast and furious, much like the woman herself. Sara and Mick left the patio to talk in private about some sort of strategy they had. It wasn't the first time that two players had left the table. For a time Mick and Tuck had struck up a partnership, but that had ended when Sara had tipped her head to the side and shamelessly flirted with her husband.

"You're staring again," Andi said, toying with the stem of her margarita glass.

"Am I?" he asked. Never before had the game of flirting been so much fun. He liked the feelings of anticipation and arousal that pooled in his gut. He was still turned on from their earlier kiss. The taste of her lingered on his tongue, and he couldn't wait to sample her skin, her pretty breasts or her feminine core. He wanted to know all the flavors that made up Andi.

"Yes. What were you thinking?" She skimmed her finger over the edge of her glass, lifting the salt from the rim before licking it off.

He swallowed, wanting to feel her tongue on him. "That someone should have told you that guys don't want to be trounced by a woman they like."

She did it again, and he realized she was aware that her little salt-licking ritual was getting to him. Never had he been forced to work so hard to keep ahead of a woman. She was toying with him and wanted him to know what she was doing.

"Really? Should I pretend that I'm not good at the game? Or that I don't like to win?"

He shrugged and casually reached across the table to take her hand in his. The salt was still there on her forefinger, and he waited patiently for her to look at him before he drew her finger to his mouth and sucked it inside.

Her pupils dilated, and goose bumps slid up her arm. Her nipples tightened, pressing against the thin layer of fabric on her top. He slowly pulled her finger from his mouth and linked their hands together in the middle of the table.

He cleared his throat. "With some guys losing to a woman might matter."

"Why would a guy want a woman who threw a game?" she asked.

He knew that she wasn't really thinking of teasing him just then. She couldn't understand a man who was like that. "Ego maybe."

"Only a guy without much self-confidence would be that insecure. Some kind of loser."

"Should I be offended?" He let go of her hands. She stared at her own hands for a moment and then pulled her arms back, wrapping them around her waist.

She was a contradiction in strength and vulnerability. Seeing her like this wasn't something he liked. He wanted her fire and passion. He wanted to see her with her eyes blazing with that gleam that said any man in her path had better guard his balls.

He pushed to his feet. "Do I look like one of those guys?"

She studied him, her eyes moving over his chest and down his legs. His body stirred to life, and he fought to keep from flexing his muscles under her gaze.

"Turn around," she said, leaning back in her chair. Studying him the way he suspected she studied every new fire she fought.

When he faced her again, she nibbled her lower lip and narrowed her eyes.

"Don't keep me in suspense. Should I flex my muscles or show you my six-pack abs?"

"Do you really have a six-pack?"

He lifted his T-shirt to show her. He worked damned hard for the body he had. And he was glad to see the flush of arousal that moved over her. He stepped closer and caught one of her hands in his. Bringing it to his abs. She flexed her fingers, her nails scraping lightly against his skin. His cock stirred, and he realized he was playing once again with fire.

"Well?" He wasn't going to last much longer at this teasing. He needed to throw her over his shoulder in the fireman's carry and take her to his truck. He'd have her shorts off and his body buried deep inside hers in thirty seconds flat.

She twirled her hand over his stomach. "You don't strike me as a loser."

"I work out twice a day, and that's all the praise I get?"

"If you're working out that much, you know you look good and don't need my praise."

But he did. He'd never say it out loud, but the look of approval in her eyes as she caressed him was making him feel invincible. He stepped away from her as he heard Sara and Mick returning to the patio. He sat down and tried to adjust his legs to find a comfortable position.

Andi winked at him as if knowing his predicament. He swept his gaze over her body, lingering on her breasts. They flexed under his gaze, and her nipples grew more prominent.

She leaned forward, her elbows resting on the table. The position framed her breasts in the skimpy bikini top. "You know what's always bothered me about that kind of thinking—aside from the obvious that throwing a game is out of the question?"

"What?" he asked. What he really wanted to know was what the hell they were doing here when they could be back at his rental unit making love.

"Why would I want a man who can't keep up with me?"

He leaned forward, reaching for one of her hands, running his thumb over the back of her knuckles. "Why indeed?"

Mick and Sara returned to the table, and the game ensued. They played for two more hours, and Andi managed to win despite being distracted by the six feet, two inches of solid testosterone sitting across from her. She helped Sara clean up the kitchen before she got ready to leave.

Mick and Tucker watched the tail end of the baseball game on ESPN. Mick was a diehard fan of the sport. He knew stats on everyone and played in some league for fantasy teams. His league used players from the past and present.

Baseball wasn't her thing. She preferred a game where she could go head-to-head with her opponents. "I'll see you tomorrow at work." She picked up her purse and headed for the door.

"Catcha later, Andi."

"Wait up, I'm leaving, too."

Andi wasn't sure she wanted to be alone with Tucker again. It had been a long night and more fun than she'd had with a man in a while. But that didn't change the fact that this had just been an innocent encounter.

Yeah, right, how many innocent encounters ended where she knew what a man's tongue tasted like and how his penis felt pressed against her. Just thinking about that kiss they'd exchanged made her feel like a flame newly formed and starting to grow. She didn't like it. She prided herself on her control. Especially around men.

There were three vehicles parked on the street other than his truck. She held back to see which one he thought was hers. The four-door late model sedan, the low-slung sports car or the Chevy quad cab truck. She'd never driven anything but trucks, and most men . . . Well, it was a test that she'd used in the past.

"I like your friends," he said quietly. The night air was warm. He tipped his head back to look up at the moon.

It was full tonight, lending the street and surrounding area enough light to see by. "They're the best. I met Mick in EMT training when we were both fresh out of high school."

"And you became friends?" he asked, showing his interest in her and her past.

"Not at first. But he liked one of my girlfriends, so he started hanging around me to get to know her."

"Sara?"

She shook her head. Mick was legendary amongst the men at the fire station. A total ladies' man who'd blazed a trail through Central Florida's most eligible women for a long time. "No. That was Tami. Mick was a total . . . player, before he met Sara."

"And Sara reformed him," Tuck said softly.

Could any woman reform Tucker? She doubted it. There was something burning in his eyes that said he knew who he was and where he was going. With Mick, Andi knew he'd been looking for the right woman to settle down with. "So he says. What about you?"

"What about me?" he asked.

She needed to hear it out loud. To remind herself that this wasn't the kind of guy that was in her league.

"Girl in every city?" she asked, trying to sound casual.

He wrapped his arm around her waist and pulled her close to him. She was sorry she'd put on her T-shirt before coming outside. She would have liked the feel of his warm arm against the skin of her back.

"Sometimes, other times no. I'm a rambling man by nature."

She nodded. It confirmed what she sensed about him. Whatever happened between them would end when he finished his investigation. Oddly, that made him more tempting. Made the chance at exploring this attraction more appealing.

"What about you?"

"Me?"

"Yeah, you and other men—dating?"

"I date when I have the time. But mostly I work or do volunteer stuff with the school system, so there's not time. I mean sometimes I—" She stopped as soon as she realized she was being long-winded.

It was just that dating was her weakness. She could never seem to find a man who made her happy for longer than a few hours in bed. She tended to overwhelm most of the guys she dated with her intensity. And even the hours in bed were iffy. For some reason she'd never been able to relinquish control in the bedroom, which would have been great if she'd been attracted to beta guys, but the men she liked didn't want to have to fight a woman for control when they were having sex.

"So you don't date," he said. Carefully, he slipped his arm around her waist and led her toward the three cars.

"Not really." Should she mention that he'd asked her out? She wasn't sure. God, she hated this. This was why she didn't date. Men made her freaking crazy.

"Well, that's about to change."

"It is?"

"Yes. I asked you out, remember?"

She bit her lower lip and nodded. "I'm working tomorrow."

"No problem. I'll pick you up the day after—around seven. Wear a skirt."

"I haven't said yes yet," she said casually. The only way that she was going to keep this thing on equal footing was to stay alert all the time. To treat Tucker Fields the way she would a tough new fire that she didn't understand. Each blaze was different. Each one reacted differently to its environment. Tucker was definitely the kind of man she wasn't sure how to handle.

"Are you really saying no?" he asked, using his grip on her waist to turn her more fully into his body. He ran his finger along the line of her jaw and tipped her head back so that she was forced to look up at him.

She shook her head. She wanted to go out with him more than she'd wanted anything else in a long time. Lust, she thought, it was just lust. But lust had never felt like this before. This was a bone-deep ache that had his name on it.

"So you're saying yes," he said.

She nodded. "I hope you know what you're letting yourself in for."

"I have an idea it'll be the ride of my life."

He led her to her truck and then waited until she climbed in and started the engine. She watched him for a minute, aware that she'd finally found a man who saw past her tough exterior. Now, what was she going to do with him?

Tucker got back to his rented duplex and pulled out the notes on the investigation. It was going as smoothly as he'd hoped. His initial look had confirmed that the fires were deliberately set. And the clues he'd found so far had been the same ones listed in Andi's report.

He took off his shirt and grabbed a beer from the refrigerator, sinking down on the cushions of the couch to let the fires play in his mind. The similarities of the blazes pointed to the same arsonist. Most fire starters worked alone.

But he didn't know this area. He'd have to start talking to the locals tomorrow. All three of the blazes had been set in abandoned citrus-packing houses. He'd asked for the insurance records on the buildings, but the policies weren't large enough to make the fires worthwhile to the owners.

That left . . . who?

He rubbed the bridge of his nose and caught the faint scent of Andi on his hand. He closed his eyes and leaned back, letting the evening replay in his head. He knew he had to handle her carefully. She was a spitfire who'd keep any man on his toes, but she was guarded.

How much of that sassy, ballsy attitude was the real Andi, and how much was the front she used to keep anyone from seeing her vulnerabilities? He promised himself he'd find out.

His cell phone rang, and he pulled it off his hip and answered it. He glanced at the caller ID, but the number wasn't one he recognized.

"Fields."

Static buzzed on the open line. He waited, knowing that only a few people had this number.

"Hello?"

"It's Andi." Her voice was low and husky, brushing over his aroused senses like a breeze stirring the edges of a wildfire.

"Missed me already?" he asked, rubbing his hand over his chest, wishing it was her caress. She had strong, capable hands and neatly trimmed nails. He wanted to feel them scraping over his chest, tangling in the hair there, and bringing him to the point where his balls felt too tight and he had to come.

"You wish," she said, sassy again. He closed his eyes, picturing her as she'd been in his arms earlier.

"Then why'd you call?" He loved the many facets of Andi and knew he was just touching the surface of who she was.

"To make sure you weren't back at your place gloating," she said. He could hear the sounds of a wind chime in the distance and the creak of a swing.

"Why would I be gloating? You won tonight." Something he'd bet she did most times. But this wasn't a call about victory. Something else was going on here, and Tuck concentrated on trying to figure her out.

"Did I? It didn't feel that way once I got home."

He picked up his beer and tipped it back, draining it in one long swallow. "I'm not playing games with you yet."

"Why do you say things like that to me? I'm going to be honest with you; I don't know how to handle you. I'm not sure what you want from me."

He wasn't sure he knew what he wanted. He wanted all the passion that she showed when playing a board game focused on him. He wanted that sassy attitude he'd glimpsed at the firehouse. He wanted every one of the secrets hidden in her big brown eyes revealed to him and only him. "I want what any red-blooded American male would want."

"*Sex.* Except since you're a guy, you'd use a different word."

"What word?" he asked.

"Don't make me say it. It's crude."

"Pussy?" he guessed. She worked around mainly men, so that made sense.

"Yeah, why do guys say that?" Her voice held not disgust, but an analytical tone.

"Most of them don't in front of women. You're dating the wrong class of men."

"I heard it growing up and around the firehouse," she said.

"I can't speak for anyone but me, but if I use that term, it's because I'm not sure of myself."

"Use it often?" she said teasingly.

"Hardly ever," he countered.

She laughed, and it betrayed her nervousness. "I'm so used to being around men. I know the way they think."

"Maybe you don't know as much as you think you do."

"There's no maybe there. I can't figure you out. Sometimes

you act the way I expect you to . . . but then sometimes you don't."

"Well, I don't think of you as just some easy lay."

"What do you think?"

"That I can't get you off my mind. That one damned kiss is still replaying in my mind. I'm so hard I could come with just the thought of your mouth on mine again."

"Oh."

"Yeah, oh. So what was this call really about?"

She was quiet for so long, he wondered if she wanted him to believe that she'd hung up. But he knew that she was still there.

"Andi?"

"I'm not sure how to say this other than just to say it. Don't talk about our date at the station house. I mean, it's only one date, and the men and I have a balance of power there that works. They've forgotten I'm a woman and treat me like some sort of androgynous older sister. That can't change."

"I understand. What happens between us stays between us. And don't kid yourself that one date is going to be enough to satisfy either one of us."

Chapter 4

It had been a busy but uneventful day. Four calls and not one of them amounting to anything more than an unattended pot on a stove that had caught fire in Ms. Granley's double-wide.

So you'd think Andi would be able to keep her mind off Tucker and the incredible kiss they'd shared the night before. But no such luck. Her mind was full of images of him.

It was what he'd said afterward that was niggling at the back of her mind. She wasn't sure she was ready for more than one date with Tuck. She walked through the firehouse. Two guys were mopping, and McMillan was standing over a pot of chili in the kitchen.

The men were restless and teasing Brown about the fact that his wife had packed him a lunch. Andrea shook her head. This was a large part of her life, and she understood it as she understood little else. Men had to tease and harass—that was what she was used to.

She missed the days of being one of the guys. Though she still was to one extent, her promotion had moved her into different territory. She was their superior and had to maintain a distance at all times.

"Phone call, Andi," Marilee called from her desk. Andi nodded and headed back to her office area.

Marilee Humphries was one of the station's dispatchers.

She was eighty if she was a day and had taken this job after retiring five years ago from the police department where she'd worked as a uniformed officer her entire career. She was seasoned by life and full of stories about danger. Sometimes Andrea looked at the never-married Marilee and saw her own future.

At least Marilee was still in pretty good shape. Of course, she lived in a small house on the lake with about a dozen dogs, cats and other assorted wildlife.

"Captain O'Roarke," she said as she picked up the phone.

"Hey, shortcake. It's Ian."

Her oldest brother was the only man alive who'd get away with calling her that stupid nickname. He'd been larger than life to her as a child and still was on most days. At six-four with more muscles than Mr. Universe and close-cropped dark brown hair, he was a menacing figure, but Andi knew that underneath that big burly exterior beat a heart of gold. Ian was a widower who was raising two teenagers.

The irony of Carin dying in a car accident had never been lost on Andi. Every day Ian went to work knowing he might not come back home. But Carin—a stay-at-home mom—should have been safe. Her brother never talked about it, but Andi knew that he still wasn't over her death.

She heard the affection in his voice. "What's up?"

"How's your arson investigation going?" he asked. She heard the sound of gulls crying and realized he must be out on his boat.

Andi picked at her cuticle. What was he getting at? Had that damned Rodney started spreading rumors that had reached her brother down in South Dade County? "Good, I think."

"You think? What's up with that? You always know every detail of what's going on in your house."

Andi felt as though she was fifteen whenever she talked

to her brother. He made her feel like a kid still trying to earn his respect. "He's not in yet today. When I talked to him yesterday about the investigation, he complimented my men and said he was working a few leads. Why am I explaining myself to you?"

"Because I'm your older brother," he said with a laugh.

"Lousy reason. Why'd you ask?"

"I wasn't grilling you, honest. We need Fields here. We've had a string of arson investigators, but none of them have been able to get results. Just a bunch of dead ends and that man is like a miracle worker with those."

Andi was reassured about Tuck's reputation. After the way he'd eyed her in the office on their first meeting, she'd had her doubts. "Want me to have him call you?"

"I left a message with his chief, but maybe you'll talk to him sooner," he said.

Silence buzzed on the line, and she thought about hanging up. Her oldest brother took his role as oldest too seriously, and she knew that he'd called about Tucker to ask her something personal. Tucker was just the thinly veiled excuse he was using to follow up on her.

She also had a sinking feeling in her gut that she wasn't going to like whatever he said next. Give her a three-alarm fire any day and she'd take it on by herself with one lousy garden hose, anything but have some sort of family conversation with Ian.

"You coming home for the old man's big birthday bash?" he asked casually.

She glanced at the photo on the wall. "Nah, summer's a tough time for me."

"You have almost two months to put yourself in a rotation that enables you to come home."

She bit her lip and said nothing. She hated going home for the big family get-togethers. She saw all four of her brothers at different times during the year. But never together. Alone they were manageable, but together and with the old man—no way. "I don't tell you how to run your station house, Ian."

"Point taken, shortcake, but the old man isn't getting any younger, and you haven't been to a bash in almost five years."

"I'm sure he doesn't miss me at the bash. I was home three weeks ago, and he didn't say anything." Now she sounded petulant, something she couldn't tolerate. "I'll try to make it."

"Good enough."

There was a rap on her door, and Andi glanced up to see Tuck standing there. She gestured for him to come in and finished up her phone conversation with her brother.

Tucker seated himself in one of her guest chairs. He wore a pair of faded slim-fitting jeans and a T-shirt that read "FDNY, 9–11." Two guys she knew had gone down that day, and her heart clenched the way it always did when she thought of the men they'd lost.

Tuck leaned back in the chair and waited for her. She realized that she liked having him sitting there clearly in her domain. "I just got off the phone with Chief O'Roarke from South Dade Firehouse Number Forty-three. They need your expertise when you're done here."

"O'Roarke, eh? Any relation?"

"My brother Ian. We're all firefighters."

"How many?" he asked.

She was glad he didn't know all the gory details of her family. Amongst some firefighters she was kind of a living legend because she was Derrick O'Roarke's daughter. He'd become somewhat of a hero fighting the muck fires in the Everglades back in the day.

"Four siblings, one father. How's the investigation coming?" she asked. God, he looked good today.

"Good. How's your mom feel about that?" he asked.

Andi knew they were heading where she didn't want them to go—ever. No one at the firehouse was allowed to ask these kinds of questions, and that went double for Tuck. "She's dead. So did you interview the property owners?"

"Stop trying to tell me how to conduct my investigation."

"It's my firehouse."

"Are you trying to start a fight with me?"

"No. I told you I don't do personal at work."

He leaned forward over the desk. The spicy smell of his aftershave surrounded her. "I'm not asking for an affidavit on your past, Andrea."

"I didn't say you were."

"Then why won't you answer a few questions. It's called getting to know a person."

"We don't need to know each other that well to work together."

He gave her a good hard glare, and she realized that she was being a little pushy, but she didn't want to talk about her family. Not at work, not with him.

Marilee poked her head in. "Good, you're both here. Another warehouse fire over on Oak. The boys called for you both."

Andi headed out of the house with Tucker on her heels. "I'll drive."

"Of course you will. But I need my gear from my truck to document the scene. Do you want me to follow you?"

She shook her head. He made her feel like an idiot. She was a quietly competent woman until he walked in the door, and then all she could think about was being a woman.

Tuck rubbed the back of his neck as he sank deeper into Andrea's office chair. She was out in the firehouse with her men doing what she did best. He sorted through her notes and the interview she'd conducted earlier in the day with the eleven-year-old boy who'd first seen the smoke and alerted 911.

He could hear a commotion going on outside the door, and he knew he was restless. The edgy sexual ache for Andrea was making work damned near impossible. He'd checked in with his boss earlier and found out he was needed in South Dade as soon as he cracked this case. But arson investigations took time.

And concentration. His was piss-poor at this moment. He heard Andi's voice again. He pushed to his feet and opened the office door. All of the six men on shift were standing in a group near the open back door of the firehouse.

There was a bar suspended in the doorway, and McMillan was doing chin-ups. Everyone clapped when he dropped down after fifty. Tuck was impressed. But he could do one hundred without breaking a sweat. Of course, he worked at it.

"Beat that, Cap," McMillan said.

"Is that all you got?"

Everyone laughed and stood back for Andi. She hopped up and stopped at fifty-five, then dropped back to the ground and took a small bow. The men groaned.

"Can't anyone beat her?"

"Marilee came close," Andi said.

The men laughed and then drifted outside to play basketball. A few of the guys were on housekeeping and did some work around the station house.

Andi glanced up and caught him watching her. "You're staring again."

"Yeah, so?"

"You're not too smooth with the ladies, are you?" she asked, walking over toward him.

He shrugged.

"Did you need something?"

"Yes."

She stopped right next to him. She smelled of the outdoors and sweat. Earthy and raw.

"Well?"

"What I need I can't take right now."

Her eyes widened, and she took half a step closer to him. "Maybe later."

"Don't tease me, Andrea. I'm not one of your boys that you can easily beat."

"I wouldn't be so sure of that, Tucker."

"Is that a challenge?"

"If you make it one. But I gotta warn you I'm feeling lucky tonight."

"So am I. What'd you have in mind?"

She gestured across the room to the bar. "There's not a person in this firehouse who has beaten me there."

"That is a brute strength event," he said.

"I've got my share of that."

"I bet you do, Amazon woman. Let's go see who wins."

They walked across the firehouse, and Andi stopped before the bar. "Don't go easy on me, Tucker."

"I won't. Like you, I don't understand why I should be attracted to someone who I have to fake being myself with."

"Did I really say that? I only said I wouldn't throw a game for a guy."

"Maybe."

But he knew what she'd meant. There'd never been a man her equal in strength that she'd been out with. He'd learned that fact from listening to the firehouse gossip and from talking to Mick.

"Bring it on," Andi said with the same glint in her eyes that she'd had when they played Risk.

She gestured to the bar. "After you."

Tuck shook his head. "My mom raised me right—ladies first."

She tipped her head to the side, and he could see her weighing her options. But then she leaped for the bar and did seventy-five before dropping to the floor. "Your turn, Fields."

"No problem, O'Roarke." Tuck did his chin-ups while watching Andi the entire time. Her eyes never left his, and he saw that hint of vulnerability again, buried beneath her confidence.

He stopped at one hundred, dropping to the ground.

"Not bad."

"Not bad? You aren't impressed."

Suddenly she grinned. "Yes, I am. Seventy-five is about all I can do at a time. You know I just did fifty-five with the boys. I can see I'm going to have to work harder . . . Then we'll have a rematch."

"Whenever you feel like it."

She started to walk away, and though they were at work and he should let her go, he couldn't.

"Andrea."

She paused, but didn't turn around. What happened next would tell him a lot about Andrea the woman. Standing his ground, he waited. Until finally she pivoted to face him.

She put her arms around her body and gave him a hard glare.

"Come here."

She hesitated. He knew in an instant that she wanted to come to him. That she wanted the same things he did. But he'd started this in the wrong place at the wrong time.

She was a few steps from her office, so he walked toward her, took her wrist in his hand and led her to her office. Once they were both inside he pushed her away from the open doorway so that her body couldn't be seen from the firehouse.

He leaned down close to her, closed his eyes and breathed

in the very essence of this strong, vibrant woman who had him tied in knots.

"What are you doing?" she asked in a whisper.

"Claiming my prize."

"There was no promise of a prize, Mr. Fields."

"Yes, there was. It has always been understood that when two warriors meet in combat, to the victor go the spoils."

"I'm the spoils?"

"I called you a prize, Andrea."

He leaned down and took her mouth with his. A quick, fierce kiss that satisfied neither of them but left his stamp of ownership on her.

He heard the men returning from outside and pulled back and away from her.

"I'll look forward to our rematch."

Andi's mouth still tingled twenty minutes later while she finished up her paperwork. She went to the filing cabinet to get the duty roster out. Ian would be on her case if she wasn't at Dad's birthday party this year.

The night was always a weird time for her. She slept in the same barracks area as the guys, but she had a curtain around her bed. She never really got a good night's sleep when she was on duty. Over the years she'd distracted herself by playing little games in her mind to help her go to sleep.

Tonight she was almost afraid to close her eyes and dream of Tuck. And she knew she'd dream of him. He was too large in her mind for her to shut him out, and that plain ticked her off.

"He's just a guy," she muttered, slamming the drawer shut and turning toward her desk.

"Who's just a guy?" Tuck said from the doorway. His hair was ruffled as if he'd run his fingers through it.

"Dammit. Don't sneak up on me."

"I wasn't sneaking," he said with a mischievous grin.

He was aware of what he'd done, but if she argued her point, she'd feel like a moron. She knew better than to talk to herself at work. Usually it was Mick who caught her. "What do you want?"

He opened his notebook. "Did you interview Roy Braley?"

"The president of the Polk County Citrus Co-op?" she asked. Roy was one of the most important men in the county. Of course they'd questioned him. But no one suspected him. He was working harder than anyone to revive a failing citrus business in the area.

"Is there really more than one Roy Braley?" Tuck asked in that smart-ass tone of voice that made her want to smack him.

"No, there isn't more than one. I talked to him at the site when we went to the first fire and suspected it was arson."

"What was your take on him?" Tuck asked.

The jokester was gone, and in his place was the arson investigator who knew how to get his job done. This was the guy she'd sent for. No matter how sexy he was or how much he made her remember she was a woman—this was why he was here. And Roy was close to this case.

"Come in and close the door," she said carefully. "We need privacy."

He raised both eyebrows at her. "I thought you'd never ask."

"Don't be a wiseass. Braley is related to McMillan."

Tuck pushed away from the doorjamb and closed the door behind him. He folded his arms over his chest and stayed there, leaning against the door.

Damn, she wanted him. He looked way too sexy standing there, just all-American testosterone waiting for some red-blooded gal to come and snap him up.

"So what'd you think?" he asked.

Damn, she was as bad as he was, and she'd called him to task for eyeing her that first day. "I think . . ." *Come on brain work.* "Roy's not telling me everything. I don't want to send Pete out there to talk to him because of the family connection. And when I called, Roy was in Tallahassee."

"Did McMillan respond to the fires?" he asked, flipping through his notebook and checking his own notes.

"Yes, the first and third fires. He was off duty when the other one was set. Why? You don't think McMillan had anything to do with the fires, do you? He's not the—"

"Slow down. I'm just getting a picture of everything, not accusing him of anything."

"Well, good. He's not your man. Have you been investigating the grove workers and the other business owners in the area?"

"Yes. As well as the other co-ops. I know how to do my job."

"I know that. Just make sure you cover all the bases."

"Are you always this bossy?" he asked.

"Always." She tried not to smile, but something about the way he asked the question made it difficult.

"Want to tell me who you were talking about when I came in?"

"Are we done discussing this case?" Great, she'd hoped he'd forgotten. But she should have known better; Tuck didn't strike her as a man to forget much.

"For now."

"Open the door."

"Not yet. Tell me what man you were talking about."

"Why do you care?" she asked. Even though he'd asked her out, she had the feeling that it was more the challenge of what she represented to him. The tomboy who could hold her own with any man. She'd had guys go after her before because they wanted to be the one man who had an edge over her—not just any edge, but an emotional one.

"I want to know who the competition is."

"For what?" she asked.

"For you."

She'd never had two men after her at the same time. Frankly, from what she knew of men, one was definitely enough. "What would you do if there was competition?" she asked.

"Make sure you realized that I was the only one who could give you what you want."

"What do I want?" she asked.

He didn't move from the door, just watched her with that electric gaze that seemed to see right through the flesh and bone of her body and straight to her shy heart. The part of herself that she hid behind an aggressive take-charge attitude.

"Was I the guy?"

"Yes. Now tell me."

He'd taken two steps toward her when she heard the bell go off. Tuck pivoted, opened the door and walked out without another word.

She pushed away from her desk, grabbing her turnout gear and going to fight a fire, but her mind wasn't on the four-car pile-up on Interstate 4. It was on the blaze in Tucker's eyes.

Chapter 5

Tuck fought the urge to go to Andi's house as soon as he knew she'd be home. Their date was at seven o'clock, and he'd waited all damn day, focusing on his investigation with only about ninety percent of his concentration. Ah, hell, it was probably more like ten percent of his concentration.

The woman haunted him. Finally it was time for their date. And not a minute too soon. He was in a constant state of arousal thanks to her.

Other than the bikini that night at Mick's house, she'd done nothing overt to turn him on except be herself. He couldn't put his finger on it, but something about Andi got to him.

Even just doing her job. He'd never been attracted to another firefighter before, and it had made for a few damned uncomfortable moments at work.

He rapped on her door with his knuckles, feeling more nervous than he should. It was just a date. He might get lucky, and they'd both want to explore the sexual tension between them. Or Andi might decide not to let him behind the wall she used to keep everyone out. Either way, he was looking forward to the evening.

The door opened a crack, letting a waft of air-conditioned air out into the humid evening. "You're late."

He put his hand up to the doorjamb and leaned in. He

could see only a glimpse of her leg. Smooth, bare and tan. Dammit, the woman had fine legs. His palm tingled, remembering the way she'd felt when he'd held her in his arms at Mick's house. "Only five minutes."

She made a *tsk*ing sound and didn't open the door any farther. "And I wore a skirt like you asked me to. That's not the best way to make a good impression."

"What is the best way?" he asked. Andi wasn't like the other women he'd dated. He had kept her waiting precisely because he'd been too anxious. To prove to himself that he was in control of this wildfire that Andi started inside him.

"Being prompt," she said.

"I can't change that. What else is on the list?"

"Dressing nice . . ."

"Check me out," he said.

The door cracked open a bit farther, and he spread his arms to the side. He'd worn a button-down shirt and his good jeans along with boots and a sport jacket.

"Not bad."

"Thanks. My sister warned me women find my "Rub My Weiner For Luck" shirt offensive."

"Smart woman."

She laughed, pushing the door wide open. She wore a short, filmy, cobalt blue skirt and a halter top that barely covered her stomach. He groaned as he saw her.

Her hair hung in soft waves to her shoulders, and her lips were glossy from some kind of lipstick. He knew he shouldn't have stereotyped, but honestly, he'd never expected her to dress like this for their date.

"You're staring."

"Am I?" he asked, but he couldn't stop looking at her legs, picturing them spread just a little wider while he caressed them. He skimmed his gaze up her body, staring at her flat stomach and the edge of her shirt.

She cleared her throat, and he tore his gaze away from her body. Damn, she rattled him. From the sparkle in her eye, she knew it.

"I'm beginning to think you have some kind of affliction."

"What kind?"

"The fixated visually kind."

"I hope not; my sister advised me that was creepy."

Andi laughed again. He liked the sound of it.

"I don't have any sisters to give me advice, but my brothers never fail to react when a woman surprises them. Do we have time for a drink?"

He'd made reservations for eight o'clock, so even though he was late, they had about twenty minutes. "Yes."

"Wanna come in?" she asked, tipping her head to the side. But she didn't move. She just stood there looking like something out of a dream.

"Stop teasing me, woman." He stepped closer to her, deliberately crowding her with his body.

"Why?" she asked, not backing up an inch.

"Because I might retaliate," he said, edging his left foot forward until his leg was between both of hers.

She shifted subtly. Not away from him, but not really closer either.

"And that's supposed to . . . ?"

"Intimidate you," he said.

She walked her fingers up the front of his shirt. Toying with the button he'd left undone at the neck. Her fingers were soft and cool as she touched him. "Ah, sorry to disappoint you, but I'm not afraid of you."

"I am disappointed."

"I thought your ego was stronger than that," she said, pulling her hand back.

"It is. I'm disappointed you'd lie."

"Who says I'm lying?"

"Your trembling fingers," he said, lifting her hand where they both could see it.

He smoothed his thumb over her knuckles and watched her eyes. They weren't shuttered as they usually were but wide open, and he saw fear there.

"What's the matter?" he asked, wishing she'd confide in him but knowing she wouldn't.

She tugged her hand free. "Nothing."

She pivoted on her heel and walked into her house, leaving the door open. He stepped inside and closed it behind him.

"Do you want a beer or not?"

"Not now."

"Let me grab my purse and we can go."

"Not yet."

"Don't push, Tuck. I'm not—"

"I'm going to push and keep on pushing until I figure out what makes you tick."

She stopped walking away and turned back toward him. Standing in the shadows just beyond the reach of her foyer lights. "That's what I'm afraid of. That you think this is just a game."

He saw then that she was telling him the truth, and he hurt deep inside that the control game he'd played with himself had in fact hurt her.

He closed the gap between them. Leaned down and took her mouth in a kiss that proved that whatever lay between them wasn't a game.

Tuck's kiss was fierce, leaving no room for the doubts that had plagued her as she'd watched the hands on the clock tick past the time he was supposed to pick her up.

She'd been stood up before, and she hated how that felt. It awakened all of her old fears and insecurities, and she didn't like it. Especially since she couldn't lie to herself and say that it didn't matter. Not with Tuck. He made her want things she'd tried very hard to forget were important.

Things like his arms around her. He wrapped her in his embrace, his hand tangled in her hair, pulling her head back farther so that he could plunder her mouth. His tongue thrust deep into her mouth, tasting her thoroughly. His fingers flexed against the back of her skull, and in an instant she was surrounded by him.

He leaned back against the wall and slid his leg between hers. His hands sweeping down her spine, rubbing over the exposed skin at the small of her back. His callused palm was a sweet abrasion there. She shivered and canted her hips closer to his. She needed more. So much more.

But he tightened his hands on her, holding her still. His tongue flicked over hers and then plunged deep to the back of her mouth.

It reminded her that he was in control of this embrace. She allowed him that dominion over her. She slipped her arms around his lean waist and held him to her.

His hand on her back slid lower, cupping her butt and pulling her more fully into him. She wedged her hands between both of them, flexing her fingernails against his chest. Her own tongue darting into his mouth, tangling with his.

She kept her grip on him strong, sure. Driving out all of the fears and doubts that had swamped her before he arrived. His kiss was dominant. He left no room for her to hedge or maneuver. This wasn't like the embrace they'd shared at Mick's house. Tuck was putting his stamp on her. Making her very aware that tonight was going to be different.

She pulled back, but he didn't loosen his grip. After a minute, he lifted his head to stare down at her. She felt her control slipping away under his intense gaze.

She reached up to cage his face between her hands. She wanted to give him back the kind of kiss he'd just given her, but she couldn't. Instead she dropped soft, gentle kisses on his face and felt deep inside a shifting of whom she'd always allowed herself to be.

Tuck traced his hand over her face, outlining her cheekbones and her jaw, before rubbing his thumb over her lips. They were swollen and sensitive from his mouth. And when he pushed his thumb between her lips, she bit him lightly.

He leaned down and took her mouth again. Kissing her deeply, anchoring her to him with his will and his calm control over both of them. She knew he was aroused, felt his erection nudging at her stomach, but he never changed the languid sweeps of his tongue or his hands. Just held her in a web of sensuality that slowly eroded all of her defenses.

Fear ate at her deep inside, not of Tuck, but of herself. She was losing her restraint. Those safety measures that had always protected her from men in the past.

"That's better," he said, his breath brushing over her face.

"What is?" she asked, forcing herself not to lean forward and rest against his shoulder. Even though that was what she craved.

"Everything's better now. I've been thinking about your mouth all day. Wanting to taste you again. Needing to really claim my prize from yesterday."

"You kissed me in my office," she reminded him. She tried to marshal her thoughts, tried to regain her footing and somehow find her balance. But it was impossible when she felt his hard-on against her lower body and his hands on her backside.

He shook his head. "Not really. Not like I wanted to."

"How was that?" she asked, but she knew what he'd wanted. She'd wanted it, too. To take his mouth completely and reach that point where both of them forgot they were separate people.

He sucked her lower lip into his mouth, before taking

her completely again. "I want to kiss you until we're both naked and I'm buried deep in that curvy body of yours."

She shivered at the images his words conjured. She knew she had a choice to make. The choice was more than having sex with Tuck, because she knew that she wasn't going to be able to keep him from her bed. She wanted him, and she saw no reason not to have him. But the real choice was how to handle the sex.

Tuck seemed to see her vulnerabilities, and she hated that. She'd have to be on her toes and aggressive with him. The same way she'd been with every man. Make sure he realized that having sex with her didn't mean she was weak.

"I don't know what to say," she replied. Honestly, no man had ever said such a thing to her before. And she wasn't sure she liked it. Tuck kept her off balance, which she suspected he did on purpose.

"Don't say anything. Just think about it while we're having dinner," he said, gently separating their bodies.

The restaurant Tuck had chosen was in Orlando about a forty-minute drive from Andi's house. He'd deliberately chosen a place where they wouldn't run into her friends. He wanted to find out her secrets for himself. Not have them joked or laughed about by the guys who made up her family at the firehouse.

Tuck had been to Orlando a few times before to help out on investigations and liked the town, which was a blend of urban and rural. A small town that had gotten big without really realizing it. (Because of the tourists who flocked there, the entire town was always a Resort casual.)

The Samba Room catered to a mix of upper-level managers from the neighboring theme parks Disney, Universal and SeaWorld and tourists. There was a very sexy atmosphere to the place, which suited Tuck's plans for the evening. The Latin food reminded him of his days in Miami, and the music was pure bossa nova-salsa. Since it was only Thursday there was no dancing tonight, but there was a small live band.

"I love this place. It reminds me of home," Andi said once they were seated.

"Where is home?"

"Miami. Well, South Dade actually, but I love Miami. I miss it sometimes."

"Then why did you choose Polk County?"

She shrugged, and the waiter came to take their drink order. Andi chose a mojito, and Tuck got a Dos Equis. She shifted back in her seat, listening to the bossa nova rhythm. He sensed she'd escaped this place and was somewhere in her own memories.

"Tell me why you left Miami," he said, once they had their drinks.

She took a sip of hers. "Why is that important?"

He shrugged. He wasn't going to tell her that all of her secrets were important to him because they kept him out. They preserved a distance between them that was becoming intolerable.

"It just is."

"My dad is larger than life, and I couldn't work for him. He's too . . ."

"What?" he asked after a few moments had passed and it became obvious she wasn't going to continue.

"I don't know how to put it into words. I just needed to get out from under his shadow. To find my own way. Being a firefighting O'Roarke in South Dade means you have to live with the old man's reputation."

"And you wanted to see if you could stand on your own," he said.

"Something like that. I didn't want to take any short-cuts."

"Really?"

"Stop teasing me."

"Why? I like it. Your men treat you like you're some kind of Amazon goddess."

"That's the only way I want to be treated."

"Really? I'd have said it's the only thing you'd tolerate because it leaves you free to stay above them."

"I don't think I'm better than my men, Tuck. That's not a fair thing to say."

"I didn't mean it that way. I meant that you keep yourself untouchable to the men."

"I have to be. We work together. I can't have them lusting after me."

She flushed as soon as the words left her mouth.

"What if one of them did lust after you?" he asked, because if it happened while he was there, he wasn't sure he'd be able to stand back and let her deal with it. Something about Andi brought all his primitive instincts to the surface. He wanted to claim her as his own.

To put a stamp on her so that every man who glanced at her would realize she belonged to him. Even if it was only temporary. And a part of Tuck acknowledged it would be only temporary. He'd never stayed in one place or with one woman long.

"No one does, so the point is moot. I've never been to the Samba Room before. Have you?" she asked.

"Yes. Don't change the subject. We were talking about lust."

"No, *we* weren't. You were."

"Hey," he said, spreading his hands. "You brought the subject up."

She rolled her eyes and took another sip of her drink. "I must have been insane."

He laughed and took a drink of his cold beer. The waiter

approached, and Tuck ordered a satay sampler platter as an appetizer. They placed their dinner orders and were once again alone.

Andi sipped her drink carefully and studied the décor in the room. The way her gaze drifted told him she was deliberately avoiding him.

He reached across the table and took her hand in his. Her fingers were long and lean. Very feminine. He knew she was strong, had seen her in action on the fire engine. But there was still that delicate, womanly grace to her.

She sighed. "I'm not talking about lust with you."

"Afraid?"

"What is it with you and fear?"

"Honestly?"

She nodded.

"I can see you retreat whenever I get close. And I'm not sure what it is I'm doing that frightens you so much."

She bit her lip, looking away.

"Don't do that."

She glanced up at him, her eyes wide. "I'm not scared of you *per se*, Tuck."

Their appetizer arrived, and Tuck smiled impatiently at the waiter, wanting him to leave. He wished now they'd stayed in where he could have her all to himself. There were too many distractions here, and he couldn't get to the heart of the matter—the heart of Andi.

She tugged on her hand, but he held tight.

"Tell me what you fear?"

"I'm not sure I can put it into words. It has something to do with the way you stare at me as if you're able to see deep into my soul."

He rubbed his thumb over her knuckles and then feathered his touch up to her wrist. "I only wish that were true."

Chapter 6

Tuck showered Andi with attention throughout the meal. There were no more probing questions, just an attention to her needs and likes that she'd never before experienced.

Something about Tuck made her remember that she liked being a woman. She didn't have to prove that she was strong and ballsy with him. Instead she just relaxed, enjoying the feelings of home that the restaurant inspired. She'd ordered pork barbacoa, which reminded her of the many backyard cookouts she'd had as a kid with the Cuban neighbors. The pork was wrapped in banana leaves and tasted utterly delicious.

She paused as she realized that by avoiding going home to see her dad, she was also cutting herself off from all the things she loved about her hometown.

"Do you like your dinner?" Tucker asked.

"It's delicious. Want to try some?"

He nodded.

She lifted her plate so he could reach it, but he shook his head.

"Feed me."

There was a sensual edge to his voice, and she knew that this was just one more layer of the evening. The one she'd been focused on when he'd come to her door and claimed her with that kiss.

She set her plate down carefully and picked up her own fork. The pork barbeque was tender, and she scooped up a piece of it as well as the gringo rice.

She lifted the fork to his mouth, he opened it and she slipped the tines inside. Their eyes met and held. She couldn't move for a second. But then she became aware of their surroundings. Of the music playing, the other diners eating and Tuck's leg brushing hers under the table. She pulled her hand back, setting her fork down.

Everything inside her was now focused on this man. Everything. What the hell was happening? How could he cause a reaction deep inside her? Did he realize what he was doing to her?

How could she keep that knowledge from him?

She put her hands in her lap, tangling them in the napkin. Her joy at rediscovering the sounds, tastes and memories of her youth began dimming due to the very real fear that this man was going to force her to face other parts of the past that she didn't want to revisit.

"Andi?"

The way he said her name. The amount of caring and concern in his voice further unnerved her, and she determined then that she couldn't let Tuck see any farther inside her. Why had she relaxed her guard around him to begin with?

She took her highball glass and finished her mojito in one swallow. Frantically searching for something to say. Some way to pull back from the edge on which she'd been hovering. "Did you like it?"

"I've always enjoyed eating from a beautiful woman's hand."

She glanced up at him. She saw something in his eyes she couldn't easily identify. Something swift and predatory. With those words he'd reduced her to one of many, and he'd taken something from her and from the evening. "Don't do that."

"What?" he asked, taking a bite of his dinner and chewing it.

He acted as if nothing had happened between them, and perhaps it hadn't. But she noticed the betraying clench of his fingers on his own fork. The tight white lines that indicated he knew she'd been trying to back away from him emotionally.

"Don't play games with me."

"You started it," he said, but not in a school-yard way.

"What game am I playing?"

"Hide-and-seek," he said, reaching across the table to take her hand in his.

"Well, I did a horrible job of it. Not only did you find me, you knew exactly what to say to make me come out fighting."

"That I did. I seem to always know with you."

"Why?"

"Why what?"

"Why you? I've dated other men, and they . . ."

"They were happy to just be out with a pretty woman."

"Yes. Why aren't you? We have to work together. We're going to see each other at different points in our careers. This could get awkward later."

"It's never going to get awkward, Andrea. I promise you that."

"How can you promise such a thing? I know that men think they can control—"

"Men think? I thought the common opinion was that men simply reacted."

"Don't. You want to joke it away, but the truth is, I'm not good at hiding my feelings, and you keep insisting on making me feel things for you."

"You say that like it's a bad thing. But I can't imagine not holding you in my arms and seeing your eyes lit with the passion you feel for me."

She shook her head at the image his words evoked. She could see that as well. Abruptly her plans for the evening changed. She couldn't go back and sleep with him because he wouldn't be content to just have sex with her. He was telling her subtly that he was going to strip her bare of not just her clothing, but of those layers she used to protect herself.

And she couldn't allow that. She also didn't want to go home to a lonely bed. Instead of leaning back in her chair and crossing her arms over her chest like she wanted to, she leaned forward and stroked her finger down the side of his face.

She watched his pupils dilate as she slipped off her sandal and stroked her foot up the inside of his calf. Andi knew a thing or two about distracting men. And now that she realized Tuck was after more than her ass, she knew how to protect it.

How to take what she wanted and still escape with her heart intact. She prayed only that her plan wouldn't backfire, because if he saw through her game . . . Well, let's just say Tuck played to win.

Tuck hadn't been sure what he'd get from Andi when they had dinner. He knew she was a very passionate woman and that it took little to get her to react. He didn't want their relationship to be based on him always daring her to do something.

"I wish the dance floor was open tonight."

"Me, too," she said. There was an aggressive sparkle in her eyes that made him pause.

This wasn't the woman whose hand had trembled when she'd fed him a bite of her dinner. Where had she gone? Or had he imagined the entire thing? Was he seeing in Andi what he needed to see? A woman hiding from her true self behind a ballsy attitude because that was the kind of woman who turned him on.

"Are we going back to Auburndale now?" she asked as they left the restaurant.

A warm breeze stirred the night air; Andi stopped walking, tipping her head back to stare up at the night sky. His whole being clenched and tightened. His blood flowing heavier in his veins, pooling in his groin. His senses tuned to this woman who was still a mystery. Every new thing he learned about her showed him only that there were more secrets hidden from him.

"Tuck?"

"What?" he asked, unable to tear his eyes from the smooth skin of her midriff. He wished he'd placed his hand at the small of her back when they were leaving. Why hadn't he?

"Are we going back home?" she asked, laughter in her voice. "It's not my legs you're staring at this time."

He gave her a rueful grin and gave up the struggle to keep her from seeing how she affected him. He put his hand on her lower back. Spreading his fingers to caress as much of her skin as possible.

His hand was large enough to almost span her waist. It emphasized what Tuck had always known, that for all her strength she was still smaller than he was. It excited him to realize that he'd have to be in control at all times. If he let his control slip for a second, he might overwhelm her.

Or would he? Andi wasn't like other women he'd dated. She was strong. Stronger than this sexy female body revealed.

"No, it's not. It's that damned smooth stomach of yours."

"Like it, do you? I've thought about getting my belly button pierced, but the guys would notice, and they'd rib me to no end."

"Why are you letting that stop you? You'd kick their butts and get them back in line in no time."

"It's just better to never let them see me as anything other than one of the guys."

"Better for whom?"

"For everyone."

"I don't think so," he said.

She shrugged, and the flirty part of her disappeared. "You never answered my question. Are we going home now?"

"Not yet. I still have a surprise or two up my sleeve."

"I bet you do."

He led her to his truck. He had a raised wheelbase and used that excuse to lift her into the truck. He kept his hands at her waist, holding her so that her legs dangled over the side of the seat in the open door.

His face was level with her breasts, and he leaned forward for a second. He ran his tongue down the vee formed by her halter top. Tasting her sweet skin. Her hands fell to his shoulders.

"What are you doing?"

"Teasing myself."

"I'm not into exhibitionism."

"Ever tried it?"

"No."

"Then you're not sure."

She shrugged, causing her breasts to brush against his face. He leaned in, inhaling deeply. Closing his eyes while he struggled for control. He could take what he wanted and end this game now. Andi wasn't saying no to sex, but he wanted more than her curvy little body. He wanted an entrée to her soul, and he wasn't going to find it without freeing her from her own fears.

He lifted his hands to the tie at the back of her neck.

"Tuck, no."

He looked into her eyes. Watched them widen, but not with fear. Her nipples were tight against the material of her shirt. He leaned closer, kissing her softly, coaxing the response he needed from her. When her fingers tightened on his shoulders he knew he'd find out if she was scared or titillated by his actions.

Glancing over his shoulder, he made sure they were alone in the dark parking lot. No cars were nearby, and no patrons stood outside. Just the two of them for a moment. Any second someone could intrude, and he counted on that fact to excite her.

He loosened the knot at the back of her neck but left the material draped over her body. Then took a small step back.

"It's your choice. Try it and see if you like it."

She brought her hands up to her own shoulders. "What if someone comes along?"

"You're protected by the door on that side. And I'm right here."

She stroked her fingers down the edge of the material. "Do you want to see me, Tuck?"

"Hell, yes. I want to see you, touch you, taste you. But I want to make sure you want it, too. Offer yourself to me, Andi. Show me those pretty breasts of yours."

She slid her fingers back up to her neck, and he waited. His erection strained the front of his jeans. The material cutting painfully into him as she tipped her head to the side and ran her tongue along her bottom lip.

Then she slowly retied the knot. "I think anticipation is one of the pure joys in life."

He groaned deep in his throat, but accepted her answer. He waited until she was seated comfortably in the truck and closed the door. He paused behind the vehicle to adjust himself and regroup.

Andi wasn't sure she'd made the right choice, but making out with Tuck . . . She wasn't ready for that yet. He steered the truck away from the interstate and instead found the quiet back roads that led behind Disney. He found a quiet area and pulled off the road.

"What are we doing?" she asked.

"I thought I'd show you some fireworks." He shifted out from under the steering wheel, unfastened her seat belt and lifted her onto his lap. A few minutes later he was leaning against the passenger door and had her cradled against his body, her back to his chest and his arm around her waist.

"I've seen your fireworks before," she said dryly. "Your kisses are fantastic, but I think calling them fireworks is a little weird."

He squeezed her for a second, feathering kisses down the side of her neck. "Not just mine this time. You get a great view of the park's show from here."

She said nothing for a few minutes, but she was pleased that he'd planned this. He still had a hard-on, but he held her against him as though he'd be content to do that for the rest of the night.

His embrace gave her a chance to regain her equilibrium. And to realize she was ready for more than just fireworks with Tuck.

"What kind of music do you like?" he asked, his hand stroking down her arm.

She clasped his other hand in hers and ran her fingers over his palm. He had a strong hand. In the moonlight spilling through the windshield she traced his lifeline and wished she knew more about palmistry. Wished she had some way of looking at his hand and divining his secrets.

He'd asked about music. That was another area where she felt as if she didn't really fit in. "Why do you ask?"

"Why do you think?"

There was a dry tone to his voice, and she realized he used it when he thought she was being contrary for no good reason.

"Um . . . I guess country." It was what most of the people she knew listened to. She'd gone to see Tim McGraw with Mick and Sara earlier in the year.

"You guess?" Tuck asked.

This time his words were spoken into her ear. His touch skimmed over her skin softly, and when he reached her head, he pushed until she rested on his shoulder. Lowering his mouth, he dropped those too-hot kisses against the length of her neck. Sending shivers of awareness coursing through her.

"So what do you like about country music?" he asked against her skin.

"Nothing really," she breathed. She turned her head toward him and found his eyes open. He watched her like . . . She didn't know how to describe it. But there was something in his eyes that said he wanted to know everything about her. It warmed her to her heart. Never had any man—not even her dad and brothers—really cared about who she was. Who she really was.

She lifted her hand and rubbed her fingers over the stubble at his jaw. She liked the way it felt under her fingers.

"Then why'd you say country?"

"That's what we listen to at work. That or heavy metal."

"We're not at work, sweetheart, and I want to know what you like."

"Don't laugh."

"Unless you say polka, I promise not to."

"Who would say polka?"

"I've been sworn to secrecy."

She laughed at his silliness and then quietly said, "Eighties. I listen to that eighties station that comes out of Tampa when no one else is around."

He reached across her and fiddled with his Sirius radio dial until the eighties station came in. Culture Club was singing "Do You Really Want To Hurt Me?" And Andi couldn't help but wonder if Tuck would end up hurting her.

"I was in love with Boy George for a while," she confessed.

"I'm not sure how to tell you this, but you're not his type."

She laughed quietly. "I know. But his voice . . . He sings about heartbreak so well."

"Yes, he does. Who broke your heart?"

"Who broke yours?"

"I asked you first."

"So?"

"I like eighties music, too."

"Chicken."

"Would you really tell me?"

"Yes. But only if you confess first. I want to keep things even between us."

"Why?"

"Because you're too cocky for your own good."

He shifted his hips, pressing his erection up against her backside. "Only around you."

She moved her behind, rubbing her body over his in a caress. "I'm not complaining. Just asking for a level playing field."

He said nothing, but his hands covered her hips, holding her still until they each were breathing calmly. She leaned back against him, feeling safe in his arms. The fireworks started to go off, and she tipped her head to the side to get a glimpse of Tuck. To try to figure out what he was doing—what kind of game he was playing—because there were times when this night felt too real and too close to her fantasies of what a man and a woman should be together.

She had a feeling that making love with Tuck would feel just as right, and she didn't know if she was ready for that with him.

Chapter 7

Tuck drove toward Andi's home without a plan. The evening had taken a few unexpected twists and turns, and he hoped he'd have enough time in Polk County with Andi. For once he wasn't eager to finish his investigation and move on to the next one.

He wanted to linger with her. He glanced over at her. She sat resting her head against the window, staring up at the moon. He'd accomplished one of his goals this evening, getting her to open up about her past. They couldn't move forward until they both had made peace with the past.

For Tuck, moving on was the way he dealt with his memories. Never committing to anything or allowing anyone to mean too much.

The Police were singing their song of devotion that bordered on obsession, "Every Breath You Take," and he was hoping that he wasn't obsessed with Andi for the wrong reasons. In the parking lot when she'd backed off, he'd let her go, but he knew that he wasn't going to be able to do that again. His control was slipping, and he wanted her.

He didn't care why she wanted him right now. He didn't care if it was just physical, and that pissed him off. Because he knew that if he weren't so turned on, it would matter.

He rolled down his window, letting the night air stir

through the cab of the truck. Andi sat up and looked over at him.

"You okay?" she asked. She turned her body so she was facing him.

"Yeah. Just needed some fresh air."

She smiled at him, her expression soft and open. His gut clenched. She wasn't making this easier.

She rolled her window down as they left the interstate and wound their way through the dark county roads that led back to her house. She put her arm out the window.

"When I was a kid my dad used to take us all out camping. He'd put us in the back of his pickup—those were the days when you could do it and no one thought you were a bad parent—and we'd all huddle in the back and let the wind rush by . . . It seemed like we never had any problems when the wind blew like that."

She closed her eyes, and he wished he had a memory like that to visit. He never thought of why he always moved on, but he knew a part of it was tied to his father.

"Did your dad do that?"

Tuck shook his head. "No. He didn't."

"One of my girlfriend's dads hated being outdoors. He'd never pitched a tent or anything like that. My dad used to call him sissy-boy. Gotta love the old man."

"Well, at least you know where you stand with him. Did the neighbor ever hear about his nickname?"

"Yes. Mr. Peters said that he could hold his own in a boardroom and make mincemeat of Dad on his own turf."

"I bet your dad saw that as a challenge."

"I thought so, too, but he surprised me by letting it go."

"What was it like being the only girl in a house full of men?" he asked. Her father's words about the neighbor were telling Tuck that Andi wasn't ever allowed to indulge in those traits that all women carried with them.

He knew from watching his mom and his sister that

women used emotions to deal with and diffuse situations. And he knew from being a guy how uncomfortable that could make a man.

"It was okay. What about you? You mentioned a sister. Any other siblings?"

He was quiet for a minute, realizing she'd changed the subject like she always did whenever he asked about her family. "Just my sister, Jayne. Where do you fall in the birth order?"

"Youngest. You?" she asked.

He knew how she felt as far as family was concerned. He didn't really want to discuss his. "Oldest."

"Well, that explains your bossy tendencies," she said, pulling her arm in and turning to face him.

He tried to keep his eyes on the road, but the moon was full tonight and he could clearly see that the hem of her skirt had risen a good inch when she'd turned. Her legs were going to be the death of him if he didn't feel them wrapped around him—soon. "I'm not bossy. I just like to get my own way."

She put her arm along the back of the seat, and he was hyperaware of her fingers just inches from his shoulder.

"Uh, hate to break it to you, but that's bossy," she said.

"No, it's not. If you'd just do what I want you to, then I wouldn't have to boss."

She chuckled, and he felt good about that because there was always such an aura of seriousness around her.

"I'll remember that," she said.

"Does your family boss you around a lot?"

"I don't know. I guess they try to, but we're known as the fighting O'Roarkes."

"Why?"

"Precisely why you'd think. We spend all of our time making our opinions heard and not backing down. We're really good at two things—fighting fires and just plain fighting."

"I think you're good at other things as well, Andi."

She tipped her head to the side. "Fireworks?"

"Yes, that. But you're also good at listening and leading."

"Those are traits of a good firefighter."

"Not every firefighter, some people are better at following."

She glanced away, out the window. He sensed her drifting away from him and had to strain to hear her when she spoke.

"Some people never get the chance to lead."

She said little else as he continued driving to her house. But those words struck a chord deep inside him. He seldom let anyone lead him. He knew she had no idea that her words cut him, and he reminded himself he wanted it that way.

Tuck pulled into her driveway and killed the lights. She was acutely aware of him sitting just a few feet from her. Acutely aware of his scent and the rhythm of his breathing. Acutely aware that this was a man who had yet to react the way she expected him to.

"So?" he said into the darkness.

Her carport blocked the light of the moon, and her small porch light wasn't strong enough to reach them where they were.

She took a deep breath and turned to face him. "Want to come in?"

"Hell, yes. But I know I'm not going to be satisfied with anything you offer me save yourself."

"Who talks like that, Tuck?" He confused her. She knew he wanted her. Twenty minutes ago she had been pressed intimately to his erection, and now he was warning her. Once again the curse of the good buddy struck. It seemed no matter how hard she tried to leave that girl in the dust, she was always there.

"Maybe I meant my words to be a caution—save yourself."

"From what?" she asked, getting a little ticked off at him. No, not really at Tuck. She was angry with herself. Just one night she wanted to be the kind of woman that a man couldn't resist. Not any man, she acknowledged. This man. She wanted him to be overcome by lust and not be spouting warnings and backing off.

"From me. I'm a rambler, Andi, and you're not. It should matter more to me, but right now . . . it doesn't."

She rolled her eyes at that. "I'm a firefighter by blood and by calling, Tucker Fields. I live for danger."

"You live for the kind of danger that you can fight with a ladder and a hose. The kind of danger that you walk into with a crew."

"Don't be so quick to isolate me. You're used to coming to the game after it's been played. To observing the way it all went down and making a decision based on what happened."

"Are you inferring that I might not be able to play this game?"

"I'd be an idiot to do that. But I think you're putting too much emphasis on my shortcomings."

He cursed under his breath with the savage intensity that she'd grown up around. She waited until he was done.

"I'm just pointing out the obvious."

"The obvious. Dammit, woman, you must know I don't think you have any shortcomings."

"Then why do you keep warning me off?"

"Because I know myself well enough to know that I'm not going to let you maintain that wall you put up between yourself and everyone. I'm not going to be satisfied with making love to the Andi O'Roarke who's everyone's pal. I'm going to make love to you until the barriers come down and you can't hide anymore."

She shivered, rubbing her hands up and down her arms. She fumbled for the door handle, then made herself stop. She wasn't going to run away from him. He had as many barriers as she did, and though she knew she wasn't necessarily the woman who could break them down, she'd always been able to help her friends find peace with their weaknesses. What was Tuck's? Because honestly, he didn't seem to have any from where she sat.

That was all she'd ever wanted, but truthfully she was afraid to reach out and find that peace. Afraid that there really wasn't anything underneath her vulnerabilities. She'd spent her entire life trying to prove she was strong enough, tough enough, man enough to be her father's daughter that being a woman had always been hard on her.

In fact, her lovers often complained she was too aggressive. Why wasn't she with Tuck?

She scooted closer to him in the cab. Slid across the bench seat until her knee bumped his thigh. She knelt there, leaning forward toward him.

She traced her fingers over his face in the dark. Traced the arch of his eyebrow and the blade of his nose. Then bent down to taste him. His mouth opened under hers, but she took her time, fanning the embers that had been banked during their companionable ride from Disney to her house.

She teased her tongue over the seam of his lips, slowly dipping inside, and when she felt him respond, she backed away. Returning again and again for brief forays into his mouth. He tasted of the beer he'd drank at dinner and something else she couldn't define.

She put her hands on his shoulders, felt the strength that he took for granted. The strength that made a mockery of her own. She kneaded his muscles, skimming her finger back toward his neck and then unfastening his buttons until her fingers could slip inside his shirt and she touched his flesh.

His mouth moved on hers then. Even though she was in

the dominant position, he took control. His tongue sweeping into her mouth. His teeth scraping along her tongue as he sucked on it.

His hands slid down her back, up under her shirt, and she felt his fingers at the tie at the back of her neck.

She knew what he wanted. Knew even that this time he wasn't going to ask. But he stopped.

"Let's go inside. I want to see you spread out in front of me."

She edged away from him, out of the truck. Fumbling in her small clutch purse for her key. But Tuck came up next to her, putting his arm around her, pulling her into his body, tucking her as it were under the curve of his shoulder. She felt so safe there that her nerves melted away.

She pulled the key from her purse and handed it to him. He took it and opened her door, leading her into her own home. He closed the door behind them and then turned to face her in her small foyer.

She reached behind him to turn on the light, and she wished for a moment she hadn't. She couldn't bear the intensely sexy look in his eyes.

Tuck leaned back against the door, happy to have her all alone at last. She nervously crossed her arms over her waist and then dropped them. He liked that he'd rattled her. He'd like nothing better than to toss her over his shoulder and carry her to her bedroom or the sofa, anywhere really. But he wanted the anticipation he'd been carefully building all night to continue working.

"Are you coming in or just going to hang out here?" she asked when he leaned back against the door.

"Maybe," he said. She'd brought him into her house despite his warnings, and he'd taken what she'd said to heart. She was a big girl and could look out for herself. Except that he kept catching glimpses of vulnerability in her eyes that made him want to protect her. Even from herself.

"Maybe?" she asked, tipping her head to the side and taking one slow step toward him. "I think I know how to change your mind."

"I know you do." Everything about her was incredibly sensual. The way she walked, the way she moved, the way she slipped her shoes off and flexed her toes against the cold tile in the foyer.

He glanced down at her bare feet. Her toes were un-painted, but she had a toe ring on her left foot, and he saw the gemstone wink at him when the light hit it.

She cocked her hip, bending one leg, and let her knee fall outward. He realized that control was the issue here. Which he'd been hanging on to just barely all evening.

She skimmed her fingers up the inside of her thigh just to the bottom of her skirt and then stopped. He groaned, un-able to help himself. A giggle escaped her, but when he glanced up she just shrugged.

She lifted her fingers to the tie at the back of her neck, and he watched it flutter out of her hands. She teasingly drew one side down, revealing the full white globe of her left breast, and then drew it back up.

"Sweetheart, I've been fantasizing about your breasts all evening."

"So that would work? Just a flash of skin and you're mine."

"Depends on the skin," he said, but he knew that he'd take her however he could get her.

She lowered the fabric again, this time revealing the outer curve of her nipple. It puckered against the skin, and he noticed she rubbed her finger over it quickly while re-turning the strap to the back of her neck.

"Am I stereotyping you as a breast man?" she asked, taking another step toward him.

There was no stereotyping about it. He was a breast man and a leg man and everything-about-them-man. He had always loved women's bodies. Their curves, their softness, their inherent differences, and tonight was no different.

"Give it a try and see," he said, wondering how long he could hold out. And that became the challenge. He sensed this was another one of her tests to see whether he'd go for the quick payoff or hang in there for the endurance run.

"Follow me," she said, pivoting on her heel and walking away. Her hips swayed with each step she took, the hem of her skirt flirting around the back of her thighs, and he fought the urge to follow for a second, then walked after her.

She stopped in the middle of her living room. Glancing back over her shoulder at him. He groaned, hoping she had no idea of the power she held over him in this moment.

"Have a seat."

"Not here. I want to see your bedroom."

"You'll have to earn that right."

"Fair enough."

He settled into a large overstuffed chair that was positioned in front of a wide plate-glass window overlooking her small patio.

"Am I where you want me?" he asked, bending down to remove his boots and socks.

"Almost. Could you take off your shirt?"

He pushed to his feet and unbuttoned his shirt and then took it off. Tossing it on the couch. He stood there for a second, then flexed his pecs and watched her eyes narrow.

"Your turn," he said.

"Whoever said this was a game of even-Steven."

"Sweetheart, you are walking a very fine line here," he said.

She smiled at him and let the left tie drop, exposing one breast. He took a step forward, but she held her hand up. "Not yet."

He kept on coming, not stopping until she was in his arms. Her one breast brushed his chest. Her nipple felt soft and smooth, like velvet against his skin. He dipped his head and caught her mouth with his.

He captured her hands in his and twisted them behind her back so that she couldn't move. Shifting his shoulders, he brought her more fully into his body, and for a moment he just held her.

Enjoyed the feel of this one woman pressed up against him. He nudged her legs apart and pushed his thigh up between hers. He grabbed her butt and pulled her closer to him. Through the fabric of her skirt he didn't feel a panty line. Which brought his head up.

"Tell me you're wearing panties," he said, his voice gruff.

"A thong," she said.

He swept his hands up under her skirt, cupping the cool bare skin of her ass and then tracing the line of fabric nestled between her curves.

He slipped his fingers lower, exploring the humid warmth of her body. Her fingernails scored his chest, and he loved the feeling of her in his arms.

He explored her folds through the silky fabric of her underwear before sliding his hands underneath and touching her skin. The curls between her legs were damp with her desire.

"I think you want me," he said.

"Is that what that means?" She rotated her shoulders, rubbing her nipples against his chest.

He hid his smile in the curve of her shoulder, biting softly at the spot where her pulse beat strongly against her neck.

He slipped his fingers inside her and bent to capture her nipple in his mouth.

Chapter 8

Andrea knew she was way out of her safe zone, but like the thrill of entering a fiery building, she couldn't resist Tucker or the games she knew he was playing. The air-conditioning clicked on, blowing cool air over her, but Tuck's body heat kept her warm. She cradled his head in her hands, held him to her breasts while he suckled from her.

He moved closer, forcing her legs wider, lifting her off the ground. She arched into him, feeling the bite of his belt buckle against her inner thighs, as she wrapped her legs around his waist.

The rhythm of the bossa nova from dinner started beating in the back of her head, and soon her heart picked up the tempo. She forgot about everything except Tuck and the feelings he was drawing from her with each tug of his mouth on her breast. The feel of his thick hair in her hands.

His hand skimmed over her, tracing random patterns as he moved his callused fingers along her skin. She tried to find her bearings, tried to find an anchor in the sensual storm he was creating within her, but could only hold tighter to his head.

For once Andi didn't feel awkward or shy in his presence. She felt as though her small breasts were enough for Tuck and that she was woman enough for this man. She closed her eyes and let the fact that she had to work with him for the next few weeks drop away. The world narrowed to only the two of them.

He let her slide down his body. His mouth on her, his one big hand holding her wrists together, the other one roaming over her, and the kind of arousal she'd always dreamed of but had never felt before flooding through her. Pumping through her body with every beat of her heart.

"Clasp your elbows behind your back so I don't have to hold your arms."

"Why?" she asked, startled out of her fantasy. She wasn't sure she could do it. She'd always been the one to take charge, but with Tuck she sensed that it was okay to let him lead.

Please, God, don't let me be wrong, Andi thought. Then she groaned inwardly as she realized it was too late to back out even if it was wrong. She was standing naked breasts to naked chest with him. He had his hands under her skirt, and she felt an orgasm building inside her.

"Because I asked you to," he said, dropping nibbling kisses along her neck. "And I don't have anything to tie your wrists with."

Wait a minute. "Uh, Tuck . . ."

She pulled back, and he reluctantly loosened his hold on her wrists. There was giving up the lead, and then there was giving up control, and no way could she do that. Everything had to be even. She couldn't be the only one to be vulnerable. "I'm not into being tied up. I'll tie you up if you want. In fact, I think I have some silk hose that would work nicely."

"Sorry, sweetheart, but I'm not good at being submissive."

"Me either," she said, suddenly very aware of her nakedness. She crossed her arms over her bare chest. "Listen, I know I'm the worst kind of tease, but I can't do this tonight."

His expression changed as he turned away from her and picked up his shirt. When he turned back around she saw something almost like tenderness in his eyes, and she wanted to cry.

She didn't know why.

He closed the distance between them and carefully tied the halter top back into place. "Can I hold you, sweetheart?"

No man, not even her father, had ever held her. Had ever wanted to hold her. Everyone said she was too much of a live wire, too independent and prickly to need a man's arms around her. And she'd longed for that.

Her fantasies had always involved a pair of big, strong shoulders, a man who just accepted her for who she was. Her gut said maybe Tuck was that man.

But her heart warned her not to trust him. That just because he was perceptive didn't mean he was really trustworthy.

She nodded, afraid to try to speak in case she spilled her feelings out. He walked past her, turning off the lights and flicking on the switch to her gas log fireplace. He adjusted the thermostat, and cooler air started to fill the room. Then he returned to her, pulling her into his arms and sinking to the floor in front of the fire.

He didn't awkwardly hold her, but settled her into the curve of his body. He moved them both around until they were sitting comfortably on the floor. He said nothing, but his hand rubbed up and down her arm in a soothing rhythm.

"I'm sorry," she said softly.

"Don't be. I like the anticipation that comes with waiting."

"You must be a masochist."

"A little. There's no pleasure in seeing you scared, Andrea."

"Why do you see me so clearly when no one else ever has?" she asked, no longer surprised that he seemed to recognize parts of her that no one else ever had.

"Because I'm looking at the real you."

"Another of those half answers that I think you say to divert me from getting to know the real *you.*"

He arched an eyebrow at her. "You're right. I see you because I grew up in a house full of women."

"It sounded even to me, you and your dad versus your mom and sister."

He tipped her chin up toward his face and gave her a sweet kiss. "It wasn't even at all. My dad left us when Jayne was three. I was eight and took on the man-of-the-house responsibilities. My grandmother came to stay with us because Mom had to work two jobs to keep bread on the table. I guess I see you clearly because I saw Mom at home when she was surrounded by those who loved her, relaxing her guard, and out in the world when she seemed so confident and sure of herself."

If he hadn't just described her fantasy family life to a tee, she would have been able to push him away. She would've been able to get to her feet and show him the door. Instead she curled closer to his warmth and felt the first inkling that Tuck might be a forever kind of man.

Tuck couldn't believe he'd spent the night on the floor, but when he woke in the morning with Andi cradled on his chest, he felt the aches and pains were worth it. His arm had fallen asleep, but he was able to move it to see his watch. Almost seven.

He had a meeting at the firehouse with McMillan at ten, so that gave him plenty of time. He turned them on their sides, anchoring her to him with his arm around her waist. He didn't want to give her time to think, because he wasn't sure he could stop again.

He wanted her. His morning erection strained against his jeans. He reached down and popped the top button and lowered the zipper a tad to give himself more room.

He pulled her thigh up over his hip and nestled the tip of his erection into the juncture of her thighs. Her skin was soft and smooth and nearly flawless in the morning sunlight. He rubbed his thumb over the bumps of her spine and buried his hand in the mass of her curly hair.

She shifted against him, blinking up at him. She leaned up and kissed him. Her hands kneaded his chest, and he let her take the lead for as long as he could. But when her tongue thrust languidly into his mouth, he couldn't resist doing the same to her.

"Good morning," she said.

"Yes, it is."

"I wish you'd left your shirt off," she said.

"Maybe now, but last night . . ."

"Thank you. I needed—"

He covered her mouth with his hand. "We both need things. Don't say any more."

She nodded, her fingers slowly unbuttoning his shirt until she pushed both sides off his chest. "You have such a strong body, Tuck. I've been wanting to touch you for a while."

"Feel free."

She pushed at his shoulder, urging him to his back. He rolled over, keeping his hands at his waist and lifting her so she was astride him. She moaned as the tip of his cock brushed her core.

She rocked against him, and he felt her warmth. While she explored his chest, with her hands and lips, he slid his hands up under her skirt and pulled her thong out of the way.

She leaned forward, rubbing her center over his length. "Do you have a condom?"

"Aren't you on the pill?"

She shook her head.

"I'm clean."

"So am I," she said. But he knew she was. He slipped his finger inside her body. She was tight around his forefinger. He pushed it farther inside, drawing out some of her wetness and spreading it up over her clitoris. She shifted over him. Her legs tightening around his hips.

"Untie your top and give me your breast."

She did what he asked of her, lowering her upper body until her nipple brushed his lips. She slipped her hands under his neck and offered him her support. Not that he needed it.

He continued to work his fingers inside her, carefully building her up. Adding another finger with each thrust, stretching her so that she'd be able to accommodate his girth inside her tight channel.

He lifted his mouth from her breast and pulled her mouth to his. Kissing her deeply while he took the wetness from between her legs and painted it over her tight nipples. She moaned into his mouth, and when he lowered his head to her breasts again, he was filled with the scent that was Andi. He lapped the wetness from her breasts. She tasted spicy and sweet at the same time. And he wanted more.

"Shift up here so I can have my breakfast," he said.

She pushed herself up, and he half slid down between her legs. Parting her opening and circling it with his tongue. He heard her little gasps as he explored every inch of her with his mouth. She was generously wet, and he knew she was on the edge of orgasm.

When he felt her hips rocking harder against him, her hands clutching in her hair, he brought his fingers to her clit and rubbed her carefully until he heard her gasp and felt her body clench.

Using his grip on her hips, he urged her down his body. Freeing his erection, he took the condom he'd put in his pocket yesterday out and sheathed himself. He held the tip of himself at her entrance until she opened her eyes and looked down at him.

Slowly she lowered herself on his length. He held her hips, letting her adjust to his cock. When he felt her start to relax around him, he pulled her down toward him as he thrust upward. Finally he was fully seated within her body, and he held still, wanting to remember this moment when he first had her.

He shifted around so that he was sitting up with his back against the couch. Using the couch for leverage, he was able to take better control of their movement.

Andi twined her arms around his neck, her nipples abrading his chest with each thrust he made. She circled her hips in motion with Tuck, her hand moving down between their bodies.

She made a circle around the root of his cock, tightening her fist around him whenever she lifted up. The added stimulation brought him very close to the edge, but he wanted her to come again before he did. So he held off, lowering his mouth to the base of her neck and sucking hard at her skin there.

He moved his hands from her hips to her butt, tracing the fine crease in the center, probing lightly while biting gently at her neck. He heard her gasp his name, and her body tightened around his as she found her release once again in his arms.

Finally he let himself surrender to the orgasm that had been building. He felt his balls draw up against his body, and he grunted as his climax roared through him.

Andi showed Tuck where the shower was and put a clean towel on the sink. She turned to leave, but he stopped her with a hand on her shoulder.

"Stay. Shower with me."

She'd never showered with anyone and wasn't sure she wanted to start now. "Umm . . . won't we be crowded?"

"Yes."

Tuck was naked, having stripped off his clothes and made love to her on her bed. His watch had beeped, and he'd apologized, saying he had a meeting at ten. So she'd shown him the shower and now was lingering in the doorway like . . . like a woman who didn't know what to do.

"Come on, drop your shirt and shower with me."

She pulled her shirt up and off. She wanted to enjoy the time she had with Tuck. She had no idea if he'd be back and wasn't going to ask him.

Was he one of those men who would be satisfied having gotten what he wanted from her body? Or was he going to come back for more? And how was she going to play it so he didn't guess she wanted him to come back?

"You have a beautiful body," he said. He closed the distance between them, taking her hands in his and stretching them up above her head. Pressing her hands to the cold, hard wall.

His gaze traveled down her body, lingering at her breasts and her nipped-in waist. He shifted her wrists to one hand and slowly caressed her. Started at her neck and followed the line of her body. Not lingering anywhere, just touching her everywhere. Making her hyperaware of herself as a woman.

Hyperaware of every spot on her body that was different from the hard planes of his. Even her arms, which were muscled from working out and having to carry ladders and equipment, weren't rock solid the way his were. There was a quiet strength in him that totally turned her on.

"I don't think I'm ever going to get enough of you," he said.

Me either, she thought, rising on her tiptoes and finding his mouth with hers. He lifted his hand to the back of her head, tangling his fingers in her hair. He stepped forward, pressing his body into hers.

He kissed and nibbled his way down her neck. As he suckled against her skin there, she arched into his body. Exquisite shivers pulsed downward. She caught a glimpse of herself in the bathroom mirror and didn't recognize the sensual woman she saw there.

Her lips were swollen and red from Tuck's kisses. Her legs were sprawled, and his lean hips were between them. She looked like a prisoner of his desire, her arms held above her head as he continued to nibble his way down her body.

He kissed her between her breasts, turning his head from side to side, scraping her with the stubble on his jaw. "I want to leave my mark all over your body."

She felt his imprint deep inside her, all the way to her bones. "Why?"

"So that you will think about me all day today while I'm working and you're . . . What will you be doing today?"

He sucked her nipple into his mouth, and she arched up into him, trying to find the words to answer his question. "Thinking of you, of course."

He grazed her nipple with the sharp edge of his teeth. The feeling was exquisite and made her tingle all the way to her toes. She lifted her leg and wrapped it around his hip, canted her body farther into his so that his erection nudged her center.

"In a hurry?"

"No, but you are."

"I am?"

"Yes," she said, pushing up on her toes until she felt him slip between her legs. Close to the entrance of her body.

He reached between them and rubbed his cock around her opening. She tugged on her hands, trying to free them, and he let them go.

She reached between their bodies and took his cock in her hand. She stroked his length and felt a small drop of moisture at the tip. She smiled up at him as she smoothed it into the head of his erection. Reaching lower, she cupped his sac, rolling his balls on the tips of her fingers. She bent and pulled a box of condoms from under the sink.

He grabbed her wrist. "Enough. I'm going to come before I get inside you."

"I don't mind."

"I do." He took the condom from her and put it on.

He lifted her up. "Wrap your legs around my waist."

She did, curling her hands over his shoulders, leaning her head against his chest. He slid inside her. She gasped a little at the feel of him there. She wasn't used to having this much sex in such a short period of time.

"Sore?"

"A little, but don't stop," she said. She had no idea how long Tuck would be around, and she didn't want to waste a single second.

"I should be a gentleman and stop . . ."

She tensed, waiting to see what he'd do. But she didn't want him to leave her. She tightened her vaginal muscles around him. He arched his eyebrow at her.

"Trying to tell me something?"

She nodded. "Don't stop."

"You'll get used to me," he said, rubbing above her mound in a circle and waiting for her to adjust to him.

She saw sincerity in his eyes and had to bite her lip to keep from saying too much. Instead she kissed him everywhere she could reach while he moved inside her. Thrusting slowly and carefully, letting her adjust to his presence in her body and gradually increasing his rhythm.

His hand on her belly moved lower, seeking the center of her pleasure. He circled her carefully, his touch there getting stronger in time to the thrusts in her body. Every nerve in her being cried out at the same time. Her release pulsing through her. She squeezed Tuck tight in her body, scoring his shoulders with her fingernails as she rode out her orgasm.

He stilled when she did, then took her hips in his powerful grip and drove into her body, going deeper than before. He thrust into her two more times before he called her name.

Chapter 9

They showered together, and for the first time in recent memory Tuck wanted to say screw-it to work and stay with Andrea. But he couldn't. And he knew she wouldn't have much respect for him as an arson investigator if he did.

When they returned to her bedroom, he sat on the bed and watched her dress. She wasn't a fussy woman at all. There was an economy of movement to her morning routine that was simple yet very feminine. The bedside clock radio came on, playing Wham's "Careless Whisper." Tuck had many happy memories of making out to that song.

He glanced at his wristwatch one more time. There wasn't time now, but he'd download a few of his most memorable eighties tunes before coming back to Andi's. Then tonight they could explore a few high school fantasies.

"George Michael helped me a lot when I was a senior. I could never understand it, but girls got hot when they heard this song."

She tossed him a look over her shoulder as she pulled a pair of white bikini panties with cherries on them out of her drawer. "I'm sure he's glad he was able to help you."

"Did this song do it for you?" he asked, watching her delicately step into her underwear.

"No. I mean, of course I loved it," she said, digging in her drawer until she found the matching bra with demicups.

Tuck groaned, knowing he was going to have many uncomfortable moments during the day when he remembered her undergarments.

"I knew you would. All girls did back then."

"Well, I was no different. I taped it off the radio and listened to it while my dad and brothers were gone. They couldn't stand it."

"What about your boyfriend; did he like it?"

"No boyfriend, I'm afraid. I was too . . . I don't know what, but a few of the guys said . . ."

He pushed to his feet and went to her side, wrapping his arms around her. She said nothing else, and he didn't urge her to. But he wanted to demand names and go find the boys who'd hurt a younger Andi. He knew she could take care of herself, but he couldn't help the well of protectiveness that was sweeping through him.

Looking at Andi, he couldn't imagine being blind where her femininity was concerned. How could the boys in her high school have missed the earthy sexuality that she exuded?

"It was a long time ago. I'd forgotten about it until you brought it up."

"Andi?"

She pushed away from him, ducking into the closet to finish dressing, and Tuck knew he'd stumbled on something. She came out wearing a pair of faded denim cutoffs and a Harley-Davidson Daytona tank top.

"Tell me about it."

"What's to tell? I was still one of the O'Roarke boys in those days. My dad took us all to the same barber and had our hair cut."

"I bet that looked cute."

"Well, thank you. But I don't think the boys at my high school noticed me in the sea of big eighties hair."

"I would have."

"Why would I have wanted you? You needed Wham to get the job done."

"When did I say that?" he asked, letting her change the subject.

"Earlier when you were thanking George."

That was a topic better off left alone. "Why did you have your alarm set?"

"I run every morning. I'm afraid my deep, dark secret is I'm not a morning person."

"That won't be an issue; I'm not either. Do you run by yourself?"

She crossed her arms under her breasts and gave him a look that could have melted steel. "I am a big girl."

He bit the inside of his lip to keep from smiling. Her sassy attitude got him every time. But this was a serious issue. A woman alone on the back roads was an accident waiting to happen.

"That is precisely why you shouldn't be running by yourself."

"I'm more than capable of taking care of myself, Tuck. I do live in this house all by myself, and gosh, the county even put me in charge of my own fire engine."

He held up his hands, realizing he'd said too much. "I'm not trying to start something. What if you land wrong on your foot and sprain your ankle?"

"Then I'd limp back here and drive myself to the doctor."

"That's not a good plan. Where's your cell phone?"

"There's not a tower nearby, and reception is spotty. I've been running every day since I moved here five years ago, and nothing has happened."

"I still don't like it."

"You don't have to, Tuck."

"Damn, I can't go with you or I'll be really late," he said.

"I'm not asking you to stay. Go on."

"Tell me you won't run by yourself. I'll get back here as soon as I can and run with you."

She flopped back on the bed. "I'm going to lie here for a while and enjoy my morning off. You wore me out," she said, but there was something in her eyes that alerted him to the fact that she was playing him.

"Say you won't run by yourself."

"Why?"

"Because I think you chose your words very carefully. You're used to saying what people want to hear, aren't you?"

"I'm the baby girl in a family of overprotective Neanderthals. Of course I am."

"It's not going to work with me. I'm an overprotective Neanderthal who's used to seeing through those kinds of womanly evasions."

"What's your sister's number?"

"Why?"

"Because I'm going to need some dirt on you if this thing is going to work between us."

"No way am I giving you that kind of ammo. Promise me you'll wait and run with me later."

"Only if you give me Jayne's number."

He knew he wasn't going to win this argument. It was there in her eyes. He gave her his sister's number and said, "I'll be back for dinner."

"I might be here."

He leaned down and kissed her long and hard and deep. Then walked out the door without a backward glance. Sometimes being a Neanderthal had its advantages.

Andi left Jayne's phone number on her kitchen counter. She wasn't going to call Tuck's sister because she had absolutely no idea what she'd say to the woman. Somehow introducing herself as Tuck's girlfriend didn't feel right.

Instead she spent the morning helping Sara and Mick dig

out a small pond in their backyard. It was hot by noon, really hot, and Mick decided he was going to have a nap and coaxed Sara to join him. So Andi drove home by herself.

Her brother, Rory, was sitting on her front porch when she pulled up. He worked in Daytona. He'd been given the opportunity to be a lieutenant but had decided he didn't want the extra responsibility. Her brothers always dropped by unannounced, so she wasn't too surprised to see him. But on top of Ian's call the other day, she figured she was in for another lecture.

"I was about to give up on you. Your phone rang twice." He pushed to his feet as she approached. Of all her siblings, Rory looked the most like their father. He had their dad's height and body structure, but his eyes were their mom's.

"Thanks, I'll check my messages. Do you want to come in for a beer or sit out here?"

"Inside, the heat's a bitch. At least at my place I get the ocean breeze."

"Is that why you chose it? I thought the proximity to Honeys was the reason." Honeys was a local bar staffed only by women in short skirts and bandanna tops.

He playfully punched her arm. "That, too."

She gave her brother a Bud Light and took one for herself, even though she really would have preferred a glass of iced tea. Rory sat on the couch after straightening one of the cushions. Andi flushed a little, remembering how they'd gotten messed up.

"What are you doing here?" she asked, hoping he wasn't planning to stay for dinner because she wasn't ready to explain Tucker to her brothers.

"I finished a training class in Orlando at noon and figured I'd stop and visit with you."

"Yeah, that sounds good except you never stop by without having a reason. I'm not driving to the beach to clean your apartment and cook a meal for Natalie's birthday."

"I don't need you to do that. My line of work was finally too much for her, and she's gone."

"I'm sorry. Did you have a close call?"

"Nah, but she wanted a guy with a regular schedule. Someone who could mingle at those chamber events she's always going to."

"You mingle just fine," she said. Of all her brothers, Rory was the most gregarious. Everyone liked Rory. "What was the real problem?"

He rubbed his hand over his jaw, draining his beer. He pushed to his feet and paced to the window. "Do you ever have . . . I swear if you say anything to our brothers, I'll deny this conversation."

"I'm not making any promises until I hear what you have to say. Remember that time Liam got locked outside Melissa's house and I had to go pick him up."

"This is different."

She'd never seen her brother like this before. "What is it, Ror? I won't repeat it."

"I'm tired of being a firefighter. I don't love it the way the rest of you do."

"Is that why Natalie left?"

"I'd been promising her I'd quit. I've been working part-time for Fidelity, the investment firm. You know how I was always good with numbers?"

"Yes."

"I still am, and they offered me a position there as an analyst."

Andi didn't really understand what her brother was saying. She knew Rory didn't want responsibility at work, but she'd always suspected he just wasn't driven like they were. "What are you saying? You don't want to be a firefighter?"

"I don't know. I mean, that's what we O'Roarkes are good at."

Andi thought about it for a minute. "Mom wasn't a fire-fighter, and she was an O'Roarke."

"Could you imagine what the old man would say to that argument?"

"We're not kids anymore, Rory. We get to make our own choices."

"Believe me, I know it, shortcake, but I still . . ."

She knew what he meant. Their old man cast a long shadow. "I've seen you with Natalie, and I think she's the one for you. I'd hate to see you throw it away because you were trying to live up to someone else's ideal of what makes a man."

Rory tipped his head to the side, studying her. Maybe she'd gone too far, said too much, but she knew Rory had come to her because he didn't know how to deal with Dad. All of her brothers did because they'd watched Andi do it her entire life.

She had never fit in and had always walked a fine line between earning his respect and being her own person. If last night with Tuck had proved anything, Andi thought she was still figuring out how to stand outside of her father's shadow.

"Nat said it was time to stop worrying about what Daddy thought. I really lost it. And said some unforgivable things."

"Why?"

"Don't make me examine this, Andi. I just want her back. If that means I'm going to have to put up with Dad calling me a sissy-man, then I guess that's what I'll have to do."

"Rory, you're six-foot-two and can bench press a small car. I think we both know you're not a sissy-man."

"Yeah, but it's different with the old man. I never want to look at him and see disappointment in his eyes. I've never let him down."

Andi knew exactly what her brother was talking about. "I have. I don't think I'm ever going to be good enough."

"That's not true. He's very proud of you. He talks about you all the time, how hard you work, how you never let the fact that you're a woman stand in your way."

Andi had never heard her father utter a single word of congratulations to her. He talked about Ian a lot. Holding Ian up as what she should try to be more like.

"Is that true?"

"Would I lie about that?"

She knew he wouldn't. He left a few minutes later, and as she watched her brother drive away, she realized that they were all trapped in the same scripts that had been running their entire lives. But she, for one, had no idea how to change it.

Tuck resisted the urge to call Andi before he left the fire station. He'd called twice and hadn't left a message either time. Instead he drove home, took a cold shower and then drove sedately to her house.

He knew she hadn't called Jayne because his mom would have called immediately to find out about Andi. Why had he given her Jayne's number? That made no sense. He was a man who kept moving. A man who didn't stay in one place or with one woman for long. Which didn't explain why he'd wanted to speed to get to her place.

He pulled into her driveway and found her truck there. He relaxed for the first time all day. He'd missed her. Thought about her way too much and knew he needed to wrap this case up and move on before it was too late.

He rapped on her front door, but there was no answer. Then he heard her footsteps. The door opened a crack. She was barefoot and had on a pair of running shorts and an exercise top that left her midriff bare.

"What are you doing back here?" she asked.

He wondered if she was going to make him stand on her porch each time he came to her house. Or if eventually she'd trust him enough to just let him in. "I told you I'd be back for dinner."

She glanced down at the black duffel bag held loosely in his left hand.

"Did you bring the meal with you?"

"Uh, no. I just assumed you'd cook."

"I can . . ." She tucked her hair behind her ear and just watched him.

"Are you deliberately provoking me?"

"So, what if I am?"

"Then I'm going to have to get some kind of revenge."

"I'm shaking in my running shoes. You promised to go with me."

"That's right, I did."

"Are you running in that?" she asked.

He'd changed into jeans and a crew-neck T-shirt after work. He'd been afraid to come dressed for running, afraid she'd gone out by herself just to prove a point.

"No. I brought a change of clothes."

"You planning on staying here for a while?" she asked, eyeing his bag.

He knew he was staying with her, and he suspected she did, too. He had his running gear in the bag. "I think I'd better wait until later to answer that."

Enough with letting her run the show. He stepped over the threshold and dropped his bag inside the door. "How about we go for that run of yours; then I'll take you to dinner?"

She smiled at him then, and his heart skipped a beat. He didn't know why this one woman affected him, but she did. "That's a very generous offer, but I'm actually prepared to make us dinner here."

"You like giving me a hard time, don't you?" he asked,

snagging her around her waist and pulling her into his arms. It felt like eons since he'd kissed her.

"Why deny it! I also like it when you give me a hard time," she said, tipping her head to the side so that the silky strands of her hair brushed his neck.

He kissed her, trying to keep things light, but unable to. He turned her in his arms, running his hands down her back and cupping her butt, hauling her closer to him. He thrust his tongue deep into her mouth. He wanted to brand her as his—completely his—so he'd be rid of this damned doubt that plagued him when they were apart.

He lifted his head after long minutes had passed. Her eyes were slumberous, her lips swollen, and her hips rubbed against him with minute movements.

He leaned down, tasting her mouth one more time. "So are we running?" he asked.

He hoped she would say no so that he could toss her over his shoulder and take her to bed.

She edged back from him. He didn't let her retreat. She'd had enough time to reerect the barriers he'd painstakingly torn down last night. He aggressively stepped toward her.

The woman was way too used to being in charge. And he'd just spent the entire day tied in knots wondering where things stood between them. He didn't like it.

"Yeah, we're running. The sun's finally going down, and the heat's not too bad. Morning's better for running."

"I'll catch you if you fall due to heat exhaustion."

"Who'll catch you?" she asked, pivoting on her heel and walking deeper into her house. She perched on the arm of her couch, crossing her legs.

"Won't you?"

"Hell, no, you're too big for me to catch. But once you fall I'll pick you up and haul you back here."

She made him laugh, and he realized suddenly that despite the intensity of his feelings for her, he really needed the lightness she brought with her.

"Seriously, I want to hear about your investigation. Did you learn anything new today?"

"I'll tell you tomorrow at work. Give me a minute to change and we'll go."

"Just because we slept together last night doesn't mean I'm not still involved in the arson investigation, Tuck. I want to know what you found out."

"I found out that you're a pain in the ass. You're the one who said that this was separate from work, weren't you?"

She pushed to her feet and paced away from him. "Yes, I did. But what will we talk about if not work?"

His heart ached when he heard her words. "Who says we have to talk?"

"Don't you want to?" she asked, glancing over her shoulder at him, her brown eyes clouded with uncertainty.

"Yes, but I also want to hold you in my arms and spend hours learning every curve of your body."

"Hours?" she asked.

He wasn't sure but it sounded as though there was a positive note in her voice.

"Yes, hours."

"Good thing I'm preparing salmon for dinner tonight."

"Why's that good."

"Lots of protein, I think we're going to need our strength."

"I've got plenty of stamina without the protein," he said, winking at her.

Chapter 10

Andi loved running. She loved the fact that the road was endless and she could just continue on, unobstructed. Her problems were behind her, and she just kept moving toward the horizon.

She wasn't the least bit surprised that Tuck easily kept pace with her. They'd gone about three miles before reaching a small lake with a park next to it. She slowed her pace. "Want to take a break?"

He nodded, and they both walked to cool down before settling on a bench overlooking the water. This was the heart of historic Auburndale, with its cute Victorian-style houses all trimmed like a girl's dream dollhouse.

"This is nice," he said, putting his arm along the back of the bench. His hand resting on her shoulder. She wasn't sure if he was talking about the two of them or the environment.

She glanced around at the small, neat neighborhood of older homes. "Yes, it is. So quiet. That's what I like best about small-town living."

"Do you think you'll stay here?" he asked, his finger stroking her shoulder.

She could barely think when he touched her. She'd had a vague plan to tease him with her skimpy running clothes and basically keep him off balance, but instead she was the one off balance. She wasn't sure what to make of him. "Yes, I've made it my home."

"I can understand that," he said.

"Where are you from? You never did say."

"Well, I keep an apartment in Tallahassee because I work for the state fire marshal, but I'm from Chicago. So I consider that home."

"Talk about your small towns, I mean Tallahassee."

"Yeah, let's say there's not much action there. I really don't spend much time there. I'm going to South Florida after I'm done here to your brother's firehouse."

"Ian has a much bigger crew, and I think he's got at least one arson guy on staff there."

"Actually, he's got two, but they want a fresh pair of eyes. Your brother's pretty savvy to call for me when he did."

"Why?"

"The serial arsonist is targeting homes on West Palm Beach, so it was only a matter of time before the governor was going to order someone from my office down there."

"Ian's smart. He's the best firefighter I know."

"You're not the least bit prejudiced either," he observed.

She was the first to admit she had a bad case of hero worship for Ian. But she also saw his faults and knew that in the firehouse he was top rate. In his personal life . . . Let's just say he ran his home the way he ran the firehouse, and her nephews were known to rebel.

"Of course I am. He's the firefighter I want to be when I grow up."

"You seem pretty grown up to me," he said, running his finger down the side of her neck, following a bead of sweat.

He brought his finger to his lips and licked her sweat from it. Immediately her awareness shifted to something totally sexual. She couldn't even remember what they'd been talking about. Her brother or something.

"What did you say?" she asked, trying not to notice that he was eyeing the scoop neckline of her top and the sweat that had beaded there during her run.

"I said—you seem grown up to me."

"I know, but I'm still not there yet."

"You're top-notch, Andi. I think your brother must be proud of you."

She felt uncomfortable. This was the second time today she'd had a conversation about pride. She didn't want to think about her family and whether or not she was living up to the name O'Roarke.

"Do your mom and sister still live in Chicago?" she asked, anything to move the topic off of her family. And she wanted to know more about Tucker. What had made him into the man he was today.

"They live in the Chicago area—Naperville. Did you call my sister to get the dirt?" he asked, turning to look at her.

"Not yet. I'm saving that to keep you in line."

"Really? Now that I'm going to meet Ian you better be careful what you do with that number."

That did worry her. She didn't want her family to ever know about her private life. Tuck wasn't going to be around forever, and if Ian and the rest of the boys found out, she'd feel like they all knew she couldn't keep a man. "You can't talk to Ian about us. He's a way overprotective brother."

"I'm the same way, so I understand that. I don't think you need to blackmail me to keep me in line."

"What should I do?" she asked, grateful that he changed the subject. Getting involved with a man in the firefighting community was a bad idea. Hadn't she learned that lesson when she'd been younger?

"Offer me sex. I'm easy. I can be had," he said, leaning down and licking carefully above her running top.

She shivered, reaching up to hold his head to her. *Just for a minute*, she thought. She knew she couldn't chain him, couldn't ever let on how much she wanted him to stay with her.

"What are you doing to me?" she asked, surprised when she heard the words out loud.

He looked up at her, his green eyes alive with the kind of fire she associated only with him. "Tasting you. You are delicious, and I feel like it has been eons instead of hours since I had my mouth on you."

She wasn't sure what to say to that. She wanted Tuck the same way. She'd missed him today, and that made her angry because she was normally very comfortable with her life. She didn't need a man to be complete. Andi was struck by the fact that she'd never enjoyed just being with another person the way she liked being with Tuck.

It's temporary, she reminded herself.

"Race you home," she said, pushing to her feet and running for her house.

Tuck waited until after dinner when they were both settled in her living room before wrapping his arms around her. There was something very elusive about Andi. The closer he got to her, the farther out of reach she seemed.

She'd put on the latest Dave Matthews Band CD before settling on the couch next to him. She'd changed into a sundress with a halter-tie top after her shower before dinner. All evening he'd caught teasing glimpses of the inner curve of her breast.

The skirt was full and ended at mid-thigh, and as she sat curled next to him the hem had ridden up. He reached down and skimmed his fingers along the edge of the fabric. He wondered what she wore under the dress.

"Have you heard this yet?" she asked, tipping her head back.

He leaned down, capturing her mouth with his. Tangling his hand in her hair, he held her head so that he could plunder her mouth. She tasted faintly of the Pinot Grigio they were drinking and a unique taste that he associated only with her.

He lifted his head and dropped several biting kisses along her neck. He was pleased to see that the love bite he'd left on her neck this morning was visible. He wanted to brand her so that any man who saw her would know she belonged to him.

Finally he lifted his head. Her eyes were wide, and she watched him the way she did sometimes. Her gaze clear yet enigmatic. He wanted to find a way past that guard she constantly kept up.

The music penetrated his senses and he realized that she had asked him about the musician who was singing. Dave Matthews.

"No, I haven't heard this CD. Are you a big fan?" he asked, keeping his hand in her hair. He loved how silky and thick it was. He wanted to feel her hair on his chest and stomach . . . lower.

"Yes. It's my secret addiction. His songs are so sexy and haunting. They make me long for something I've never had."

"What?" he asked. But he couldn't help thinking that Andrea was becoming his addiction, and he was afraid it wasn't all that secret. Today at work a couple of the guys had asked him if everything was okay when he'd become distracted by thoughts of her.

"I don't know for sure," she said, then took a deep breath. "But something that is missing from my sex life."

He knew exactly what was missing from her sex life . . . him. But now that he was with her, he'd be happy to make sure that the problem was gone. "I think I know what you're missing."

"Do you? You think you know everything," she said, pushing up and taking a sip of her glass of wine.

"True. But sometimes I really do."

"Ha."

He'd made her nervous. She'd shifted her body a little away from his, and now there was a distance between them. She'd been in an odd mood since he'd come to her place, and he wanted to get to the bottom of it but knew he wouldn't be able to until she was honest with them both. Until she stopped being the woman he thought she was and became the woman she was meant to be. His woman . . .

"*Ha?* That's the best response you can come up with? I can't believe this is the same woman who beat my socks off at Risk."

She smiled at him, but he saw trepidation in her eyes and realized that he may have pushed too hard. If there was one area where Andrea didn't feel confident, it was this one. "I can't be supersharp twenty-four/seven."

"Thank God for small favors."

She punched his arm and took a sip of her wine. "What did you mean before?"

"Just that when we had sex last night I felt . . . like you weren't sure you should give up control."

"So?" She pushed out of his arms and moved away.

Tuck debated shutting up and leaving it alone, but he knew deep inside that Andi was too used to denying a big part of herself. She tried to pretend she was just one of the guys. She tried to convince herself and everyone else that she was happy being one of the guys. She tried too hard to make sure no one ever saw a crack in that one-of-the-guys image. But he saw that crack and the woman hiding behind it.

"I think you need to let go of your restraint."

"How?" she asked. "It's not like I haven't tried, Tuck. Men expect me to be a certain way."

"Or do you expect yourself to be that way with men?"

She pushed to her feet and paced to the glass door. Staring out at her own backyard. His heart ached for Andrea. Because he saw her vulnerabilities so clearly. He knew that she was a strong, capable woman, but she thought any hint of fragility was a weakness, a detriment. And he was determined to make her see otherwise.

Plus, his ego said he could be the man to break her out of the shell she'd been happily living in all these years. But first he had to peel back the layers with which she surrounded herself. And he couldn't do that unless she agreed to give herself to him. One hundred percent to him, no safe-words or backing out.

"I don't know. A big part of it is . . . I can't do this. If I say it, you'll . . ."

He went to her, put his arms around her and pulled her back against his chest. "I won't think less of you. Remember how you said that Ian didn't know how to act outside the fire station?"

She nodded.

"Neither do you. Let me help you."

"How?"

He stepped away from her. "Just for tonight do everything that I say."

"Everything?" she asked, her voice dropping an octave.

"Everything."

"Okay, but I reserve the right to back out if—"

"No, sweetheart. I won't ask you to do anything you can't."

She bit her lower lip, and he saw excitement and arousal in her eyes as she looked over her shoulder at him. She nodded.

"Good," he said, retreating to the couch and seating himself. "Turn around."

Andi had never been so excited. She'd felt that jingling of eagerness mixed with nerves when she entered a burning building. She'd felt tingling of enthusiasm in the pit of her stomach when she'd gotten her last promotion, but this was something different.

This was a total cessation of her own will to Tuck. For once she didn't have to worry if she was acting the right way or if she'd do something that he didn't like. He wouldn't let her.

But by the same token, it was a little scary. Tuck saw her deeper than anyone else did. "This is just for tonight, right?"

"If you want it to be. But I doubt seriously one night will be enough for me."

"So what do you want me to do?" she asked, to change the subject.

"Are you wearing panties?" he asked.

"Why wouldn't I be?"

"Sweetheart, anything other than a yes or no answer is going to get you in trouble."

"Uh . . . Yes, I am."

"Take them off."

Slowly she lifted the hem of her skirt, careful to watch his reaction. His eyes narrowed, and his hands tightened on the chair. She knew Tuck liked her legs. From the first moment they met he'd been unable to keep his eyes from them.

She took her time, drawing the skirt slowly higher until her cream-colored mesh thong was visible to him. Then she hooked her fingers into the sides and slowly drew it down her hips.

He'd sat up in his chair before forcibly making himself relax and sink back. She bit her lip to keep from smiling as she realized that sometimes power wasn't in the hands of the one who seemed stronger. It was a heady realization as she watched Tuck react.

She was having a profound effect on him just by standing in front of him. The full skirt dropped as she bent to remove her thong. She held it in one hand, dangling on her finger.

He was staring at the scrap of fabric the way a hungry

man looked at food. She tossed it to him. He caught it one-handed. He brought her panties to his nose and sniffed. She felt a trickle of wetness between her thighs, watching him. He pushed her thong into the front pocket of his pants and then glanced back at her.

"You seem to have a thing for halter tops," he said.

"I like them because I don't have to worry about a bra."

"Do you like the texture of the material on your nipples?" he asked.

"Yes."

"Do you like that only one tie at the back of your neck is keeping you decent?"

She flushed a little at hearing her secret thrill from his lips. She did like it. She always felt sexy when she wore one of these tops. Knowing that only a thin layer of material covered her breasts.

"Yes."

He nodded. "I want you to go to the kitchen and bring me a cup of ice."

"What—"

"Yes or no only."

She nodded. "Yes."

She walked down the short hall to the kitchen. Taking a glass from the cabinet, she went to the refrigerator and filled it, but didn't hurry back to Tuck. She needed to re-group and . . .

"Andi, come back here."

She walked slowly back down the hall. When she entered the room she saw he'd removed his shirt and still reclined in her armchair.

"Come here."

She stood next to his chair. Her hand was frozen from holding the cup of ice.

"Put the glass on the table."

She placed it where he said.

"Lower your top and sit here on my knees."

She perched on his lap, but felt as if she was going to fall. He caught her waist and helped her get settled. She felt his erection against her butt and sensed that these games weren't going to last too much longer.

"Lift your skirt, sweetheart."

She shifted up and slipped the back of her skirt from under her butt. Now her bare cheeks were pressed to the rough denim that encased his legs. She shifted on his legs, rubbing her butt against him, liking the rough stimulation of the cloth.

Though she was enjoying playing with him, she wanted to be held in his arms. Wanted to feel him deep inside her and wanted to wrap her arms and legs around him. Hold him to her so she could pretend she never had to let him go.

"Your top," he reminded her.

"I'm going to take a turn being in charge; you realize that, don't you?"

He arched one eyebrow at her. "Do you want me to spank you?"

The walls of her vagina clenched at the thought. She'd never really thought about a man spanking her. She wasn't sure if she'd like the real thing, but the threat . . .

"No."

He leaned forward, kissing her, his hands sprawling down her bare back. He slipped his fingers under her skirt and began skimming them along her bare butt. He squeezed each cheek. At first just some light pressure, but then she felt it grow stronger. His finger slipped along the crease in her backside, moving lower, probing at her opening.

"Then lower your top. I want to see your breasts."

She couldn't think with the tip of his finger buried in her body. She shifted on his finger, and it moved deeper still.

She reached back to unfasten the top of her sundress. His

fingers continued moving inside her body, keeping her on the edge of madness.

"Cup your breasts, Andi."

She smoothed her hands up her torso from her waist. She rarely touched herself, so the feeling of her hands on her own body was forbidden and slightly erotic. She cupped her breasts and then skimmed her thumb over her nipple.

It hardened instantly. She glanced up at Tuck and noticed he watched her with narrowed eyes. His fingers kept moving inside her body, his thumb nestling between her cheeks.

He lifted the glass with his free hand and pulled one of the ice cubes into his mouth. She watched him suck on it for a second. "Lean forward."

As she did, he lowered his head, taking her nipple into his mouth. She shivered at the combination of the ice-cold water and the heat of his tongue. He held her nipple between his teeth and suckled at her while his fingers thrust deeper into her body. She rocked harder against him. Moving her hips almost frantically when he switched breasts and suckled her other nipple.

Everything inside her clenched and released. Stars danced behind her eyes, and she clutched his shoulders as her orgasm rolled through her body.

He kept stroking her between her legs and suckling at her breast until she collapsed against his chest, eyes closed. Then her arms came around him to hold him tightly to her.

Chapter 11

Tuck carried Andi down the hall to her bedroom. He needed to be inside her or he'd go crazy. He set her on her feet next to her bed and pushed her dress off. Then he lifted her, laying her in the center of the bed.

She smiled up at him. Stretching her arms out to the sides, her legs falling open. This was how he always wanted to see her—hair spread across the pillow, her body soft, wet and ready. He'd hoped to put a little distance between them by ordering her around. By treating her the way he'd treated other lovers in the past. But he couldn't ever forget that this was Andrea. That this woman was different to him.

He loved the way she got so hot for him so fast. He couldn't wait to be inside her legs again. To have her wrapped completely around him.

Though he'd never admit it, when he was in her arms he felt as if he'd found something that had been missing for a long time.

"Hurry."

He grabbed a condom from the box he'd put on her nightstand earlier and tossed it to her. It landed on her stomach, but she made no move to retrieve it. He unfastened his pants and carefully lowered his zipper.

He stroked his erection as she watched him. Lifting her

arm toward him, she brushed the head of his cock with her fingertips.

"I love the way you feel," she said. Her voice soft and husky. Wrapping her fingers around him, she tugged until he stepped closer to her. She stroked him up and down, her fingers sweeping under his body to cup his balls with each caress. He groaned deep in his throat as her strokes grew harder and stronger with each pass. He didn't want to come in her hand. He wanted to be buried in her body when he did that.

Reluctantly he pulled her hand away just as a drop of pre-come glistened on the head of his cock. She swiped her finger over it and brought it to her lips, sucking his essence into her mouth.

He swallowed hard and grabbed the condom, ripping the packet open and sheathing himself. "Put your arms over your head and hold on to the headboard."

She lifted her arms, making her breasts shift upward. He leaned down to suckle her nipple into his mouth again. He loved the way she felt in his mouth. He sucked harder at her breast, felt her hips move on the bed.

"Don't let go."

"Yes."

He pushed her thighs apart with his hands, staring down at her center. He remembered the scent of her from her thong and wanted to taste her now. There was always so much he wanted to do with her body. And he had the feeling when he was in her bed that he might never make it back into it again.

He leaned down, just inhaling the scent of her. Resting his head on her mound and looking up her body. She had her hands above her head as he'd ordered, but she was watching him. He reached up and massaged her breasts while dropping biting kisses along her stomach.

He teased her belly button with his tongue and then traced the line of her pubic hair at the top of her mound, before lowering his head and rubbing his cheek over her. Her hips lifted.

He turned his face into her body, touching her with his tongue. He brought his hands to her nether lips, parting them so that he could see her fully engorged and wanting him.

He teased her with the tip of his tongue, then carefully sucked her into his mouth. She screamed his name, her hips arching off the bed. She grabbed his head and held him to her while she rode his mouth.

While she was still climaxing, he grabbed her ankles, pushed her legs farther apart. "Hands on the headboard."

She lifted her arms again. He grabbed one of the pillows and shoved it under her hips. "Watch me take you."

She nodded. He positioned his penis against her opening. Bending his legs toward her body, he held himself at the entrance until her hips rose toward him, seeking his penetration. "Wait for it."

"No. Take me now, Tuck. I need you."

She started to move her hands.

"Don't do it," he warned. He was on the knife's edge and loved it. Her entire body was flushed. Her mouth open, her pupils dilated, her breasts full, her thighs trembling. He knew she wanted him. And he couldn't wait another second to be inside her.

He forced himself to enter her slowly. But when her walls tightened around him, his control snapped, and he thrust all the way to the hilt. He rested there for a second, his forehead to hers. Looking deep into her eyes as his hips moved, thrusting in and out, searching for release.

He bent his head, craning his neck to capture her nipple between his teeth. He applied pressure there before suckling her. He twisted his hips with each thrust, catching her clitoris. Her breath started to catch. And her hips moved almost frantically against his.

He reached down, holding her still, slowing his pace and leaning up so he could see her eyes. Watching her as he changed his angle of penetration until he hit her secret spot. Felt the way her body clenched on his and the way she almost stopped breathing and cried his name.

He thrust harder and deeper, feeling his balls slap against the back of her butt with each thrust. He wanted to go deeper, to get farther inside her silky body before . . . Everything convulsed, and his climax ripped through him, leaving him shuddering in her arms.

He felt her legs slide down his hips and her arms come around his shoulders. He shifted his weight and settled between her legs and slightly off her chest, resting at her bosom, finally realizing that what he wanted from Andi was this. Peace, contentment and a kind of sexual satisfaction that touched him all the way to his soul.

Andi woke before her alarm and stared at the ceiling. Something had changed last night when they were making love, something inside her that had never been touched before, and it scared her.

She was almost forty; when was life going to be easy? She'd thought as a teenager that being an adult and getting away from her dad and brothers was the answer. She'd thought finding peace with being single in her twenties was the answer, and now, she'd thought . . . She'd thought she could have sex with Tuck and it wouldn't make a big difference.

Little did she know that Tuck wasn't going to fit easily into any place she put him. She'd never undergone the range of emotions she'd felt with him last night. Never had she let any guy tell her what to do. But she'd experienced with him the kind of sexual fulfillment she'd always wanted in bed.

She eased from between the sheets, trying not to disturb Tuck. Carefully she tugged her robe from the bottom of the bed and wrapped it around her body. He was sprawled on his stomach, the sheets tangled around his waist and legs. Her body ached from last night.

She sat in the stuffed armchair in the corner of her bedroom and watched Tuck. What would today bring? Should she wake him and kick him out before she left for work? She hoped he wouldn't be like . . .

"What are you doing over there?" Tuck asked, startling her.

She stared at him through the weak light of dawn that spilled through her open windows. The air was damp, and the sheer curtains stirred in the faint breeze. "Thinking."

"You can't think in bed?" he asked, pushing up and leaning on one elbow to watch her.

His gaze was steady and intent, but she couldn't read his emotions. She didn't know what he was thinking, and that made her uneasy. She was comfortable around men when she knew what to expect, and she was reminded that she rarely knew what to expect from Tuck.

"Not while you're there," she said honestly. He permeated all of her senses. She could still feel the beard burn he'd left on her stomach sometime during the night.

He held his hand out to her. "Come back to bed, sweetheart. Everything will be okay."

She wanted to go to him so badly that she forced herself to stay in the chair, feigning nonchalance. "What makes you think I'm worrying?"

"Am I wrong?" he asked, in that arrogant way of his that was beginning to make her want to prove him mistaken.

"What makes you think you aren't?" she asked.

She wasn't going to tell him he was right. The man already thought he knew too much.

"My gut."

"What gut?"

"Stop trying to change the subject. Come back to bed."

She pushed to her feet and walked back to the bed, settling herself next to his hip, facing him. She traced his bicep on the arm holding his head up. There was a lot of strength in Tuck, the kind she always wanted to project, but she had the feeling she fell woefully short.

He rubbed his hand up and down her arm. "You're a little chilled; come here and let me warm you up."

He pushed her robe from her shoulders and pulled her down next to him on the bed. Wrapping his arms around her, he placed her head on his shoulder and rubbed his hands up and down her back.

"What's going on in that head of yours?" he asked softly. He stroked his jaw over the top of her head.

She liked the way he did that. Just reached out for her whenever he needed her. Or whenever he sensed she needed him. And being wrapped up in his arms was comforting, though she didn't want to admit she needed to be reassured.

"I didn't know if I should wake you up before I left for work. You're not coming in the same time I am."

"No, I'm not. I asked Marilee to put me on your calendar for ten. I finally got Braley pinned down for an interview."

"I can't go with you. I can't leave the firehouse. Mick is out today, so there's no lieutenant on the engine. I'll have to stay."

"No problem. Can you spare one of the guys?"

"I won't know until I get in. I wish you'd mentioned this last night," she said, pushing away from him.

"Why? Last night we were two lovers, not coworkers."

"Is it really that easy for you to switch between the two?" she asked, not sure how he did it.

"No. But I thought that was what you wanted."

"What I want is to know what's going on in my firehouse."

"Are you trying to start a fight with me?" he asked.

She took a deep breath. She was. She'd feel a lot better if he left angry. Because then at least she'd know what to expect from him when she saw him at work. She pushed away from him, but he held her still. Rolled until she was under his body, taking her hands in his and stretching them above her head.

"Let me up, Tuck." She pulled at her wrists, trying to free herself. Last night she'd played his games, but this morning she wasn't going to. She'd held back some of her strength because she didn't want to hurt him and because she'd enjoyed what they were doing. But she didn't want to be held captive in her own bed this morning.

"Not until you answer the question," he said.

"You're starting to really tick me off with this dominant crap you keep pulling."

"It's not crap, babe. This is the way I am. So tell me why you're trying so hard to make me mad."

"Who said I was?" she asked. Maybe she could keep him talking and get him out of bed that way.

"I did. I'm not an idiot."

"You just act like one sometimes."

He kissed her then, not a fierce kiss, but one that was soft and gentle and spoke of understanding. She shivered in his arms and closed her eyes so he wouldn't see the uncertainty there.

Tuck found the Polk County Citrus Co-op offices easily. They were in Haines City near the old train station. Haines City was a small town like Auburndale, but Tuck could tell that at one time this city had been a town of some prestige.

He parked his black pickup on the main street and walked into the building. Despite the cold breeze they'd had early this morning, the day was already pushing eighty, and the humidity hung heavily in the air.

He brushed the sweat from the back of his neck, wishing he was still in Andi's bed. He pushed open the door and stepped inside.

The receptionist, a pretty blond woman, looked up as he entered. "Can I help you?"

"I have an appointment with Roy Braley."

"Your name is?"

"Tucker Fields, ma'am. I'm here to talk to him about the warehouse fires."

"Have a seat, Mr. Fields. I'll let him know you are here."

Tuck seated himself in one of the faux-leather chairs. He rubbed the bridge of his nose. Focusing on his investigation had never been a bigger challenge. Andi consumed his thoughts, and he wanted to spend all of his energy on her.

He carefully shoved those thoughts to the back of his mind. Something about this case was making the back of his neck itch. His gut said that Braley held the key.

"Sorry to keep you waiting, Fields. I'm Roy Braley."

Tuck stood up and shook hands with Braley. The man was a few inches shorter than Tuck. He had a salesman's smile and an easy air about him. "Can I get you something to drink—coffee, water, soda, orange juice?"

"Coffee if it's fresh."

"We'll see that it is." Roy led the way down a series of hallways and then into an office.

"This is Rachael, my secretary. Rachael, this is Tucker Fields from the fire department. He'd like a coffee." Roy glanced over at him. "Cream or sugar?"

"No. Black is fine."

"I'll have the same."

"I thought we talked about me getting coffee," she said.

"Not now."

Tuck wanted to smile as Rachael walked away. "Sorry about that. Rachael is more of an office manager than a secretary."

"No problem. I'm just glad you had time for me today."

"Me, too. So tell me what I can do for you?"

"Tell me about the locations of the fires. What were those buildings used for?"

"Well, we were just starting to renovate them. We are putting in an attraction at the first location. Kind of a museum of the citrus history in the area. The other two warehouses are near enough that we're in development to make them working juicing and packing houses. We're going to offer tours."

There was a knock on the door, and Rachael walked in, setting both mugs on Roy's desk.

"Thanks," Tuck said.

"Thank you, Rachael. Tomorrow I'll get the coffee."

"That's right you will. Is there anything else?"

Roy glanced over at Tuck. "Do you want to see the mock-up of the development plans?"

"Yes, but I have a few more questions first."

"No problem," Roy said. "Rach, would you make sure the models are in the conference room?"

"Yes," she said, leaving quietly.

Tuck asked a few more questions and then got to the point of most arson investigations—money. "So who stands to lose if the place goes up in flames?"

"The area loses because of the revenue the tourism would generate. But also the co-op. We're partnering with several other citrus grove co-ops in Central Florida."

"Were there any other bidders on the museum?"

"As a matter of fact, Indian River County bid. They still do a lot of citrus production down there. Up here most of the land is worth more when they subdivide and sell it for real estate. So having the citrus museum and attraction here gives us small co-ops a shot at keeping our heads above the water financially."

Tuck made a few more notes, then looked at Braley. The guy was slick and seemed friendly and up front, but Tuck never took anything at face value.

"Where were you when the fires broke out?"

Braley smiled at him. "Like I told Andi, I was at home every time."

Tuck nodded. He'd double-check with Andi and see Braley's statement from the night of the first fire.

"Who do you think started them?" Tuck asked. He always asked the question because often you could tell a lot by what a man didn't say.

"I'm not sure. It was spring, and you know how cold it gets here in March . . . I think maybe the first fire was started by a homeless person."

Which they'd already ruled out. There was no barrel drum in the building. And the fire had been started using gas. Most homeless didn't have access to a gas can.

"We've already looked into that. Any other theories?"

"Frankly, no. I can't understand why anyone would try to stop the work we are doing there."

"Did they hurt the project?"

Braley hesitated, and Tuck knew that something had happened with the project. "A little, but we're back on track now. In fact, all the fires did was slow us down by a few weeks."

Tuck nodded. "I'm ready to see your models now."

"Great. While we're in the conference room I'll get you a glass of Florida's best orange juice."

"Thanks," Tuck said.

He took photos of the model with his digital camera. Then double-checked the architecture plans on the wall. He noted who the architect was. He knew that he was missing something but couldn't put his finger on it.

Chapter 12

Throwing ladders was one of the drills that most of the guys didn't mind. They liked to keep in top shape. Plus they needed to know what Brown could do. So Andi assembled them in the yard and got them moving.

Throwing ladders was a timed exercise where they got the ladders from the engine and to their fire tower. Then climbed up and entered the building in full gear.

Johnson, McMillan, and Powell had worked together for a while now and had a shorthand that even Andi wasn't a part of. They moved together as a team, and she watched them with a sense of pride as they drilled.

They included Brown as far as anyone would without knowing his skills. She teamed up McMillan and Brown and watched them. Brown would fit in, she thought, because he had that same internal passion that all good firefighters had. That self-knowledge that they were called to fight fires.

When the drills ended she went back into her office, trying to keep her focus on work and not on the man who'd spent the last two nights in her bed. She'd toyed with putting on lipstick this morning. Just a light coating of make-up over her evenly tanned skin.

Would he even notice? Heck, would she know how to do it right?

She checked her e-mail and then glanced at the open door. She heard the television on and knew most of the guys would be watching ESPN2. Opening her Internet browser, she typed in Cosmopolitan.com before she could change her mind. If any place could give dating advice, it was Cosmo. And no one would be the wiser. There would be no magazine lying around for the guys to catch a glimpse of and tease her about.

Man, was she really doing this? She kept one eye on the door while the magazine loaded in her browser.

Once there she had no idea what to do. What the hell was she thinking? She wasn't going to change for Tuck. She wasn't going to make herself into some sort of femme fatale in the hopes that it would make him stay.

Someone rapped on her door, and she minimized the browser before looking up. Of course it was Tuck. She should have closed the window instead of minimizing it. What if he saw that she was on Cosmo. She glanced at the bottom of her screen.

Oh, no, it said sex quiz. What would he think if he saw it?

"Got a sec?"

"Sure, have a seat. Did you talk to Roy this morning?"

"Yes. Do you mind if I close the door?" he asked.

She shook her head. "No, go ahead. I think the guys are all watching TV."

She tried to forget that the last time she'd seen him he'd been lying in her bed, hair rumpled and a sheet tangled around him. She shivered as memories washed over her. Here was a perfect reason not to be sleeping with Tuck.

"McMillan was washing the truck with Brown," Tuck said. "Which is good because I wanted to talk to you before I speak to him."

Tuck was all business, and she should be, too. Normally she would be, but she was . . . unsure of him. She closed her eyes for a brief second and thought about the fires. The warehouses and the surrounding grove area had been devastated by them. Someone had deliberately set them.

Make that matter, Andi. Make that the focus of your attention instead of Tuck and his skin-tight jeans.

"Did you find something to implicate Roy?" she asked, reaching for a pen to take notes. She thought better when she wrote things down.

Tuck pulled the guest chair closer to her desk and sat down. He put his booted feet on the corner of her desk and took out his notebook, flipping through the pages. "Not exactly, but I have the feeling he's not telling me something. I thought we could both go over my notes. You know the people involved better than I do."

"Let me get this straight . . . You need me?" she asked.

"Yes, I need you."

"For your investigation?" she asked just to tease him. He seemed so cool and confident, and she felt like an inferno burning out of control.

"Yes, and other things. Do you want me to go into them now?"

"Not necessary. I'm content to wallow in the fact that you require my help."

"Stop gloating or I'll have to come over there and remind you that you need me, too. Tell me what you know about the citrus museum-slash-attraction that Roy is working on."

"Not much. There have been a few articles in the local papers."

"Is there a lot of support for it?" he asked. He seemed completely at ease in her office, but she could tell that he was running facts and variables through his mind. Trying to find the answers to the case.

She wished she could be of more help. But she didn't pay much attention to the local political climate. "I don't know.

I haven't heard of anyone protesting it or anything. Maybe a few developers who wanted to subdivide the land. I think that Roy's museum made a few real estate deals go sour. Most of the grove owners would rather see the land stay undeveloped."

"Who were the players in the land deal?" he asked, letting his feet drop to the floor.

"I have no idea. Let me make a few calls. Marilee still has some connections at the sheriff's office. She might be a good source for us. But if I call her in here, everyone else is going to want to know what's up."

"I'll talk to her later. I guess that's all the business I have with you for now."

"Thanks for all your hard work on this case, Tucker. Keep me posted. You can leave the door open on your way out," she said, congratulating herself on treating him like she would anyone else. Tucker Fields had no idea how deeply the last two days had affected her, and she hoped he never would.

"What if I'm not ready to leave?"

Tuck watched her flush. Though he had no business starting anything personal at work, she was so cool, so unflappable, that he couldn't resist.

She leaned forward on her desk, arms crossed on the surface. Her image was one of poise and of total control. He wondered how her men made it through the day without wanting to kiss her. Her will and the way she wielded it were a huge turn-on for him. But also her sharp mind and her sassy tongue. She knew that she was in a position of power, and she didn't abuse it but exerted it carefully.

"Then I guess I'll have to make you," she said.

"Really? That sounds interesting. How?" He liked the sound of that. And the fact that she was no longer treating him the way he'd seen her treat her crew the first day they'd met. He needed to know that he wasn't just another man to her.

"I don't know, maybe by challenging you to the chin-up bar again."

"Are you sure you want to do that? Your guys are all inside this time. I'd hate to have to beat you in front of them."

"Bet you'd hate for me to best you even more, right?"

He grinned. "Hell, yeah, but I don't think that would be the result."

"What makes you think I can't take you today?" she asked, lifting one arm and flexing her muscles.

He studied her arm. He walked around her desk and tested her muscle. She held herself still, but he noticed that her breath increased just the tiniest bit. Not so immune to him after all.

"It's only been three days; strength training takes weeks not days as I'm sure you know. Did you spend yesterday working out like a madwoman."

"I'm not going to give away any of my secrets."

She put her hand on his thigh, walked her fingers up toward his belt. He liked the feel of her fingers on him a little too much. His intent had been to tease her and maybe himself, not to start something now, because he knew that the ramifications for Andi would be long lasting. He caught her hand in his, lifted it from his thigh to his chest.

"What are you doing?" he asked, unable to help the husky catch in his voice.

"What I said I would do," she replied in the silky tone of hers that warned him she was up to no good.

"And that is?"

"Convincing you to leave."

He leaned down and kissed her. Her mouth had been driving him crazy during their entire meeting. And it felt like days instead of hours since he'd tasted her. He caught her bottom lip between his teeth and then slipped his tongue through the seam of her lips. "I thought you were trying to find a way to convince me you could beat me at chin-ups."

She smiled up at him. "I was counting on the fact that I wore you out last night to lessen your strength."

He smiled at that. He had felt worn-out this morning. His body ached in places it hadn't in a long time. And the thing was he shouldn't be feeling anything close to this kind of lust so soon after last night, but he was. "Babe, you so didn't wear me out."

"*Babe*, you were so sleeping like a baby when I left my place."

"Do you really want to go there?" he asked. He loved being in her bed. Had slept better last night than he had any other night in recent memory.

"Why not? That's what you meant when you refused to open the door."

"Maybe I did. Or maybe I just wanted to remind you that we are more than just an arson investigator and a fire chief."

"As if I'd forget that."

"You act like you already have."

"I'm not going to fawn all over you, Tuck. Even if you weren't here in an official capacity."

"I don't want you to fawn."

"What do you want, then?"

Honestly, he had no idea what he wanted from her, but he had wanted to needle her and to get some sort of reaction. "I want to know that you're mine."

"For how long?" she asked.

"Do we have to discuss that now?"

"When would you like to discuss it?" she asked.

He slipped his hands around her waist and lifted her from her chair. She rested her head on his shoulder. "Sweetheart?"

"Sometimes this entire thing with you seems unreal."

To him, too. But he was used to hiding what he really felt and did so now. "Because the sex was incredible."

She punched his arm and stepped away from him. Watching her put the distance of the room between them, he knew he'd screwed up. His arms felt empty now that she wasn't in them. Really empty, as if he'd never hold her again.

"I wasn't thinking about the sex," she said. "But that was a bit unreal."

He crossed to her and put his hands on her shoulders. Tucked her up against his chest and rested his chin on the top of her head. "That's the one thing I'm sure is real. The one part of our relationship that I'm really confident in."

"You must be to use the word relationship." There was a smile in her voice, a hint of lightness that hadn't been there before.

"You like the thought of a relationship with me?"

"I don't know for sure, Tucker. But there are times when the thought of having a deeper bond with you is very . . . reassuring."

"For me, too," he admitted. Realizing that he'd seen in her what he'd wanted to see. A woman who was cool. Used to dealing with her affairs and not showing any emotion. But she'd seen in him the same thing. They both were very unused to showing any weakness, and that left them both with a vulnerability that neither wanted to admit.

The evening was quiet up until midnight when they were called to a car accident on I–4. It was an SUV versus an eighteen-wheeler. A family on their way home from a weekend at Disney, based on the balloons in the backseat. By the time the crew got back to the firehouse, there was only an hour and a half until their shift ended, and everyone was in that overtired mode.

Andi really wanted a shower in which she could stand and let the water drown her sorrow at the lives that had been taken by impatience. Her eyes felt gritty, and her stomach was almost queasy. She put on her game face, but it was more difficult today.

She went into the kitchen to make the coffee and found McMillan standing at the sink, the water overflowing the glass pot in his hands. She reached around him and turned off the faucet.

"Sorry, Andi. Don't know where my mind went."

She nodded and took the pot from him. She knew where his mind was. With those three little boys in the back of the SUV that had crossed the median and flipped. Three boys that would never grow up and play ball or tour the fire station with their kindergarten class.

"It's okay," she said at last.

"Dammit, Andi, it's not okay. It is never going to be okay for that family again. Did you see the mother? Did you see her eyes?"

Andi turned away from Pete. She understood what he was saying, but she couldn't deal with the mother's grief. Her own feelings were perilously close to the surface, and she had always been able to keep up the façade of being just like the guys. When they were raw—when she was raw—it was hard.

She knew she couldn't start crying here. She'd done that only once, when she'd been sixteen and her father had responded to a car accident off duty. She'd been with him and had seen her first fatality. The face of that woman still haunted her . . . Jennifer Montgomery. An eighteen-year-old whose Harley had possessed too much power for her.

Andi had been unprepared for death and had started sobbing when she realized that Rory had actually dated Jennifer for three months. Her father had told her to get back in the truck in that gruff way of his, and the look in his eyes had told her to suck it up. She'd never forgotten that.

Never forgotten how she'd felt sad and mad and unsure that she'd reacted in the right way.

"It just makes me think about how random life is. How we don't know if when we leave here, one of us won't make it home."

She turned toward Pete. Knowing what she had to do, she pushed her own grief, her own painful emotions, aside. For a moment everything she'd been trying to figure out about Tuck crystallized in her mind. She'd been focusing on the fact that he'd leave her. Every man she'd ever dated had and not because they were bad people, but just because she had absolutely no idea how to live day-in and day-out with anyone.

She pushed that away for the moment. She had to get McMillan's head turned around. Had to get him away from the dangerous rage that she sensed boiled just below the surface. "How do we know that one of us might not win the lotto on Wednesday?"

He tipped his head to the side. Saying nothing. The only noise in the kitchen was the automatic drip pot. "Yeah, who's to say? But why them?"

"Pete, you know I'm not going to tell you how to feel, but you need to get their faces out of your head. I think that Johnson is in the weight room using the punching bag . . . Why don't you go take a turn?"

He stalked past her, stopping in the doorway. "How do you do it? How do you just shut off everything and function like that?"

His words hurt because they were an accusation. "I have to, McMillan. I'm not like you guys. I don't have the luxury of expressing my emotions the way I need to."

"How's that, Cap?"

She shook her head, swallowed hard and just stared at him. She knew the moment he realized what she meant. He turned his back and blocked the kitchen doorway. "Go ahead. I won't let anyone in."

She smiled. Pete was a great guy, a good firefighter and the kind of friend she'd had too few of in her life. She went up behind him. Wanted to hug him but knew she couldn't. Instead she put her hand on his shoulder. "That's the sweetest thing you've ever said to me."

"Don't let it go to your head. It's just that sometimes I really do forget you're a woman."

"Are you trying to be a jerk?" she asked, teasing him because he'd caught a glimpse of her vulnerability. The chink in her armor that she didn't want anyone to realize she had.

"Yes, but only so you won't think I'm less a man than you are."

She squeezed his shoulder. "I never could."

He walked away, and she went back to the coffeemaker, watching it finish its cycle before she could grab a cup. She took her mug into the weight room and watched the guys all silently working on the machines. She'd seen them do this before, and to be honest, it seemed to work.

For herself, working out provided the kind of physical exhaustion she'd need to hopefully fall asleep when she got home. She put her mug on the floor and went to the stairclimber machine.

Danny Brown was on the rowing machine, and from the look in his eyes he wasn't getting off until their shift ended. McMillan was holding the punching bag for Johnson. They both continued trading off, holding and punching.

She climbed on the machine until her thighs started to burn, and she thought about climbing mountains, climbing stairs, maybe in the Sears Tower. Climbing away from the reality that being a firefighter brought. Climbing away from Rory and his not wanting to be a firefighter anymore. Climbing high enough that she would be safe to indulge in her affair with Tuck and not have to worry about what the ending would be.

At some point someone switched on the CD player in the room. AC/DC blasted with "Back in Black," and Andi felt herself drift farther away from the firehouse as she continued climbing.

Chapter 13

Tuck had deliberately left his day open. He'd spent the evening at the county archives, looking into who owned the land surrounding Braley's and who had the most to gain if a residential project went in instead of that citrus museum.

The knock on the door brought him up from the couch. He took his time walking into the bedroom of his rented duplex and pulling a pair of jeans on to cover his nakedness. He took another swallow of his coffee as he walked through the living room.

He opened the door to Andi's back. "Well, this is a surprise."

She turned around, and he saw tears streaking down her face. He'd never expected to see her cry. A thousand questions sprang to mind.

She stepped forward. "Thank God you're home."

"Andrea—"

She put her fingers over his lips. "I don't want to talk or think. Make love to me, Tuck."

He opened his arms, and she stepped into them. Her breath caught on a hiccup as he wrapped her in his embrace. He bent his head to her shoulder and rocked her back and forth. Wishing he could take away whatever it was that had upset her.

He framed her face with his hands. She still clung to his

waist. Questions rose again, but she shook her head. "Please don't ask."

He wiped the tears from her face with his thumbs and then bent and licked up the remaining salt trails with his tongue. Her hands skimmed over his bare chest. Sliding around to the small of his back. He felt her fingers slip beneath the waistband of his jeans as he held her closer.

She wrapped one of her legs around his hip and turned her head to find his mouth. He pulled her inside the house and closed the door. There was a look in her eyes that couldn't be described. His first and only thought was to make sure she was okay. Rubbing his hands up and down her back, he realized she was chilled. He lifted her into his arms and carried her through the small living area and sank down on the couch.

Cradling her in his arms, he closed his eyes and held her closer. "Rough night?"

"No talking, Tuck. I'm not kidding," she said, her fingers moving down the buttons of her blouse with smooth efficiency. She shrugged it off her shoulders and immediately reached behind her back to unclasp her bra.

Her pretty breasts spilled free, and he brought his hands up to cover her. Immediately his blood began flowing heavier, and he started to get a hard-on. She shifted around to straddle him. Hands in his hair, breasts brushing his chest. Hips rocking against him.

"Not like this, Andi. Tell me what's going on."

"Tuck, I'm making a note that you tried to be a good guy, but I really need you to just be a guy right now. Just make this about sex."

"Okay, baby," he said, framing her face in his hands and kissing her. He wanted to take his time, but she wouldn't let him. She bit at his mouth, soft nips as she reached between their bodies and lowered his zipper.

She stroked his naked erection and murmured his name softly as she explored him. "Were you expecting me?"

"Nah, if I was, I'd have tied myself to the bed."

She smiled, and his heart turned over because it was so sad. "Don't make me laugh, Tuck. I don't want to do anything but feel you. Inside me . . ."

She stood and shimmied out of her pants and underwear. But she'd forgotten her boots and cursed.

Bending over, she quickly pulled the laces and kicked them off, then her pants. She still had her work socks on, but nothing else. She looked so heartbreakingly beautiful with her hair falling around her shoulders and her trim, fit body nude that his breath caught.

"Pants on or off?" she asked.

He lifted his hips and kicked his jeans off. He didn't want to feel anything but her silky skin against his. She straddled him again, pulling his head back and ramming her mouth down on his. She thrust her tongue deep inside, tasting and taking him. There was nothing passive in Andi at this moment, and he was so hard he thought he'd come in the next heartbeat.

He tested her between her legs, found her wet and smoothed some of the moisture on his fingers and up between her labia. She moaned and threw her head back. "Harder, Tuck."

"Shift up here so I can get your breast, baby."

She moved, and he suckled her nipple into his mouth while his fingers massaged between her legs. Her hips rocked harder against him. "I want you inside me."

"Let me up," he said. He needed a condom.

"Not now," she said.

"I need a condom."

"Just be careful. Don't come inside me. I need you."

He didn't know if he'd be able to pull out at the last second, but was determined to give Andi what she wanted. She'd asked him for so little, and he wanted to give her the world.

She reached between them, held his erection in her hand,

waiting. He couldn't deny her. His hand slipped over hers, positioning himself to enter her body. She moved her hands to his shoulders and lowered herself slowly onto him.

He had never felt anything better than her warm body wrapping around him. He gripped her hips, holding her still so he could just feel her. She moaned his name and tried to rock her hips, but he held her off, wanting to enjoy his time in her silky body.

He lowered his head, finding her nipple with his teeth, biting carefully. He felt her tighten around him, and he skimmed his hands up her back, thrusting up into her body. She moved on him with the same frantic energy she'd had since he opened his door. She rocked harder until he felt her fingernails bite into his shoulders and her mouth on his neck. She tightened around him, clenching him in her body.

He grew harder, fuller, as she rocked through her climax. He felt his balls draw up tight against his body and subtly shifted her off his cock. She sat back on his thighs and reached for him, using her hands to milk him as his orgasm rocked through him.

Tuck wrapped his arms around her and stood up. Carrying her down the hall to his bedroom and placing her on the center of his unmade bed. She wiped her hands on her stomach, rubbing in the essence of him so that she'd have that small part of Tuck with her. He watched her moving her hands over her stomach, and his cock twitched.

He reached for a tissue on the nightstand and wiped his own body clean before lying down next to her and pulling her into his arms. "Talk."

"What?" she asked, totally stalling for time. There was a shrewd look in his eyes that told her she couldn't escape any longer. She felt confident she could seduce him again. That with very little effort she could have him back inside her body and that talking would be the last thing on his mind.

"Tell me what that was about," he said, running his finger

over her cheekbones. He touched her so gently sometimes that she forgot she was a tough-ass woman who could easily best most men. He treated her as if she were some kind of princess.

She felt so mellow now, the last thing she wanted to do was visit those emotions again. She wanted to just stay in his arms and make love to him over and over again until she fell asleep.

"Not yet. I want to pretend that you and I are the only two people in the world."

He nuzzled the top of her head and pulled her on top of him. She lined her feet up on top of his and tucked her head into his shoulder, covering him from neck to toes.

She hadn't thought about coming here. Not until she was in her truck and realized that if she went home, she wasn't going to ever stop crying. She thought about what Pete had said about how none of them knew if they'd live through the day, and she'd needed to see Tuck again.

She'd needed to see him and hold him because she knew life was precarious. She knew that as soon as she felt comfortable with each new stage of life, something would happen and force her to change.

So she'd come to his house. And as she stood on his porch, the doubts and fears she'd been harboring about . . . about having a relationship with him had completely disappeared.

"Sweetheart—"

"Why do you call me sweetheart? I'm not sweet."

"You can be very sweet," he said, tracing his fingertips down her back. He cupped her rump and shifted underneath her so that the tip of his erection nestled between her legs. Though she'd just had him, she wanted him again. Wished she were on the pill so she could shift her legs and take him inside her body. Let him spill his seed deep within her. So that later when life intruded and they were both on their own again, she'd have the memories of how it had felt to have him inside her.

"That doesn't explain the nickname." She wished she had a name to call him. She'd never use an endearment because she'd feel silly calling him by anything other than his name. But she liked that he used one for her.

"I want to call you that. I've never had a sweetheart before, but you . . . Well, you are one. You try not to let the world see, but inside you're this very feminine person who just wants to be coddled."

"Do you want me to call you something like that?"

"Do you want to?"

"I don't know. I've never . . ."

"Sweetheart, just holding you in my arms, just having you here, is an endearment."

She turned her face away from his. Lying naked on top of him should have protected her, should have made it so she didn't feel so vulnerable, but she did. He'd reduced all of her protective maneuvering to nothing with those few words. Did she really want what he'd said? She thought maybe she did, but only with Tucker.

She was glad that he felt that way about her. She'd never say the words out loud, but Tuck made her feel as though she was whole for the first time. That every part of Andrea was acceptable.

"Did I scare you?" he asked.

She pushed up on her elbows and felt him hot and hard between her legs. "Did you want to?"

"Maybe. I like to keep you guessing about me. I don't want to be like the other men in your life."

She cupped his face in her hands and leaned down. She rubbed her lips back and forth over his and then sucked his lower lip into her mouth. Sucked on it for a long minute before tasting him with languid sweeps of her tongue.

She pulled back when his cock began rocking against her. "You are not like any other man in my life, Tucker."

"Tell me," he said, tracing light patterns over her breasts with his fingers.

"No other man sees me. No other man . . . Let's just say normally I would have just gone home and locked myself in the shower, but today . . ."

"You came to me. I loved that you were so turned on, baby. I loved that you needed me that much, but I think you might be using sex and the fact that I let you use me as an escape from whatever is bothering you."

She looked down at him. She felt so safe in Tuck's arms—safe in an emotional place where she'd never ventured before. "If I tell you, you have to just drop it afterward. Okay?"

"What if I can help?"

"You can't. This is something I have to deal with myself."

"Okay, tell me. I'll let it go after, I promise," he said.

She knew Tucker was a man of his word and closed her eyes, lying back on his chest and turning her face away from him again. "We had a late night call to a traffic fatality. We had to help cut three kids out of a crashed SUV. Three little boys. I . . . I don't like it when I react like a female at work. Most of the time it's not an issue. But when I saw that—hell, when the guys saw it—it was rough on everyone, and I held it together as long as I could."

Tuck, true to his word, didn't say a thing. But he wrapped his arms around her and rocked her in his embrace, before he rolled her under him, put a condom on his body and made tender love to her.

Tuck had to go to work, but he had his arms full of a warm, soft woman, so he was naturally reluctant. He hadn't called in sick in over three years and figured the state owed him a day.

But he sensed that Andi would need some space. She'd been pretending to sleep for the last twenty minutes or so, and that had suited him. He liked holding her. His cell phone rang, and she looked at him with those wide brown eyes. "Do you have to work today?"

"You know I do," he said, patting her backside. He felt too lethargic to move. His alarm had beeped, and he knew that the cell call would be Marilee with the name of a county commissioner in Bartow who could help him.

"You should have said something," she said, pushing out of his arms and sitting up. Her eyes were sleepy; her body language indicated she was ready for sleep instead of pulsing with her normal energy. He traced his finger down her back. It amazed him that she was his lover now. That she'd let him into her soft body.

He couldn't explain why he hadn't said something earlier, except he hadn't wanted to leave their bed. She rarely needed anyone. Perhaps at one time she had needed someone and they hadn't been there. The trust between them was a new and fragile thing.

"I'll go get dressed and leave," she said.

He snagged her around the waist and pulled her back to him. Held her loosely in his arms when what he really wanted to do was bind her to him. He knew he couldn't do that. Knew that he had to give her the room to be herself . . . to stand on her own as she always had.

"Don't."

"Don't what?"

He sighed, burying his face in her hair. "Don't leave. You're tired, and I like the thought of you naked in my bed waiting for me to return."

She rolled over to face him. One of her legs curving over his, her hands slipping up around his neck. "Is this another macho fantasy, like your game the other night?"

"I don't like the way you said macho. But I guess it is a fantasy."

"I knew it. I like that about you, Tuck. You have no problem telling me exactly what you want."

"What else do you like about me?" he asked, only half joking. He wanted to know what it was he'd done right so he could keep doing it.

"You're a good lover."

"Goes without saying, but thanks for saying it," he replied.

She tugged at his chest hair and laughed, but sadness lingered in the back of her eyes. "I also like the way you keep things even between us."

"I do?" he asked, rubbing his stinging chest. He liked the way that Andi didn't fight fair. That she wasn't above using any means at her disposal to keep things even.

"Well, you're going to," she said. She stacked her hands on his chest and rested her chin on them.

He tried to concentrate on what she was saying. He should just keep his eyes steady on hers, but her nipples abraded his chest. And he couldn't help glancing down at those ripe little berries and remembering how they'd felt in his mouth.

"How?" he asked, while he could still think. Yeah, right. The only thing he was thinking about at this moment was shifting her legs a little so he could thrust inside her again.

"By giving me a fantasy," she said, licking her lips.

He hardened immediately against her belly. Her eyes widened, and she adjusted her legs on either side of him. She shifted against him, riding the ridge of his erection.

"I thought having a stud like me in your bed was your fantasy."

"Keep dreaming that dream."

And it was a dream to have her with him. A wet dream. Andi was the kind of fantasy woman he'd given up on finding. "What's this fantasy of yours?"

"That's just it, whatever I want."

"When are you going to claim it? When I get back from work?"

"Maybe . . . You'll never know when I'll ask or what I'll ask for, but someday I'm going to ask you to do something sexy like this for me."

"And I'm going to agree to this why?" he asked.

She slipped her arms around his neck and brought her mouth to his, just barely touching, and let her breath mingle with his. She watched him, building the anticipation, and then slowly kissed him. Tasting him deeply and making sure he knew that she wanted him. That kiss made him realize that leaving her today or any day was going to be very hard.

"Because I could tell by the catch in your voice that you've thought about me naked here."

"I have and more."

She smiled at him, totally losing her cool negotiator face. "Really?"

Any doubts he harbored that she had started making a place for herself in his heart disappeared. There was something so endearing about the joy on her face as she thought of being the object of his fantasies.

"Yes. If you're good while I'm gone, maybe I'll share a few when I get back."

"What if I'm bad?"

"Hell, woman, that'd be a dream come true."

"So we have a deal?" she asked.

"What are you going to—"

She leaned down and kissed him. "Whatever I feel like. I'd be worried if I were you."

"I'm sure whatever you have in mind, I'll be happy to play."

And he meant it. He took a record shower, dressed and left her sleeping in his bed.

Chapter 14

Tuck's house was very much a bachelor's temporary residence. So after sleeping most of the day she woke to find nothing to do but watch television. That didn't appeal to her, so she scoured his house and found three books. They were popular fiction, and two of the authors, she knew from her own secret reading addiction, were romance authors.

She picked a book and looked around for something to wear while she was reading. But remembered that she'd given Tuck her word she'd stay naked in his bed. Naked . . . She'd never spent that much time without clothing. She didn't hate her body; she just never really felt as though she fit in it.

There was a crooked mirror over the dresser, and Andi studied her own form. What was it that Tuck saw in her that made him want her? She didn't understand it.

She'd taken a shower and didn't feel so blue anymore. Tuck had helped more than she ever wanted him to know. He'd given her a way of dealing with her grief and respected the boundaries she'd put up.

A part of her wondered why it was so easy for him to let her have that space. Was that a precursor to his leaving? Their meeting yesterday and the report he'd given her indicated that he was close to wrapping up his case.

Then he'd be off to his next assignment. In Miami with

Ian. She couldn't still see him—not down there. Her brothers and father . . . No, she couldn't deal with Tuck and all of the boys at the same time. So she had at most a week left with him.

Such a short time with a man who made her want forever. Was that true? She looked at herself in the mirror, seeking answers. But they weren't there.

The phone rang, and she wondered if she should answer it. She glanced at the instrument and then heard the answering machine click on. "Hey, sweetheart, you still sleeping?"

She picked up the phone, watching herself in the mirror. "I'm awake."

"Still naked?" he asked.

"Yes."

"Do you like it?"

"I'm not sure. I've never just sat around without clothes on. What about you?"

"I do it all the time. Sometimes you have to strip away the layers of civilization to get to know a fire."

"Does that really work?"

"It doesn't hurt."

"Do all investigators do that?"

"I have no idea . . . It's one of my trade secrets."

"Ah, before you know it I'll know all of your secrets."

"I'm not too worried about you revealing them."

"Why not?"

"Truth?"

"Yeah."

"You'd have to admit to a personal relationship with me, and I can't see you doing that."

She said nothing. She'd never thought of how Tuck was affected by her choices. She wasn't changing them or changing her mind. Her life worked precisely because there were limits. There were areas of her life that no one ever intruded into because she'd marked them off-limits.

"Does that bother you?" she asked.

"Yes. But that's my issue. Don't you worry about it."

She wished she were a different kind of woman. Hell, it wasn't the first time she'd had that thought. Always when she tried to have anything like a relationship her inadequacies seemed to stand out. "I don't want to be responsible for making you feel . . . What do you feel, Tuck?"

He said nothing for a few long minutes, static echoed over the open line and she knew he hadn't hung up, but maybe he wished he could.

"More than you're ready to hear now," he said at last.

What did that mean? Now she wanted to know, had to know, but she couldn't ask him. She had to hope that it slipped out sometime when he wasn't expecting his emotions to get the better of him. "What makes you so sure?"

"Because it's more than lust."

"Oh," she said. What else? She wanted to know more but was afraid to push. From years of living and working with men she knew that emotions weren't up for discussion. But for once she wanted to rock the boat.

"I was calling to tell you that I'm going to be home later than I anticipated. There's some food in the fridge and a couple of books in my suitcase."

"I found the books. Maybe I should go home, and you can meet me there later."

"I don't think so; you shouldn't be driving naked. And you promised a day in my bed."

"Did your fantasy involve me being bored?" she asked. If this were his real home and not a temporary place, then she'd probably indulge in hours of exploring. Really seeing what he surrounded himself with.

"Not at all. I imagined you laying there thinking about me and pleasuring yourself."

"What?" She'd never . . .

"Have you ever masturbated?" he asked. His voice

dropped an entire octave, going so low and gravelly that she could feel the vibrations of it through the phone.

"Maybe." No way was she having this conversation with him. Sure she'd done it, but talking about it was different—way different—and it felt too intimate to ever speak of out loud.

"Maybe? That's so a yes."

"That's a very personal thing, Tucker."

"I'd tell you."

"Like that's any secret. Guys always do."

"That's not nice; some men might not."

"Did you really think I'd do that in your bed?"

"I hoped. What about you? Do you like thinking of me getting off just by thinking about you?"

"Yes," she said, still staring at her body.

Tuck drove effortlessly through the traffic while talking to Andi. As usual she'd thrown him off. He'd called to check on her and figured she'd resent that, but she'd been so sleepy and sad this morning despite the fact that he'd made love to her. And he didn't want her to wake up alone and be stuck in his house with only those sad memories.

Tuck had been an investigator on the police force before becoming an arson investigator, and he'd seen his share of fatalities. They were tough. Everyone had a different way of getting through them. And he knew that Andi's burden was stronger because she was a woman and a leader. But word at the firehouse this morning had been about how Andi handled tragedy better than most. Tuck had felt a swell of pride hearing that.

"Want to have some fun?" he asked her. He was almost to the county records office. He pulled into a parking lot on one of the many oak-lined streets. He rolled down his window and turned off his truck. He couldn't drive and listen to her at the same time. She drove him out of his mind.

"What kind?" she asked.

"The kind Clinton made famous."

She paused, and then said, "You want me to do something with a cigar?"

He hardened immediately as the visual assaulted him. Andi was a walking wet dream, and everything she did turned him on. "Damn, I'll have to stop and get one on the way home. I was thinking of phone sex."

"Do I have to call you Mr. President?"

"Only if it turns you on."

"I don't have to pretend you're someone else," she said softly.

"Me either."

"Really?"

"Hell, yes. I haven't been this horny since I was a teenager."

"Good."

"You like keeping me in a state of arousal?"

"Yes. I think you're too cocky for your own good most of the time. Pun intended."

"I'm going to be coming home eventually." It was the first time he'd said those words to a woman. He'd never lived with a woman. He'd had one long-term relationship that had lasted three months, but Carin had kept her place and never let him sleep over at hers.

"But until then, what's this about phone sex?" she asked.

"Wanna try it?" He just wanted to hear her come again. He loved the sounds she made.

"What does it entail? Me moaning and saying stuff like 'do me harder'?"

"No. I thought you could start by getting one of my ties out of my suitcase and then getting on the bed."

He heard the light pad of her footsteps and then his suitcase open. "Which one?"

"The blue-striped one."

"Got it."

"Are you on the bed?"

"Just a second. Okay, now I am. Should I lie flat or prop myself on the pillows?"

"Do you masturbate on your back or stomach?"

"Both."

"Which would you prefer?"

"Back," she said.

He heard the bed squeak as she adjusted herself on the mattress. "I'm ready."

"Okay, rub the tie over your body. It's silk; does it feel good?"

"Yes, it's soft and a little cool from the air-conditioning. It reminds me of how your mouth felt on my nipple when you had the ice cube."

"Rub your nipples with my tie and then tug on them. Make sure they are good and hard for my mouth."

"They are hard. I like the way they feel in my fingers. I'm imagining your hands with that rough callus you have on your palm rubbing over me."

Her breathing was audible now, and he knew she was getting close. "Rub my tie down your body. I love your belly, baby. Make small circles there, dip your finger into your belly button."

Her breath hitched in her throat, and so did his. He was hot and hard. His erection painfully tight against the zipper of his jeans.

He straightened his leg to give himself some room, but knew that he was just going to have to suffer for now. "Now, go lower, Andi. Hold yourself open and test your body. Are you wet for me?"

"Yes, Tuck. I'm really wet."

"Good, baby. That's so good. Take some of that cream and rub it on your stomach and nipples."

She moaned softly.

"What are you doing?"

"Pushing my finger into my body."

"Just one?"

"Yes," she said, her breath catching again.

"Add a second one," he said.

She moaned again. "That feels so good. Almost like I do when you come inside me."

"Move them in and out slowly."

"I wish you were here, Tuck. This is fine, but I want you inside me."

"Me, too, sweetheart. Pretend it's me. Use your other hand to pinch your nipples."

"Ah, Tuck . . . I'm so close."

"Put your thumb on your clit and circle it. Alternate your touches light and then hard. As hard as you can—"

He broke off as he heard her gasp his name. Her breath coming in heavy exhalations. She said nothing for a minute, and then he heard her. "Thank you, Tucker."

And she quietly hung up the phone. He put his head forward on the steering wheel and sat there until a cop knocked on the window and asked him if he was okay.

Andi woke to the feel of Tuck's arms around her. She opened her eyes and stared into his deep green ones. "Hello."

"Sleep good?" he asked.

"Yes, that phone sex did the trick. Put me out for the rest of the afternoon. What'd you find in Bartow?"

"I'll tell you after."

She realized he was naked and felt the latex tip of his condom-covered erection nudging her. She spread her legs a little wider and drew him closer. He slipped inside her body, and she wrapped her arms and legs around him.

For the moment she felt so content. So . . . perfect, she thought. Tuck's thrusts were slow and steady. Easy, as if he had all evening to rock inside her body.

Surprised, she felt her body tightening around him. Her

climax was a gentle wave that washed over her. Tuck must have been waiting for that because he quickened his pace and shouted her name as he climaxed.

He rolled to his side and pulled her into the curve of his body. With one hand he dealt with the condom, tossing it in the trash can next to the bed. He rubbed her back, and she cuddled closer to him. Her eyes closed as she thought about where this could possibly go. There was no future for them. And that saddened her.

She could leave Auburndale if he asked her to, but Tuck never stayed in one place very long. Always traveling around the state to solve arsons for rural firehouses.

"Want to tell me what you found out?" she asked, after a few minutes. There was something reassuring about being able to talk shop with Tuck. She'd been involved with another firefighter a long time ago, and it hadn't been anything like this. In fact, Lloyd had seen her as some kind of freaky sex trophy.

"I'm not sure it's anything solid. But I have a few leads at last," he said. He cupped her backside and pulled her leg up over his hip. So that she wrapped him.

"Who?" she asked. The arsonist had to be someone in the community because of the nature of the fires and the fact that vagrants had been ruled out. It worried her that someone she knew may be responsible.

Tuck leaned down to kiss her. Leisurely exploring her mouth. He was turning her into a sex fiend. She pulled back before she totally forgot what they were discussing.

"Well, Braley's partners for one. They were set to go through with a development company—Jameson Homes— when Roy got the state to kick in some bond money to aid the economy in the area."

"What about Jameson Homes?" she asked. It may sound bad, but she hoped it was the developer. Anything to put another layer between the fires and Pete's family. She'd hate to be McMillan if it turned out Roy was the one behind the arson.

"I'm not sure yet. So far it doesn't seem like they were affected when Braley backed out. They bought some neighboring property, so they were able to break ground on their new subdivision a few days later than scheduled." She'd seen their signs on the cutoff road that led from I–4. A modest bedroom community with lots that backed up to the lake. The sad thing about the development and about Roy's museum was that a part of Florida's rich agricultural history was being lost with the citrus groves.

"Who are Roy's partners? I hope that Pete's dad isn't one of them."

"There was a McMillan listed—Brian—I'm not sure if it's Pete's dad or not."

"No, that's Pete's uncle. I hope it doesn't turn out to be one of his family members."

"Me, too. There are four other partners. I'm going to be busy the next few days following all these leads."

"I'll go with you tomorrow."

"That's not necessary."

"Yes, it is. I might pick up something that you miss."

"I've been doing this job for a while—"

"Hush," she said, covering his mouth with her hand. "I didn't mean that disparagingly. I just meant that sometimes with two people observing, one of them sees something the other doesn't."

"Sorry," he said.

"That's okay. I didn't realize you were so sensitive."

"I'm not sensitive. You're just so ultraefficient that I have the constant need to beat on my chest and prove myself."

"It's a very nice chest."

"Don't try to flirt your way out of this."

"I wasn't." But she liked that she could use her wiles to influence him. She liked that Tuck was so honest about the way she affected him. It made her more comfortable being herself around him.

"So I can come with you tomorrow?"

"I don't know . . ."

"Don't make me pull rank."

"Would you?"

"Yes. I want to be involved. Sitting at home isn't how I want to spend the day."

"You can stay at my place tomorrow, do the whole naked thing again."

"Thanks for that generous offer, but one day is enough for now."

"Didn't you like it?" he asked, genuine caring in his voice.

"Yes, I did. I think . . . I think I needed this today. Just to be in your bed and not have to deal with anything outside this room. But this isn't reality, and I'm the fire chief for a reason."

"I guess I have no choice, then. What do you say we shower and then go get dinner?"

"Sounds good. Are you staying at my place tonight?"

"If you'll let me."

"I think that could be arranged," she said, following him into the bathroom. She tried to forget about what he'd found in Bartow, but the niggling feeling in her gut said that the McMillan family was more involved in this arson case than she'd previously thought.

Chapter 15

Tuck worked alone. He'd always resented having another person close to a case other than to get the information he needed. And today was no different. His investigative methods weren't always orthodox, and he felt an added pressure to not miss anything with Andrea riding along with him.

Their first stop was at the law offices of Johnson, Pillmon and Terric. Jon Terric had been one of Roy Braley's partners in the land. They were a few minutes early. The office was right off of Main Street, close to the park where young mothers and their kids played. There was a nice easy feeling to Auburndale.

"Wouldn't it be nice if we walked in and found a gas can?" Andi said.

"Yes, but a little too pat," he said. The fire had definitely been started using gasoline, and the lab was still analyzing the results to try to determine where it had been bought.

"What kind of questions are you going to ask?" Andi asked, taking a sip from her Styrofoam coffee cup.

"Just general ones. I want to get a feel for the kind of man he is. What he thought about the real estate deal going the way it did. He's not under suspicion of anything yet."

"He's not listed as an owner on the warehouse property," she said.

"He doesn't have to be to want to get even with Roy."

Tuck didn't add that he'd asked Marilee to check and see if any of the investors had financial problems. Marilee had been excited to have something to do. She said she'd missed the investigative work she used to do on the force.

"Do you think that's what was going on?"

"I have no idea. It'd be nice if one of these guys had some connection to fire starting."

"I doubt any of them do other than maybe a barbeque pit in their backyard."

"That's why I'm leaning toward an investor. This is no fire obsessive that has always had a fascination with watching things burn."

"Good thing, because all my guys would be suspects then. Did you ever wonder about that fine line between firefighter and arsonist?"

"Sometimes. Most of the time I don't think about it because then I'd have to be suspicious of everyone I know."

"Ha!"

"Yeah, just kidding. Arsonists have a different profile than firemen. Though they both share a love of fire. What about you, Andi?"

"Yeah, I like to watch the fire burn, but only because I know how to put it out. It's like having control over something that I know is uncontrollable. Like at any second it could burn in another direction, and unless I'm concentrating a hundred and fifty percent, the fire's going to get the better of me."

"You ever set a fire?" he asked, curious. What she said about being in control was something he understood. He felt that way about an investigation, when he got to a site and determined what the flash pattern was or how the fire had accelerated.

"Couple of controlled burns. When I was a kid, Dad used to make us run drills at home. I probably knew more about putting out a fire than most rookies do by the time I was ten."

"What was that like? I mean, I learned how to put out a kitchen fire, but that was only because my mom wasn't home when it happened."

"Where was your mom?" she asked. "You don't really talk much about your family."

"I don't dwell on the past much. I'd rather look forward."

"Me, too," she said with a quiet smile that seemed to acknowledge another thing they had in common.

"My mom was working . . . She worked a lot when I was growing up. But I'd rather hear about your dad."

"He's the best at what he does," she said. The simplicity in her words belied the fact that her father, in Tuck's opinion, didn't sound like a great father.

"At everything?"

"He'd say yes, but only with this big flash of ego. Then he'd admit there are a few areas he could be better at."

"Are there?" Tuck asked.

"Yes, but he is good at a lot of stuff. Mainly he doesn't see the point in doing something if you're not going to do it right."

Tuck saw a lot of that same attitude in Andi. It explained the dogged determination she displayed in everything she did.

"You sound like you respect him a lot."

"Of course I do. He made us a family after Mom died, and that took a lot of effort. There are five of us, and Dad worked twenty-four on forty-eight off like everyone else; but he had a herd at home, and he'd never been the disciplinarian in the house."

"Really? Did he change?"

"Yes. I mean, he always had rules, and we knew to follow them; but Mom was the one who we got into mischief with, and suddenly she wasn't there. Dad had to deal with that. He did a good job. I really admire him."

Tuck was going to let it go, let the subject drop because she hadn't really brought it up, but he couldn't resist. "Was he a good father to his daughter?"

She turned away like he knew she would. Stared out the window so silently that he cursed himself for asking the question. But he sometimes felt as though Andi was another case he was on. Every answer he got led to more questions.

"Look, their offices are open now. We should be going."

"Aren't you going to answer?"

She gave him a hard glare. "I'm a functioning adult and successful in the career I've chosen. I think that's a yes."

Andi hung back, letting Tuck do his thing. And it was impressive. He was still the easygoing man she'd come to know, but a steel that was leashed underlined his every movement.

They spent about thirty minutes talking to Jon, who was funny and friendly and admitted he'd been in charge of the Auburndale High School bonfires in the park for a few years.

"I guess that means you know how to start a fire," Tuck said wryly.

"Yes, it does."

They left Jon's office.

"I liked him," Andi said.

"Me, too. He was very honest about everything which helps. I want to check out the fire sites again. Make sure I didn't miss anything. Want to come with me?"

"Yes."

He drove to the first warehouse, and they both got out of his truck. She hated how buildings looked after a blaze had ripped through them. At least in nature you knew that fire was part of the regrowth process, but with buildings . . . It was total destruction of what had once been.

"What are we looking for? Didn't you find the burn pattern already?"

"Yes, but I want to verify everything and match it to what the lab found."

"Why?"

"To make sure there was no cross contamination of samples."

"The investigator from the insurance company took most of them. Pete Farnsworth, do you know him?"

"Yes. I've been in touch on this case. I've made a computer model of the warehouse, and I want to check the different burn patterns and see which one matches the exact patterns here."

He took his laptop from behind the seat and opened it on the hood of his truck. Andi walked around the perimeter, checking for anything they may have missed. She remembered the night they'd arrived. The smoke had been billowing up in the air. They'd all gone into action and had been focused on getting control of the blaze, putting it out. The accelerant they used in the hoses had helped them make a huge dent in the fire, and slowly they'd won the battle.

She was aware of Tuck walking around the site as well, bending to examine the ground or to take a picture with his digital camera. Watching him, seeing him in action, was something of a turn-on, and she had a flash of him wearing turn-out gear and nothing else.

She wondered if he'd do it. He hadn't been a firefighter before going to the fire marshal's office. He'd been an investigator for the police force.

Her cell phone rang. She saw that it was Sara. "Hey, what's up?"

She heard the sounds of Alanis Morrisette in the background, which was never a good sign. Sara always played the *Jagged Little Pill* CD when she and Mick were fighting. "Can you do lunch today?"

Sara was closer to her than a sister. But she wanted to spend the day with Tuck. Wanted to spend as much time with him as she could before he had to move on. *God, that didn't sound pathetic.* "Maybe."

"Maybe? What are you doing that's more exciting than lunch with me?"

Andi took a deep breath. She wanted to keep Tuck her private secret. She didn't want anyone else to realize how involved she was with him. And there was no pretending with Sara and Mick. They always saw through her when she said that love was something that the Disney films had made everyone believe was real when in truth it was just a fairy tale.

"Andi?"

"Don't tell Mick."

"Okay, now I've got to know what you're doing."

Andi waited. Heard Sara sigh.

"I won't tell Mick."

Andi dug her sunglasses out of her purse and put them on. "Even when you're over being mad at him."

"Right now I don't know if that's going to happen, but yeah, even then I won't say anything."

Sara sounded more than mad. And that bothered Andi. Though most people thought she gave good advice and was a good listener, she honestly had no idea how to help out. Dumb luck had been on her side for a long time. What if she couldn't help her friends? "Well, I'm helping out with the arson investigation."

"With Tuck?" Sara asked in a low voice.

"Yes, so?"

"Who won the dare?" she asked with a little laugh in her voice.

"You're impossible when you're like this."

"So Mick tells me. Can you get free for lunch?" Sara asked.

She didn't want to let Tuck into any other area of her life. Right now, he was separated from all the other areas . . . at least by public knowledge. "I'd have to bring him with me."

"Why?"

"Because we're in one vehicle."

"Oh, my, this is serious. You let a man drive?"

"Stop being a pain. It's not nearly as cute as you think it is."

"I'll have to remember that. I can drag Mick along. I really need to talk to you."

"About?"

"Can't say."

"Mick's there?"

"Yes."

"Is it serious?" She hated it when Sara and Mick fought. They were her solid duo, the couple she counted on to always keep it together.

"I'm not sure. I just need to talk to another woman."

"Let me call you back about lunch."

"Thanks, Andi."

She hung up the phone and walked over to Tuck.

"Who was on the phone?"

"Sara—Mick's wife."

"I remember who she is," he said.

"Um . . . Something's come up. I'm not going to be able to spend the rest of the day out here."

"I'm sorry to hear that," he said. And she thought she saw genuine regret in his eyes.

Tuck rubbed the back of his neck and pushed away from the desk. His computer simulations confirmed what he'd determined at the site and through questioning. He now knew how the fires were started, and how they spread. Pete, the insurance investigator, concurred with Tuck's findings, so he was as positive as he could be that this was what actually happened.

Pete's list of suspects matched Tuck's and . . . That was it. He was at a standstill. He knew he was missing something. That one detail that would send his mind down the right track. That one fact that would put just the right spin on what he had found so he could figure out who had set the blazes.

And he knew with whom the blame for his distraction lay. Andrea. He'd driven her back to her house, and she'd left him without even a kiss.

Just a vague wave that told him her mind was somewhere else. On her friends. One of the things that he liked about Andi was the way she cared about her circle of friends. And he'd bet more people were in that circle than realized it. Like her crew on the engine, who probably thought that she was just a thorough captain. But he knew better.

He'd seen the way she cared and how she hid it deep inside.

He checked his watch; it was almost dinnertime. He logged off his computer and debated for about thirty seconds not calling her. But he was days away from wrapping up his investigation, days away from leaving Auburndale.

The phone rang before he could call Andi. He reached for it. "Fields."

"Tuck, it's Mom."

She always identified herself, which cracked him up. "I know your voice, Mom."

"Just making sure you knew it was me. Do you think you can come home at the end of the month?"

He glanced at the calendar. "I think so. I'm close to finishing up this investigation, and then I'm supposed to go to South Florida. How long do you want me home?" he asked. He toyed with inviting Andi to go with him. They could stay at the Hilton Towers on the Magnificent Mile. Go to dinner with his mom, shop, eat and just enjoy each other.

"Just for the weekend. Jayne's dating a new guy."

Jayne's dating record was fifty-fifty. Sometimes she found a great guy, others not so much. And when a guy pushed her to settle down she drove him away. About like him— neither of them ever settled down. They moved on. For Jayne, he suspected that it was because she was afraid of being too much like their mother, who cared to the point that she exhausted herself.

For Tuck, he was too afraid of being like his dad, who'd been unable to stick around. He'd gone over every memory in his head leading up to when his father had walked away and could never figure out what had driven him away.

He knew why his mom wanted him to come home now. For some reason, with Jayne's men, Tuck had been right about the guys who ended up being losers. "Uh-oh, you want me to do the big brother thing?"

"Yes. He seems nice, but you have a better radar . . ."

"Want me to come home sooner?" he asked. The last man Jayne had dated had really been a jerk and left his sister pretty shaken.

"No, then Jayne would guess—"

"That you asked me to."

"Exactly. The key to being a meddling mother is to never let your kids know what you're doing."

"News flash, Mom, we know." She'd always been like that. Even working two jobs didn't keep her from being aware of everything that happened in their lives. He had never felt alone, even when she'd been on long shifts. She'd called, she'd rushed home for lunch . . . She'd mothered them and made them feel safe.

Who had done that for Andi? He heard what she'd said about her father—that he was a good dad—but men, himself included, didn't do the emotional support thing the same way women did.

"Sweetie, I know that, but if I don't do anything overt, you can't call me on it."

"Well, I'm on to you. I might even warn Jayne about it."

"Whatever you want to do. How's your investigation going?"

"Good. Like I said, I've almost wrapped it all up."

"Are you dating anyone?" she asked.

Was he dating Andi? He wondered how she'd answer that question. He wanted to know the answer as much as his mom. But he was too old to put up with that kind of interfering from his mother. "Mom, that's overt meddling."

She made a *tsk*ing sound that made him feel about eight years old again. "It was just a question.

"Aren't you going to answer it?" she asked, after a few minutes had passed.

"No, I'm not answering the question."

She sighed. "That means either yes, you are and don't want me to know about it—which I can respect. Or you're not."

"Mom, you're a mastermind. I'll call you when I know the exact weekend I can come home."

"I'm betting that you are dating someone."

"Goodbye, Mom."

"Bye, son."

Tuck leaned back in his chair, staring at the bed. He had so many images of Andi on it. He missed her. He missed her out of his bed and in it. He wanted to submerge himself forever in her, and he didn't know how that would work because she was too used to being independent.

And what did the future hold for them, because he was a man used to walking away and not looking back? And this time he wasn't sure he could do it. But at the same time he was afraid to stay.

Chapter 16

Mick had gone a little crazy when Sara had announced she was pregnant. Sara, an oncology nurse, was herself a cancer survivor who'd been in remission for the last eight years. But her doctors had warned her time and again that pregnancy could trigger a regrowth of the cancer. And last week she'd had the test that determined her cancer was back, but so far she hadn't told Andi what the results were.

"I just don't know what to do. Mick was already upset about the baby. He's starting to come to terms with it, but he... He's worried about the jobs the both of us have. Worried he might not make it home one day. And what can I say... Now I have to add this to the mix."

"How did you get pregnant?"

Sara sighed. "I... tricked him. I know it's wrong, and you might not understand this, Andi, because you've never seemed to want kids, but I dream of having a family. I dream of it so often that I wake up crying. On the nights Mick's home... I try to keep it from him, but he knows... He knew what I wanted."

"Then how did you trick him?"

Sara looked away. They'd been here all afternoon, and Andi had just now gotten Sara to talk. And she didn't know what she was going to say or how to make this better. Sara might think Andi didn't want kids, and it was true, she'd said it often enough, but the reasons why she'd ruled them out were so personal. She'd never been the maternal type. Her entire life people had commented on how strong, how capable, how good she was at getting things done, and as an adult she'd heard time and again how lucky she was to have a career she loved since having a family didn't seem important.

"I lied about my cancer. I lied about the percentage of risk involved."

"Why would you do that? You know that if it returns you won't live to see your baby born. Do you really want that for Mick?"

"Oh, Andi."

She knew in an instant what was going on. "Your cancer's back?"

"Yes, and I can't treat it. It was back before the pregnancy."

"What are you going to do?"

"I have no idea. Mick said to get rid of the baby . . . but I can't."

"You know you'll die. It's not like there's going to be a miracle."

"There's a small chance that won't happen."

"Honey, this is real life and not a made-for-TV movie. You're a nurse; you've seen people who had a lot to live for die."

Sara turned back to her. "What would you do?"

"Seriously? I thought you didn't think I wanted a family."

"Sometimes it's easier for me to think of you as a superwoman who is above all the doubts and fears the rest of us have, but I know the truth, Andi. I saw it in your eyes when I mentioned the baby."

Andi hated that she wasn't a superwoman. That she did have the same doubts and fears as other women. And that she had no advice for her friend. She'd never have gotten pregnant like Sara had. "Why didn't you consider adoption?"

"We did. It's just that I really wanted Mick's baby. I know it doesn't make sense. But I wanted a little bit of him and a little bit of me."

Andi bit her lip to keep from crying with Sara. She knew exactly what her friend meant. Maybe from a different angle. If she had Tuck's baby, then once he was gone, she'd still have a living reminder of a time when things had been good. A time when she'd been like everyone else. Not that being like everyone else was her goal, but she'd always been so out of step with the rest of the world that having a baby . . .

"What am I going to do?"

Andi hugged her friend, holding her close. "Talk to Mick. Listen to what he has to say. He loves you, Sara; don't make him choose between you and a child."

"He's not being rational."

"Would you be? What if Mick came to you and said he was going to die in nine months but you'd have a kid?"

Sara pushed away from her, got to her feet and walked around the bench in a jerky sort of pacing that made Andi wonder if she'd gone too far. But it was easy to insulate your emotions when you didn't have to think about reality. Lord knew she'd done it a time or two herself, but she always forced herself out of the hole.

Finally Sara stopped. "I guess you're right. That's a different way of looking at it. I . . . I don't know what to do."

"Go home to Mick. Talk to him, fight with him, do whatever you have to do to get to that place where you can both figure this out."

Sara sat back down next to her. "When I was a little girl all I wanted to do was grow up. I was so sure that as a grown-up my life would be . . . easier."

Andi sighed. "Me, too. I thought once I got out of the

O'Roarke house my life would be this kind of dreamlike thing."

Sara patted her arm in a gesture of understanding, and that epitomized what made Sara different from Andi. Even in her own chaos Sara was aware of others around her and could react to them. Andi never had been able to act on those feelings.

"I wish there was some kind of magic that would work."

Sara sighed. "Thanks, Andi."

"Anytime. Of all the things that I've found in life, I'm glad to have friends like you and Mick."

She smiled over at Andi. "Me, too."

"Are you going to be okay to drive home?"

"I don't know," Sara said. Andi saw she was drained and drove her friend back to her house. Mick was standing in the doorway when they got there, and Andi had the feeling he'd been standing there all day. He didn't say anything to either woman, but when Sara got out of Andi's truck he opened their front door and opened his arms to her.

Andi swallowed on a lump of emotion too strong to identify and backed out of their driveway, heading to her house where she could be alone.

At nine o'clock Tuck acknowledged the fact that Andi wasn't going to call, so he got in his truck and drove over to her place. The lights were out, but her truck was in the driveway, so he parked on the street and went to the door.

He rapped on the frame and rang the doorbell, and after about five minutes the door cracked open. "Tuck."

"Andi."

"What are you doing here?" she asked.

"I wanted to see you."

"Oh."

"Can I come in?"

She stepped back, and he entered. There was an open

pizza box on the coffee table and a pitcher of drinks next to it. From the smell of her breath, he knew it was alcohol.

"Did you eat yet?" she asked.

"Nah, didn't have time."

She went into the kitchen and came back a second later with a plate, napkin and cutlery. "Work?"

He took them and sat on the couch, fixing himself some food. "Yes, and worry."

"Worry?" she asked, settling down next to him. She leaned against him while he ate, and he realized that this was what he'd wanted. Sitting alone in his quiet place, he'd just wanted to be near her.

"About you," he said, putting down his plate and wrapping an arm around her. The television played softly in the background, some movie or television show he didn't recognize.

"Why were you worried about me?" she asked, tipping her head back.

He leaned down and dropped a quick kiss on her lips. "Because you didn't call or anything. I know it's stupid, but that's the way I am."

"What could happen to me?" she asked. A slight smile teased the corners of her mouth.

He knew that he should never have opened this can of worms. Now he was going to have to verbalize the things he'd thought. And to be truthful, until this moment he'd never considered that physically she might have been in danger. He worried more that she'd finally decide that being with him wasn't worth the risk to changed perceptions at work.

"A million things. Your car could have broken down and your cell phone was dead."

"That didn't happen and isn't likely to. I take good care of my truck."

Of course she would. She was the most self-sufficient

person he'd ever met. It made him feel lacking in an odd way. As though there was nothing he could offer her that she couldn't do for herself.

"You do. You could have realized that I wasn't the kind of man you wanted to spend your nights with."

She put her hands on his face, brought his mouth to hers and kissed him. In that tender-aggressive way she had. "I didn't. I just needed to be alone to think."

"Because of the accident the other day?" he asked. He felt as if she wasn't really over it yet. He knew he wouldn't be. He'd seen a grisly homicide on the force. Actually, it had been part of the reason why he'd decided to apply to the fire marshal's office.

"No. Sara's . . . I don't know how to say this, but Sara is having some health problems."

"And?"

"And she and Mick are fighting about it."

"Is it life-threatening?"

"Yes."

"And?"

"I don't know. It gave me a lot to think about. I don't have any sisters . . ."

He reached out and pulled her onto his lap, hugging her tightly. "Want to talk about it?"

She snuggled closer to him. "I don't know. I really wanted to cry, but couldn't. I feel like a loser sometimes when that happens. It's almost too much emotion for me to finally let go and cry."

"You don't have to cry to feel things," Tuck pointed out. He seldom cried, but deep inside he had felt a lot of pain and sadness. Especially after his dad had left them. But he'd never cried. He didn't know if it was because society said boys don't cry, but he didn't think so. He thought it was more the fact that his mom and Jayne had needed someone to be the dry-eyed one.

"Do you ever cry?" she asked.

"No."

"I suppose your life has been . . . What has your life been? You've never said."

"My life has been my own. I've had my share of disappointments."

"That heartbreak you spoke of?"

"Amongst other things."

"Ian cried when his wife died. It was the saddest moment of my life. I'd never seen my brother look like that before. To be honest, I didn't want to see him like that. That's kind of how it was with Sara today. She's always so sunny and upbeat, and I didn't want to have to be the one to cheer her up."

"Maybe she was glad you were there, just to listen."

She shifted around on his lap. "I think she was. Everyone always says to me that I'm a good listener. But to be honest, I don't feel like one. I feel like a fraud."

"Today?"

"Every day, Tuck. Every damned day of my life I feel like a fraud, and then every night I thank God no one saw through it."

"I don't think you're a fraud, sweetheart. I think that it's easier for you to pretend that the real you isn't who you are."

"Why?"

"Because then you don't have to admit that you care. It's easier to pretend that you're aloof."

"Is that the voice of experience?"

"I guess." He'd never really thought about it, but instead of pretending he didn't care, he always just moved on. Left before anyone could make him stay. Left before he became the man his father had been.

Andi woke around two A.M. Tuck wasn't in bed with her, and for a minute she wondered if she'd dreamed the entire conversation. Something Sara had said earlier made her realize that her fantasies of what life could be like weren't all that different from every other little girl's in the world.

She wondered if she was building something in her head around Tuck that simply wasn't there. Making Tuck into some kind of mythical perfect man because he had so many of the qualities she admired, along with a few she didn't think most men possessed.

He was strong and funny, able to hold his own, smart enough to not have a fit when she beat him at something, and savvy enough to treat her with respect when he beat her. He was everything . . . and that worried her because no one man could be that right for her. What was she missing?

Or was it her own fear that kept her from grabbing on to Tuck with both hands? She'd had a hard time falling asleep after Tuck had made love to her. Her mind had been full of the conversation with Sara, the fires and Tuck. The three of them spinning around in a macabre dance.

She envied Sara her bravery because she'd taken a risk to have her baby. Andrea knew she'd never have taken it. If she ever had Tuck's love, she wouldn't risk it in any way.

No, that doesn't sound pitiful, she thought scornfully.

She pushed out of bed and grabbed her robe. She found him in the living room with the TV on, sound muted, and a notepad in his lap. He glanced up when she entered the room.

"Did I wake you?" he asked, his voice a low rasp.

"I don't think so." It wasn't that he'd made any noise; it was just that she'd realized he wasn't in bed with her. "Why aren't you sleeping?"

"The investigation—I'm missing a detail and can't put my finger on what it is."

"Maybe I can help," she suggested. She needed something to distract her from her own thoughts. She had to work tomorrow, but there was no way to shut off her mind.

She hated when she got like this and thought it was nice to have Tucker here in the middle of the night. He was just the kind of distraction she needed.

"Maybe," he said in that low drawl of his that meant he was up to no good.

"Tell me what to do," she said, edging farther into the room. The only light was the glow of the television.

"Take off your robe."

She stared at him at first but then had to laugh. No matter what Tuck did, he always surprised her. But she should know better. He was the sexiest man she'd ever met. "Ah, how is that going to help with the fire?"

"I need a distraction," he said. He put his notepad down and leaned back on her couch, spreading his arms along the back. He wore only a pair of faded jeans. He looked like . . . her lover, she thought.

"I'm waiting."

And a man who liked to play games when it came to sex. A man who didn't want to admit he liked to always be in control, so he shaded it in these little scenes they played. But she was coming to realize that he made love to her like this only when things had turned a corner between them. Was he running like she was?

She toyed with the sash on her robe, loosened it and then let the ends fall toward the floor. The fabric gaped open down her center, and underneath she wore his T-shirt, so it wasn't as if he was getting any kind of peep show.

"There you go."

"I said off."

"What's the magic word?"

"Now."

"That's not the magic word. Did you get that box checked in school—does not play well with others?"

"No. Everyone always listened to me."

"Then it's a good thing I don't."

"Andi . . ."

"What . . . ?"

"I thought you wanted to help."

"Yes, with my mind, not my body."

"The mind is a sex organ."

"So you need me naked to have sex with my mind."

"Stop messing around, Andrea. I said to take the robe off."

She slipped it off.

"When did I give you permission to put my shirt on?"

She liked it when he got this way. The sparkle in his eyes let her know that he was just playing, but the steel in his voice said that right now, their play was serious. "I don't remember asking."

Damn, her voice was too husky. Now he'd know that she was turned on, and she wanted him to have to work harder. He arched one eyebrow at her and snapped his fingers.

She started to sass him, but he was in a strange mood tonight. She was willing to play with him, but only so far. So she caught the edge of the shirt in her hands and slowly lifted it up. She deliberately got it tangled in her arms and shimmied, trying to free herself.

She pulled the shirt off and found him standing right in front of her. He'd shed his jeans while she'd removed the shirt. "Here's your shirt."

"Thanks," he said, taking it from her and tossing it on the ground.

"Now what?"

"This," he said, lifting her by her waist. "Put your legs around my hips."

She did.

"Bring me inside you, Andrea."

She reached between their bodies and found he'd taken time to put on a condom before coming over to her. She rubbed the tip of his hard-on against her opening, teasing both of them. But then she just wanted him inside her. She wanted to feel that sweet solitude that she found only while lying in his arms. That peace from her worries about her friends, her job and her future with Tucker.

Chapter 17

Tuck arrived at the firehouse well after Andi did. He'd spent the morning on the phone with the police. Tuck needed search warrants, and Phil DeMarco, the detective in charge of the fires, was more than happy to help out. He wanted the case closed as soon as possible.

Tuck hated sneaking around. He'd had a few affairs where he'd needed to be circumspect and hadn't minded them, but for some reason with Andrea it bothered him more. To be honest, it chafed a little that they were still hiding their relationship. He heard the men in full joking mode as soon as he approached the open door.

"Hot date?" McMillan asked. McMillan was the ringleader as Tuck had observed. The rest of the crew followed him. Mick was in charge when they worked, but because of his rank he was left out of much of the mischief the younger guys got into.

"I like that color. You should wear it more often," Johnson added.

Tuck's gut tightened as he realized there were only two women in the place and only two people who'd be the target of this type of teasing. Marilee, who wore a bright red lipstick every day, and his Andi.

"Kissing contest?" Powell asked with a laugh.

"If there was one, boys, I'm afraid none of you would be worthy."

"I might be," Tuck said.

She turned on him, every inch the fire chief and not a speck of the sweet, loving woman he'd held in his arms just a few short hours ago.

"Only in your dreams, Fields."

The men laughed and slowly dispersed as they realized they'd gotten as much of a rise out of Andi as she'd let them. He thought about his dreams, which had been plagued and troubled. Visions of fire and Jayne and his mom and then Andrea. The complication that seemed to intensify everything else. She made all of his emotions sharper, and he didn't like it.

"Can I see you for a minute?"

She nodded.

"Need some privacy for your kiss-off?" Johnson asked.

The guys snickered, and for the first time Tuck saw the reality of what being Andrea entailed. Saw that she wore her façade not because she didn't want to let people in, but because letting them in—letting them see the feminine side of her personality—was too painful.

He took a step toward Johnson, but Mick came out of the office. "Back off, Johnson. You know that Fields is conducting the arson investigation."

"No offense meant, Lieutenant."

"I think you boys have too much time on your hands. Let's get the truck washed."

"We just washed it yesterday."

"And I'm saying to do it again."

There was a chorus of gripes and moans as they went to work. Tuck realized Andi had disappeared into her office. Mick gave him a hard glare.

"Don't draw attention to it. She's got to work here after you leave."

"It's not in my nature to walk away when someone insults my woman." Tuck realized then that no matter how circumspect the situation, his gut instinct was to brand her. To stake a claim that every man in the vicinity would recognize. And he had absolutely no idea how to curb that.

Mick walked closer. His voice low, he said, "But no one knows she's your woman, and if you really care for her, you'll keep it that way."

"If either of you wants to survive, you'll stop discussing me like I don't exist and can't make my own choices. Fields, get in here if you want to talk about your investigation."

Tuck walked into her office, knowing there was little else to do, but once that door was closed he planned to have a few words with her.

"Thanks, Mick."

"Anytime, Andi." Palmer walked away, and Andi closed her door.

"Why are you wearing make-up today?" he asked, because he realized she had on more than lipstick.

"Somehow I woke with beard burn on my neck and cheeks. I thought lipstick would be a better distraction."

"Should I apologize?"

"Did you do it intentionally?"

"Maybe."

"Maybe? You don't strike me as a man who doesn't know why he acts."

"I'm not. But in this case . . . With you everything is different. I'd like to say 'no, I didn't think of the consequences,' and to be truthful, when you're naked I think of nothing but touching and claiming you."

"So then it wasn't intentional."

"I can't say that. I want my mark on you. I want those guys to know you're mine."

"That's so . . . primitive. I know you're a fairly civilized man."

"Usually."

"Well, what did you want to talk about?"

"That's it. End of subject."

"Sure, what can I say to that? It's flattering to think I make you react in a primal way. I think that's a first for me."

"Well, it's not meant to be flattering. It's damned uncomfortable, and I'm not sure I like it."

"Why not?"

"Because the woman I'm involved with doesn't seem to have the same instinctive reaction to me."

"Who says that?"

"Do you, Andi? All kidding and joking aside, how do you feel about me?"

She took a deep breath, and for a second he wished he'd dropped the subject, let her turn it back to work. But he had to know.

"I feel the same. In fact, if the situation were reversed and you worked with a bunch of women, I'd probably make sure you arrived at work every day with traces of my lipstick on your lips."

Andi had a hard time concentrating on work after her conversation with Tuck. He'd gone over the investigation, telling her that he'd requested search warrants for the three suspects on his list. He'd left the firehouse around lunchtime when they had to take the truck on one of those weird calls only the fire department got. A man had his hand stuck in the drain of his bathroom sink.

His neighbors had called when they'd heard him pounding on the wall of his apartment. Since firefighters' first mandate was to rescue, to solve the problem and get out, they weren't usually neat and orderly when they went on a call. True to form, Andi's men tramped through the living room and into the bathroom.

Andi paused in the doorway, taking in the scene of a naked man with his hand in the sink. The man flushed bright red when she came through the door. She turned her back politely while Mick helped him wrap a towel around his waist.

"This is Captain O'Roarke, and I'm Lieutenant Palmer," Mick said. "We're from the fire department."

"I'm Terry Phillips."

"What have we got here, Mr. Phillips?" Andi asked, to focus them back on the job.

"My wedding ring fell down the drain, and I thought I could reach it." Phillips looked to be in his early twenties.

Andi got closer to the sink to assess the situation. Sometimes you could free a person by just applying force. His fingers were twisted in the drain, and it was blocked by the rest of his hand and a lot of pink lotion.

"What exactly is stuck in here?"

"My fingers are wedged from the knuckle down."

Andi didn't turn on the water because the bottom of the basin already had standing water in it up to Phillips' wrist. "I'm guessing the drain is blocked?"

"Yes. I think the baby lotion I stuck in there along with my fingers is to blame."

"Can you still feel your fingers?" Mick asked. He was taking Phillips' pulse.

"Kind of."

"Are you in pain?" Andi asked as Mick wrote down his heart rate.

"Not too much. I just want to get out of here."

"That's why we're here," Mick said, patting the man on the back.

"How long have you been in here?" Andi asked before she made the decision.

"Since about eight this morning."

It was almost four. "That's a long time. Do you want us to get you something to eat?"

"Can't you just get me free?" he asked in a panicked voice.

Seeing Mick here in control, she was reminded of how he'd looked last night. How he must have felt learning his wife was sick once again with a disease that neither of them could control as easily as they both did their everyday lives.

Mick arched an eyebrow at her. God, what the hell was happening to her lately? She'd never spaced on the job before. Thank God this wasn't a fire. But in all fairness, she didn't have the time to think in a fire that she had now.

"Andi?"

"Hmm . . . ?"

"How do you think we can get Mr. Phillips free?"

"Probably have to take out the sink."

"What? No way, my wife will kill me. We're moving into a house next month, and she's planning to use our security deposit for some new furniture."

"Do you want to wait for her to get home?" Andi asked. "Because this is the only way."

"Can't you pull me?"

Andi looked at Mick. "Sure, we'll do it."

Andi grabbed his wrist while Mick grabbed his shoulders, and they counted to three and then yanked backward.

"Stop!" Phillips yelled.

They did.

"What happened?" Andi asked.

"It hurt a lot."

"Well, we can leave the sink intact and pull you out that way and probably end up injuring you further, or we can take the sink. It's up to you."

"The sink." Phillips said. "It is going to take a little while. Mick, keep him company while I talk to the boys."

"Will do, Cap."

Andi walked out into the living room to find Johnson

and Powell trying not to laugh. "Boys, be nice. He was trying to save his wedding ring."

"We know. How are we going to get him out of there?"

"His hand's not coming out on its own. I think we're going to have to take out the sink."

"Ugh. I knew I should have called in today. I hate construction."

"This is more like destruction," Johnson said. "I'll go get the equipment we need."

"Listen, let's make this as clean as possible. He's worried about his security deposit."

"Would he rather lose his hand?" Powell asked.

Andi thought he might. But she didn't say anything, just pointed to the door so that the men would get what they needed.

Twenty minutes later, they'd tried everything they could, and even Mr. Phillips agreed the sink would have to come out.

Andi made sure none of the men mentioned the fact that they were going to have to cut the sink in half to free his hand. Braced around Phillips, Powell got under the sink and turned off the water. Then he used their steel cutters to snip through the drain.

"Ready down here."

Johnson cut through the caulking holding the basin to the vanity and pried it loose. Andi held the left side, and Johnson got the right. They lifted the sink free and then tried one more time to release his hand.

"Just break it," Phillips said, and Johnson used the sledgehammer to break the porcelain and free Phillips.

Andi watched her guys as they headed back to the truck, thinking about how life was full of the unexpected. No matter what you planned for, something always got in the way. In this case, Mr. Phillips and his wife weren't going to have the money they'd hoped for their new furniture. She tried to divorce herself from her line of thinking. Tried to make it be about Mr. Phillips and not herself.

But she couldn't help the feeling that no matter what she did, her affair with Tucker was going to end, and she was going to be hurt.

Tuck went with Detective DeMarco to deliver the search warrants. Neither man was sure what they'd find, but they had enough circumstantial evidence to warrant a search. The first house was unfortunately Roy Braley's. He was good-natured about it and followed them through the house, garage and small guest cottage on his property. They found several items of evidence that they tagged to take away.

They also impounded his two desktop computers, his laptop and PDA. His wife stood in the doorway with tears in her eyes as they pulled away. Tuck hated this part of his job.

"Makes you feel like a creep when it's a nice guy, doesn't it?" DeMarco said.

"Yeah, it's easier to work on a case where the suspects have a rap sheet or a history of priors with fire."

"If it helps, I've known Braley for a dog's age."

"It doesn't. One of his kin is one of the firefighters who was at the scene."

"Pete McMillan?"

"You know him?"

DeMarco nodded. But didn't elaborate as the miles flew past.

"How are they related?"

"Braley's wife is McMillan's mom's sister."

Tuck slipped that information into the back of his mind. "Does everyone know they are related?"

"Just about. The McMillans have been here forever, old citrus family."

"What'd they think of Roy's idea to build a museum?"

"They were very enthusiastic about it. After all, it'll be mostly about their family."

"Anyone else?"

"The Adams family."

Tuck started laughing.

"Oh, I forgot about the TV ones. But the truth is Adams and McMillan own most of the groves in this area."

"What about citrus packing, any families there?"

"Braley is involved in that. Along with Terric, his defense attorney." DeMarco said it with the same disdain many cops had for defense attorneys.

"Got off a few of your busts?"

"More than a few, but I always get them by the book the second time."

Tuck laughed to himself. "Being a defense attorney doesn't make him a criminal."

"No, but it does tell us he has a liberal interpretation of justice," DeMarco said.

"What do you know about Jack Bell?" Tuck asked, because he'd been unable to find out any information on the man. No one knew anything about him.

DeMarco rubbed the back of his neck. "He's not from around here. I think he's with the Indian River Co-op."

"Does he have a second residence?" Tuck asked. The Auburndale address was the only one he'd asked for a warrant to search.

"I don't know. Braley might be able to tell you."

"I'll check into that." Normally, Tuck wouldn't have missed a detail like that. In fact, he thought he needed to go out of town for a few days and figure out this entire Indian River connection. What was the deal there?

Tuck and DeMarco dropped the evidence off at the police lab. Tuck stuck around for a couple of hours doing his own analysis, but that wasn't his area of expertise, so in the end he got out of their hair so they could get him some results.

He wanted to call Andi but knew she was working, and he needed to stay out of her way. He didn't like the fact that there were certain times when she was unavailable to him. Didn't like the fact that she had a career that would almost always keep her occupied.

He checked his watch and then gave Marilee a call. "Can you run Jack Bell's name through your databases and see if you can find a second residence?"

"Will do. Everyone's in for the night, and we're settling in to watch that Dennis Leary television show . . . *Rescue Me*. Why don't you drop in?"

"Why don't you butt out?" Tuck suggested. Marilee had told him she considered herself the information hub . . . not just for the station, but for the firefighting community. So she liked to keep tabs on everyone on the different shifts and then make sure that the information was disseminated. The way she'd said it made it seem like a complex information-sharing system. Instead of just plain old water-cooler gossip.

"Because I'm a busybody. It's my job."

"Well, bother someone else."

"I got my head handed to me by Lieutenant Palmer earlier; you're a lot safer."

Marilee must have asked about Sara. Tuck had an uncomfortable moment as he realized he knew more about Mick's personal life than the other man realized. That was the thing about women. They created this bond that men were unaware of. "Cut the guy a break."

"Why should I have to do that?"

Tuck couldn't say. It wasn't his secret to share. "Just do it. You won't die if you're nice to him."

"He might from the shock."

Tuck laughed and hung up the phone. He liked the firehouse. Liked everyone there and could easily see himself as part of that family. He knew it was only because he associated the firehouse with Andi.

Somehow she'd carved a place for herself deep inside him. He didn't understand it and was afraid to really think about it too much, but he needed her. He wanted to be surrounded by her all the time. Man, he sounded like a stalker.

But if she asked him to leave, he'd do it. He'd do whatever it took to make her happy. To keep her happy. To keep her smiling, even though he might be the only one who saw that smile.

Chapter 18

Andi was pretty sure she'd never been so cranky at work before. Tuck had left a brief message on her answering machine five days ago saying he had to go out of town to follow the investigation. That was it. No call to say where he was or what he was doing. And it pissed her off.

She'd buried herself in trying to help Sara and Mick. Mick was walking on eggshells around his wife, and that was so unlike him that both women were worried. And yesterday at work, Mick had spaced during a routine run. He'd never done it before, and she knew that his mind had to be on Sara and the baby.

She had to speak to him about it. She hated this part of her job. Life had been so much less complicated before Tucker Fields showed up in her firehouse.

"Hey, Andi, what are you doing here?" Sara asked as she opened the door. Her friend looked tired, but her eyes were happy.

"I need to talk to Mick about work," Andi said. She wasn't sure what his reaction would be. But Mick was one of the most levelheaded and together men she knew. She understood why he was not himself, but in an emergency situation, they all needed to be one hundred percent. Otherwise mistakes were made, and men died.

"You just missed him. He ran into Richie's to pick up a

pizza. Want to stay for dinner?" Sara tucked a strand of her hair behind her ear and stepped back, gesturing for Andi to enter.

She nodded. Sara led the way to the kitchen. Both women sat at the table. There was a bouquet of flowers in the center, and she suspected Mick had bought them for Sara.

"I thought you were spending your days off with your hot new lover."

Definitely not what she wanted to talk about. But Sara was the one person she could actually trust to listen and not judge. "He's not here."

"Where is he?" Sara asked.

Andi shrugged. She knew the realities of his job. Knew that the investigation was his first priority and understood it. It made her realize what a long-term relationship with Tuck would entail, and she wasn't sure she was cut out for it. "Somewhere in Indian River County."

"You mean, you don't know?"

"He didn't say in the message he left me." The message Marilee had delivered just after dinner. That Tuck would be out of town following a lead. When she'd gone home the next morning, she'd hoped for a personal message on her machine, but there'd been nothing. It was as if having let her see a little bit of his soul, he'd had to retreat.

She could appreciate that; she acted the same way every time he edged closer. But she had hoped for more. Hoped that he'd be unable to leave her.

"Phone lines work both ways, you know. You can call him, and he can call you."

"Thanks, smart-ass, I hadn't realized that." Until this moment Andi had honestly expected to feel uncomfortable around Sara. To have to walk on eggshells around her because her cancer had come back. But the disease hadn't changed their friendship as far as Sara was concerned. Andi knew that she had to be careful not to let the cancer matter.

"No problem. So why haven't you called him?"

Andi leaned her elbows on the table and rested her forehead on her hands. She thought about her two long days off. She'd been so angry that he hadn't called her, she refused to even think of calling him. Instead she'd gone running by herself, her way of thumbing her nose at him. But in her bed that night she'd felt so empty and alone. It wasn't anger but a deep hurt, and she didn't know how to deal with it.

Then finally being back at work and forcing herself to concentrate on the job and not her personal life. It was how she'd always survived, but she no longer wanted to just survive. She'd had a glimpse of what life could be like, a life where she was involved not just in her job, but with another person, and she'd liked it.

Sara put her hand on Andi's shoulder, and Andi glanced up at her. "I've dialed his number more times than you can imagine. But I don't want him to think . . ."

She couldn't say the words out loud. The men she'd been involved with before had been different. Andi had aggressively pursued them, and she'd been in control of everything from the beginning, but with Tuck it had never been that way.

"You need him more than he needs you?" Sara suggested.

Put out loud, it sounded as if she was vulnerable where he was concerned. She didn't want to be. It didn't matter what the truth was; she didn't want to be that defenseless with anyone—especially Tuck.

"How's things with you?" Andi asked, wanting to forget about her problems and deal with Sara's. After all, when compared to Sara's situation, a man not calling wasn't all that big a deal.

"I feel fine today and don't change the subject."

"Was there really anything left to pursue?" Andi asked.

"Yes. Call him and ask him when he's coming back."

She turned away from Sara. She wasn't here to talk about her problems, but somehow they'd just spilled out. She did want to talk to Tuck, but not while Sara was there.

Her friend stood up. "Why don't you go out on the patio while I finish making the iced tea and lemonade?"

"Stop trying to boss me around," she said.

"I'm the only one who's not afraid to do it."

That was the truth. Sara had never been intimidated by Andi. Sara had taken one look at her and somehow seen a woman she wanted to have as a friend.

"What am I going to say to him?"

"Remember how you told me to be honest with Mick?"

"Ugh. You're not going to throw my words back at me, are you?"

"That's exactly what I'm going to do. We can't go through life hiding."

Andi walked out onto the patio and sat down in the chair, letting Sara's words echo in her mind. And hoping she showed half of her friend's strength and courage. A blazing fire, she could face; emotional nakedness scared her.

Tuck was on the Florida Turnpike heading north toward Auburndale when his cell phone rang. It was Andi's number, and he hesitated to answer it. He wasn't ready to talk to her.

"Fields."

Static crackled on the line, and he wondered if she'd speak or hang up. "It's Andi."

"What's up?" he asked, trying to sound casual, but fearing that he hadn't succeeded. He wished they were together so he could take her in his arms and make love to her. He'd hold her arms over her head and just take her. He wouldn't have to talk or think or feel anything other than her silky limbs wrapped around his body.

"I . . . Where are you?"

He rubbed the back of his neck. "On my way back to your neck of the woods."

"Oh. Did you find what you were looking for?" she asked.

No, he hadn't found it because he hadn't felt the way he had when he'd moved on from other women in the past. He'd thought that his emotions for her would lessen and he'd realize that the intensity he'd experienced in Auburndale was only due to sexual chemistry.

Instead he'd spent every night in the hotel room aching for her. Not just sexually—though that was a big part of it. He'd wanted to hold her. To feel her breath on his neck as she slept and wake to her shy smile.

"Tuck? Did you get the information you needed from Jack Bell?" she asked.

"Yes. Bell's our guy. We've formally filed charges against him."

"Well, then there's no reason for you to come back here, is there?"

"I have to close up my duplex and file a final report. Can I use your office?"

"Yes," she said.

He heard the sound of her breathing and the rustle of the wind through the trees.

"Will I see you again?" she asked.

"Hell, yes. I'll be getting in late; can I come by your place?" he asked. He wasn't sure what her answer would be. He should have called, but the investigation had progressed too quickly, and he wasn't sure what he'd say. He felt as if he'd told her too much, felt too raw from their last encounter, and he'd retreated.

"Sure. I'm at Sara and Mick's for dinner."

There was an odd note in her voice, and he jumped on it to talk about something other than their last conversation when he'd confessed that he needed her. Was this the same kind of panic that had driven his old man to disappear? "Is everything okay?"

"Sara looks tired, but otherwise she's the same. I'm worried about Mick."

"Why?"

"I'll tell you later when you come home."

And he was coming home. But could he stay? Did he want to? Did she want him to? It worried him that he might not be able to stay if she asked him to. Not because of his job. He could travel or even apply for a job in Orlando, which would put him closer to her. But could he stay as her man?

Taking a deep breath, he said, "I like the sound of that, Andi."

"Sound of what?" she asked.

The weariness in her voice made him feel sad and mad at the same time. She should know him better by now. Should be able to read the emotions that he'd never be able to put into words.

"Coming home . . . to you." He didn't know how to express it well, but his home had always been a vague black-and-white memory of a time before his father had left, changing their lives. But when he held Andi in his arms he found it again. And that was what scared him. He knew exactly how easy it was to lose that feeling. To lose the home that he'd been searching for since that day long ago.

"I can hear a 'but' in there, Tuck. What are you trying to tell me?"

He should tell her. She needed to know that he'd never stuck around. She needed to understand that even though she felt like home to him, he wasn't sure he could stay there.

"Nothing I want to say over the phone. But we have to talk."

"Listen, let's not do that. I don't want to ruin what time we have left together."

"I don't hear a clock ticking, do you?"

She didn't respond, but then he hadn't expected her to. Andi wasn't going to bare her soul to him. Wasn't going to leave herself open for that kind of rejection. And he knew she'd consider it a rejection. It ticked him off that she'd let him have control of her body, that she'd let him dominate her completely in their sex lives, but not trust him with her emotions.

He couldn't let it drop. "Do you see our relationship ending in a few days?"

"Don't you? This is an affair, remember. Not a long-term committed relationship."

"Maybe you give yourself easily, but I don't."

He heard her sharp intake of breath and hated himself for letting his temper get the better of him.

"If that's what you really think, then maybe there's nothing left to say."

"Well, you're wrong. And not for the first time, I might add. No matter what you think, Andrea O'Roarke, we're not through, and I'm not letting you go that easily."

He hung up before she could. Realizing that dealing with her insecurities was so much easier for him than facing his own.

Dinner with Mick and Sara wasn't relaxing. There was an underlying tension between her friends, but more than that was her own discord with Tuck. That sick feeling in the pit of her stomach wouldn't go away, and she just wanted to get back to her house where she could let her guard down.

"Can I talk to you alone?" she asked Mick after the pizza was gone.

He nodded.

"Walk me out to my truck. Good night, Sara."

"Bye, Andi, thanks for stopping by."

Andi led the way out of the house and down the path to the sidewalk next to her truck. She leaned back against the frame and stared at Mick. It would be so much easier if he somehow knew what she was going to say, and she could just nod and remind him to not let it happen again.

"Thanks for talking to Sara the other day. I don't know what you said to her, but thank you."

"To be honest, I have no idea if I said the right thing. She surprised me."

Mick rubbed the back of his neck and turned to look at his own home. "Me, too. What'd you need to say to me?"

"It's about your performance at work yesterday."

"What about it?"

"Mick, you were distracted. Your entry time was slow, and I saw you pause before we entered that house. This is unofficial, but the other guys noticed, too."

He cursed savagely, and Andi said nothing to him. What could she say? *I know your wife is pregnant and might not live through childbirth, but a fire is serious business.* Mick knew these things.

"I've never been afraid of what we do. I know some guys worry about not making it back, but I've always felt . . . kind of arrogant. Like there's not a fire out there I can't get a handle on."

She nodded, but realized he wasn't looking at her. He still watched his house. "I've noticed that about you, which is why I'm bringing this up."

"But the stakes are raised for me. If I don't make it back, who'll take care of Sara and the baby?"

She had no answer for him, knew he didn't expect one,

but she was torn. She'd help Sara if something happened to Mick, but she knew that wouldn't be enough. Wouldn't be the same.

"Do you want to transfer to a different job?"

"No. Being a firefighter is my life."

His words didn't surprise her. "We are part of the lucky few who knew this was our calling."

"Yeah, we are," he said. "You know that doing the job has always been where I felt like I was my real self. The place where I can forget all the other crap. But this thing with Sara—I can't get free of it. Not even for a minute."

"What were you thinking?" she asked. When they got to a fire she always thought of her dad's words: *There's no fire an O'Roarke can't figure out and put down.* And then because she was always a little scared at that moment behind her mask with her blood pumping, watching the flames billow up, she added her own mental goad: *But you're a girl, and that means you have to work harder.*

"I was thinking that I'd promised her I'd never die in a fire. You know, when I said those words, there was a little doubt in the back of my mind. You know, a niggle of worry that I might be lying to my new wife."

Her father's words aside, after four weeks on her first fire engine she and Mick had bonded in their first big fire. "We made a vow to each other, Mick, to never leave the other behind. I'm still willing to do my part," she said.

"Me, too. But now with the baby. Yesterday was the first time that felt real, and I thought about how I grew up. I don't want that for my kid."

Mick had grown up in the foster care system. He'd been left in a hospital cafeteria when he was six weeks old. He'd never known his real folks, never had any family.

She put her hand on his shoulder, squeezing gently. "I understand."

"How can you?"

"Because I care about Sara, too."

"She's not your life, Andi. In fact, no one is your life. You glide through the surface of relationships. You can't understand this."

His words hurt. She knew he was upset and angry over Sara, but she hadn't expected him to snap at her like that. To go right for her own weakness. "I might not have any-one who's my life, but that doesn't mean I don't care, Mick."

"Whatever. I won't screw up on the job again, Captain."

He pushed away from the truck and walked away. Not into the house, but down the street. She glanced back at the small house and saw the front door open. Sara stood on the porch.

Was Mick right? Did she just glide through all her rela-tionships? She didn't think so. She was hurting at the thought of Sara being sick again. At the thought of her losing her friend to a disease she couldn't fight.

"Andi?"

"Sorry, Sara. It was a work thing. He'll be back when he cools down."

Andi climbed into her truck and drove away without looking back. She felt raw inside, as if she'd scraped every emotion she had out of her own body.

Her house looked small and lonely when she pulled up in front of it. Her porch light had burned out, and it was dark. She sat there in front of her house for a few minutes.

Tuck pulled into her driveway behind her. He shut off his engine, and she got out of her truck. Suddenly she didn't feel as lonely as she had just a few moments ago.

Mick didn't know her. She was silly to let his words hurt her. She might appear to glide over the surface of life, but everything . . . everyone she met had a profound impact on her. She'd just learned not to show it.

"Hey, sweetheart," he said, opening his arms.

She hesitated for one second, but didn't care if she looked needy or weak. She wanted his arms around her. She'd missed him.

She ran to him and jumped, wrapping her arms and legs around his body. He embraced her with a fierceness that made it almost impossible to breathe, but that was okay because she needed to be held that tightly.

Chapter 19

Tuck left Andi sleeping in her bed. He had that strange rest-lessness that had always plagued him. The urge to move on. To sneak off in the middle of the night.

He knew that he'd changed since he'd come here. He'd changed in more ways than he wanted to acknowledge, but he'd never been good at lying, especially to himself.

He pulled on his jeans and unlocked her patio door, step-ping outside into the night. Since it was summer in Florida it was warm, even though it was close to three in the morn-ing. He rubbed his bare chest and walked off the cement pad that made up her patio onto the grass of her backyard.

Unlike Chicago the grass here was hearty and tough, not soft. But he liked it. He liked a lot of stuff about Florida. He sank to the ground, stacked his hands behind his head and leaned back to stare up at the sky.

He really liked the woman inside that house. Liked her enough to not want to ever see her hurt the way his mom had been when his father left.

He wasn't the same man his father was, but genetically there was a fairly strong chance that he could be a leaver. He'd carved a nomadic life for himself. Only now he real-ized that by always leaving he had nothing to go home to . . . until now.

He'd swept Andi into her house and into the bedroom.

He'd held her under his body, holding off his own climax until she'd come three times, screaming his name and begging him. But it hadn't been enough. He wanted more from her. He wanted that emotional distance that she kept between them to disappear. And he'd been unable to shatter it with his body.

She'd fallen into an exhausted sleep, but he'd been left awake staring at her in the dim light provided by the moon. Her features were soft in sleep, and with all her determination dimmed, she seemed to need him. Staring down at her, he realized what he'd tried to do. What kind of man was he? Did he really have to make her admit her vulnerabilities so his unstated affection for her wouldn't leave him at a disadvantage?

"Tuck?"

"Out here," he said, not sitting up. He didn't like himself much at the moment and wasn't really ready to talk to her.

"What are you doing?" she asked, sitting down next to him on the ground. She had a Mexican blanket wrapped around her and handed him a beach towel. "This will be more comfortable."

"I don't want to be comfortable."

"Why not?"

He couldn't tell her that he'd had sex with her to try to control her. To try to force her past her barriers until she admitted feeling something for him. To try to make sure she knew that he was still in charge.

He shrugged. Then stood up. She shook the towel out, and he sat back down on it. Despite the way she always acted as though he was just a guy in her life temporarily, she always made him feel cared for.

"I'm sorry I was an ass," he said, hauling her into his arms. He slid his legs outside hers and pulled her closer until her back nestled against his chest.

He leaned forward, closing his eyes and breathing in the

floral scent of her shampoo and the natural scent of her skin.

"When were you an ass?"

"On the phone earlier."

"Well, I probably said a few things I shouldn't have."

"Really? I think you should have ripped me a new one after the way I left without calling."

"Why did you?" she asked.

She'd tipped her head back on his shoulder and looked up at him. He had his hands braced next to his hips, but she took them in hers and wrapped them around her waist. With her arms over his, he felt as if he was a part of something. Something special and something permanent. God, there that word was again. He closed his eyes and rubbed his chin against the top of her head.

"Tuck?"

"Hmm?"

"Why did you leave a message with the dispatcher instead of calling me?"

He took a deep breath. He needed to tell her about his past. Needed to make her understand that when he hurt her it wasn't because of anything she did. That it was all him. Because of the choices he'd made for his life. "To prove something to myself."

"What was that?" she asked. Her fingers rubbed up and down his forearms, toying with the hair there. She caressed in a circular motion that was meant to be soothing but was actually turning him on.

He shifted her on his lap, pulling her blanket from her shoulders and realizing she wore only his shirt. He tugged her back against his chest again, and she shifted her hips until the ridge of his erection was nestled along her buttocks.

He reached down to unzip his jeans but stopped at the last minute. They needed to talk, and he wouldn't be able to string two words together if he felt her warmth against his naked flesh. Instead he slipped his hands under her shirt and held her closer.

"What did you hope to prove?" she asked again.

There was a husky catch to her voice, and he was grateful for how well matched they were physically. Both of them entirely insatiable for each other. He wondered if she'd ever experienced that with a lover before. He never had.

"That I could leave," he said at last.

"Oh, to me?"

"No, sweetheart, to myself."

"Why would you want to do that?" she asked.

"Because I'm a nomad."

Andi wanted to make a joke about him. Something about being a fire marshal and following the trail of smoke, because it was a trail that never ended. But she also sensed that there was more to this. That it had more to do with Tuck than his job.

"But you came back," she said, very carefully because she'd repeated those words over and over to herself. Trying to make that mean more than perhaps it did.

But she'd felt so alone. Alone in her soul where it had never mattered before. Driving away from her friends, seeing their lives in chaos. Needing Tuck and knowing that things weren't settled between them. Fearing what the coming days would hold. It had shaken her.

"Yes, I did," he said.

"That has to count for something." She hoped it didn't sound as if she was trying to convince herself, but she knew she was. How much more could she handle before she just retreated back into herself? She needed to find her center again. To make her world return to its nice safe axis, and Tuck . . . She hoped he was part of that, but if he'd left to prove something, how could she count on him?

"It counts for everything," he said, his arms tightening around her.

She sensed Tuck was more comfortable showing her physically how he felt. And maybe she was making things up or pretending to read signs that weren't there, but from her father and brothers she'd learned that a quick hug often masked intense feelings—joy, fear, pride. Feelings they could never put into words.

But there was a tone in his voice that told her he wasn't sure. "There's more to it, isn't there?"

"Yes," he said abruptly, dropping his arms and scooting away from her.

"Tell me." She turned to face him and came up on her knees. With the dark of the night around them, it felt as if they were the only two people in the world, and whatever their problems were, they could be solved. The impact of their troubles was just on the two of them . . . and . . . Oh, God, Andi thought, if she cared enough about Tuck, the problems would go away.

"Talking makes me feel like some kind of wimpy guy."

"Tuck, you aren't. And I'd never think of you like that."

Had he come back to prove something to her? Had her words on the phone been a gauntlet thrown down that he couldn't ignore? Had he come back to her only to leave her again?

"Self-perception is all that matters. Haven't you found that to be true?"

She had agreed with that at one time. She'd always believed herself unlovable to a strong man. Unequal to the kind of man who'd always attracted her because she'd come up short so many times in the eyes of her father. But Tuck had changed all that. He made her feel as though she was more than worthy. And if he was playing a head game with her, she wasn't going to take it calmly.

"Yes. But you can't really believe that about yourself."

He ran his finger down the side of her face. That familiar gesture made her feel safe, but there was something in his eyes that warned her not to get too cozy right yet.

"Sometimes I know I'm not an admirable man. Close your eyes."

"Why?" she asked, because closing her eyes was going to make her feel very vulnerable, and she hated it. She'd never been able to do it in workshops or seminars. She always had to have one eye cracked open.

"Because I don't want you to see me while I tell you," he said.

"I don't think I can do it. What could you have to say that's so bad?" she asked.

"Nothing. But I don't want to see pity in your eyes," he said, brushing his lips over both of her lids.

She immediately opened them back up. "You're one of the strongest, smartest, sexiest men I know. I doubt you'll see pity."

"Trust me on this," he said, putting his fingers over her eyes, and she closed them.

She hated it immediately and kept them closed only because she sensed how important this was to Tuck. And he hadn't asked her for a lot outside the bedroom.

"Do it quick. I'm not sure how long I can keep my eyes closed," she said.

He squeezed her shoulder, and then his touch dropped away. She strained to hear him. His breathing, some kind of movement on the blanket, anything. But only silence surrounded her.

"You know my old man walked out on us when I was eight."

She remembered what he'd said, about having to be the man in the family when he wasn't ready to be, about having to watch out for his mom and his sister, and she could easily see why that would make him the kind of man who wouldn't want to leave. Or had it made him another kind of man?

"Is that what this is about?" she asked, to distract herself from the conclusion she'd reached in her mind. That Tucker Fields was the type of man who left. Left before he had a chance to hurt anyone by staying.

"I promised myself I'd never be responsible for another person's happiness. I'd never make a woman look the way my mother did."

Andrea opened her eyes because she couldn't stand it anymore. She needed to see him. To watch his face for clues so she could guard herself. "You can't be responsible for my happiness, Tuck. You aren't. You can make me mad or sad, but I'm the only one who can control my happiness."

"That's not altogether true," he said. "I can hurt you with my actions and my words."

"What do you mean?" she asked, sensing he had a specific action or word in mind. Earlier on the phone he had hurt her, and she'd wanted to lash right back at him. Saying not to come back at all.

"I left to prove that you weren't different from all the other women I'd slept with."

His words hurt and cut her deeper than she'd expected. Her breath caught in her chest, and she stood and walked away so she couldn't see him anymore.

Watching her turn away convinced Tuck he still knew nothing about women in general or Andi. He should have chosen his words more carefully. He reached for her but let his hand drop before he touched her. "I came back because I realized that playing those kinds of games with myself and with you was pointless."

She said nothing. Her shoulders weren't shaking, so he hoped she wasn't crying. She had her arms wrapped around herself. He went up behind her and pulled her back against his chest and just held her. She didn't struggle, but made no move to embrace him as she had earlier.

"I came back because you are different. I wanted to see for myself if I could leave you."

But even out loud the words weren't good enough. Could never really make up for what he'd said. He couldn't stand the distance, even though he was responsible for it. At least she didn't push him away.

"Listen, Andrea. I'm trying here, but you aren't what I expected."

"What did you expect?" she asked, her voice a thready whisper. "Did you expect me to be some kind of freaky story to share in the next firehouse? Did you expect me to smile while other firefighters and fire marshals joked behind my back?"

"Never."

"Listen, Tuck. You're not the only one with a past here. And I thought . . . I don't know that thinking had much to do with it. Maybe we've taken this as far as we can and it's time . . . to both just move on."

"I know. But in the past leaving . . . I could have done it and did do it. And in the end I was glad for the memories, but that was it."

"And this time?"

He turned her in his arms, forced her face up to his so that their eyes met. "This time I couldn't sleep because you weren't in my arms. This time I couldn't eat because I wasn't hungry for food, only for you. This time my life coalesced into two important moments."

"What were they?" she asked.

He didn't want to answer. He'd come outside to escape and find the truth buried somewhere deep inside him. Actually, he didn't need to find it. He needed to face it, and he wasn't sure he was ready to share that truth with Andrea before he had accepted it himself.

"Tuck?"

He took a deep breath, knowing the truth of who he was and what he wanted was right here. He needed Andrea in a way he'd never needed a woman before. Sure, he had his mom and his sister, but that was different. Their bonds had been forged through being forced to survive together in difficult times. The bonds of family.

Andi was different. She completed him in a way that was seamless and integral. A way he'd always hoped a woman never would because then the damaged part of his soul would be tied to hers.

"What did you figure out while you were gone?" she asked again.

He took a deep breath. These next few moments would determine the type of future he'd have and if she'd be a part of it.

"That being a fire marshal and being your man were the only important things to me."

She gave him a smile that was heartbreakingly sad and stood on her tiptoes to kiss him. It was a sweet and thorough kiss that left him aroused and afraid to let the conversation continue.

"You can't be both. I'm not the kind of woman who can be—"

"Be what?" he interrupted. He couldn't continue to hide from the world. That was part of what he'd discovered on his trip south, the fact that if Andi had been injured on the job, no one would call him. If he was hurt, no one would think to notify her. They were lovers, but no one knew, and he wasn't the kind of man to skulk about when he cared for someone.

"You know," she said. She dropped her hands from his shoulders and stepped back.

He let her go, needing the distance she'd provided by retreating. It wasn't lost on him that when things got tough she always backed away. She wasn't afraid of a challenge or a fight when it was physical or in front of her men, but one-on-one and dealing with emotion she always ran.

"No, I don't. You're a woman who has an important job that doesn't have to be your entire life. The men you work with might give you a hard time at first, but when they see you're serious about me they'll back off."

He saw her shake her head and withdraw. Not physically, but emotionally. And he had the feeling in the pit of his stomach that he was losing her. Not because he'd tried to leave, testing himself and her. But because Andi wasn't ready to leave behind the comfortable niche she'd found for herself.

"You're not even sure you want to stick around," she said, sounding very defensive.

"At least I'm willing to try. Give me something to stay for. You have to give me a reason." If she indicated that she'd try an open relationship with him, let him be her man in every sense of the word, he'd stay. He'd change jobs and figure out a way to make a life with her.

"What reason? You just said you left to prove you could. I'm not sure we're on the same page."

"So I was too honest with you. Give me a reason to stay."

"Sex is a reason."

"Is that all we have?"

"I don't know."

"Is that all you want?"

She said nothing and walked back into the house. He followed her, not ready to let go. Not willing to believe that she hadn't felt the same way he had. He'd found the one woman he wanted to spend the rest of his life with, and if he could just get through to Andi, she'd acknowledge she felt the same way. There was only one way they really communicated, and that was in bed.

Chapter 20

Andi knew this was it, the last time that she'd have Tuck in her house, and decided not to waste time talking or rehashing things. She couldn't ask him to stay. She just couldn't do it. Not that he'd know, but she'd once asked Lloyd to stay, and he'd left anyway.

She knew Tucker wasn't the same as Lloyd, but she couldn't do it. She'd once been on her knees begging a man not to go, and it had gotten her nowhere.

So when Tuck followed her into the house, she pulled her shirt over her head and tossed it on the floor. She reached one hand toward him and beckoned him closer.

He locked the patio door and then pushed his jeans down his legs and off. Coming naked toward her. She knew he was aroused, but she wanted more than that. She wanted to reach the hidden layers deep inside. The part of Tuck that he kept private from her even when they were both naked and sharing one body.

"Andi—"

"No talking, Tuck. I think we've both said everything there is to say. Come to bed with me."

He hesitated for less than a second and then scooped her up in his arms and carried her into the bedroom. She wrapped her arms around his chest, resting her face against him.

He set her in the center of the bed and then turned on the lamp on the nightstand.

"You're so beautiful."

In his arms she'd always felt so. She thought about that. How much he'd given her and that maybe she was making a mistake in not taking a chance on him.

He traced his hand slowly down her body. Fingers brushing so lightly over her skin that she almost felt she'd imagined his touch.

The second time he traced his hand down her body he lingered over her. She caressed his chest, gently exploring every inch of him. Coming up on her legs, she pushed him to his back, leaning over him and kissing his chest.

Tasting every inch of his flesh. Trying to memorize the way he looked here in her bed. The way he tasted under her lips. She closed her eyes, breathing deeply the musky scent of his skin and the smell of their arousal as it grew.

Each touch was a slow building of the fire that burned between them. Each stroke echoed in her mind and body . . . last time. Last time with Tuck. It was too much. She pushed away the thought and made love to him with all the walled-off emotion that she'd felt since the first moment she looked up and saw him standing in her doorway.

His hands roamed down her back as she bent over him. Taking her time with each bit of his body. His muscled form was too taut to allow her to nibble at him the way he did to her. So she scraped her teeth around his belly button and then lower. Her tongue tracing over the line. He groaned her name; his hands tightened in her hair as she reached the tip of his erection.

She glanced up his body and saw him watching her through half-closed eyes. She blew gently on his aroused flesh and then kissed the tip. He moaned.

"More, sweetheart."

She ran her tongue all over him. Tasting him with long swipes of her tongue until she settled over him and sucked him deep in her mouth. He framed her head with his hands and held her close to him. She suckled on his length, pulling him more deeply into her mouth.

She loved the way he tasted. His grip on her head tightened, and his hips lifted toward her mouth. He tugged on her, urging her up his body, but she didn't want to move. She wanted to suckle him until he came. Wanted to give him this release. To be in control of the way he reacted for just the one time.

"Andi, I need to be inside your body," he said. She lifted her head and allowed him to pull her up over him. He urged her head down to his and kissed her thoroughly. His lips and tongue taking complete control of her mouth.

He anchored one arm around her waist and rolled them over. Wedging his feet between hers, he spread her legs and settled into the notch there. He suckled her nipple in his mouth. His hand plumping her breast for him.

She arched her back, her hands in his hair. She felt him suckling on the globe of her breast and knew he was leaving his mark on her. The way he always did.

She reached for the nightstand, but they were on the wrong end of the bed. "Get a condom, Tuck. I need you inside me."

Reluctantly, he pulled away from her. Turned and grabbed a condom from the nightstand. He handed it to her.

She opened it and stroked him with one hand before placing the condom at his tip and rolling it on. He stood there next to the bed, watching her with that intense green gaze of his. She opened her arms and her legs.

He lowered his body slowly over hers. And she savored the feeling of him on top of her. Their eyes met and held. His hands skimmed down her sides and gripped her thighs, pulling her legs farther apart. Opening her totally to him. He bent her legs back toward her body and then leaned up to position the tip of his cock at her entrance.

She lifted her head to watch him take her, this last time. He slid slowly inside, and then his hands left her legs.

She wrapped them high around his back as he plunged deep within her. She ran her arms down his body, cupping his ass and pulling him toward her. "Stay still for a minute."

He stilled, and she closed her eyes. Savoring the stretched, too-full feeling of him inside her. Savoring the rough texture of the hair on his chest against her breasts. Savoring . . . him.

She tightened her inner muscles, and he began to move. Slowly at first, building the tension with each thrust of his hips until everything in her body was tensing with each withdrawal and she climaxed, calling his name.

He shouted her name and held her close. Thrusting a few more times until they were both still. He rolled over, holding her to his side, and she closed her eyes, afraid to open them and let this moment end.

Tuck held Andi in his arms until dawn crept through the window and painted the room in its bright light. The reprieve he'd enjoyed during the night was gone. There was no way to stay and pretend that things hadn't changed. He got out of the bed and was surprised when Andi didn't move.

He had two choices, and walking away without a word wasn't his style, so he sat back down on the bed, hard. His weight jarred the mattress, and she rolled toward him. Opening her eyes to stare up at him.

"Sorry, did I wake you?" he asked, brushing his finger down her face. What if that really had been the last time he'd have rights to her body? He didn't want to believe it, but a part of him feared it.

"No, I think the earthquake did that," she said, turning her face into his palm and kissing him.

"Why?" he asked, he wasn't going to push. He knew women, had lived with and protected his mother and sister for many years. He wasn't going to be the guy who couldn't just go. But he needed a reason. Because from where he sat, it felt as if there were grounds to stay.

She pushed her hair out of her eyes and pulled the sheet higher on her chest. Rolled to her side, propping her head on her elbow, the pose was a relaxed one, but he saw the tension in her shoulders and in her face.

"It's kind of early in the morning, barely six. I was sleeping."

He wasn't going to let her play any games this morning. They'd played enough of them. "You must be joking. I know you weren't sleeping any better than I was."

She bit her lower lip, and for the first time since they'd met he saw her shrink from him. "Maybe I didn't want to talk this morning."

Let it go, man. But he couldn't. He'd never needed a woman the way he needed Andi, and he didn't for a second believe she didn't need him, too. "I do. I don't want to walk away from you without—"

She sat up, gesturing with her hands wide open. "Without what? Rehashing what's already been said? It's no use. There's nothing left to discuss."

He reached for her, and she drew back, pulled her legs to her chest and hugged them tight. He felt like a creep when she did that.

"Don't touch me, Tuck. That only leads to one place, and there are no solutions there."

He pushed to his feet and paced away from Andrea and the temptation she offered. "I think sex is where we are both most honest—where we get down to the real communication."

She arched both eyebrows at him and gave him her staunch feminist glare. "You would."

"Don't say that like I'm a guy and I can't relate to you unless you're having sex with me. I said there was honesty when we are in bed."

"Honesty? Then why did we play so many of those games?"

"Because you were afraid to be yourself without them," he said.

Her eyes widened, and he knew he'd said too much. She thought her fears were hidden, but from the first he'd seen them all too clearly.

"Sorry you thought you had to be so kinky for me," she said after a minute. But there was no heat to her words, and she huddled deeper into her own body.

"I wasn't kinky. I was trying to get you to unlock that part of yourself you'd forgotten."

"What part? And don't you dare say the womanly part. Because I'm always aware of the fact that I'm a woman."

"I know, sweetheart. You are aware of it, and you fear that part of yourself because it's what makes you different from everyone else at the firehouse."

"What about you? You have issues, too," she said. "Why don't we talk about them?"

"We did last night."

"You're right, we did. I don't think anything changed since three this morning."

"We had soul sex, woman. That has to count for something."

She blinked her eyes and then rolled away from him. The sheet dipped low to her waist, and he was distracted by the curve of her back and hips. What he really wanted was to be so distracted that he wrapped his body around her again.

"Andi?"

"Soul sex isn't something real."

He put his hand on her shoulder and shook her. "Yes, it is."

Leaning over her, he waited until she opened her eyes and looked at him.

"Well, maybe it felt like soul sex to you, but to me it was just . . ."

"Do you want me to leave?"

"Yes."

He turned on his heel and stalked into the bathroom, showering and shaving. When he came back into the room she was curled on her side.

He dressed and packed his bag. Then sat down next to her on the bed, resting his hand on her hip. She didn't stir or move.

"Andrea?"

She rolled over to her back and glanced up at him. "Yes?"

"I'm leaving."

"I know."

He should leave it at that, should just walk away, but he couldn't. Last night had changed him. "That's it. That's all you have to say?"

"What should I say, Tuck? Tell me what you want to hear?"

"I want to hear that you need me," he said, wishing he was still in bed with her. He should have forced her to say the words he wanted to hear when they were having sex. Except he didn't want to stay unless she asked him. It was stupid and juvenile, but he didn't want to need her more than she needed him.

"Why?" she asked.

Because I need you, he thought. "Forget it."

He kissed her one last time and picked up his bag, walking out without looking back. He'd left so many times that this shouldn't have hurt, but it did. For the first time he'd wanted to stay, and Andrea didn't want him to.

Andi couldn't move as she heard Tuck's truck start and then pull out of her driveway. She huddled deeper into herself, holding her legs tighter. She had always thought if she made herself small enough, the pain couldn't touch her. But somehow that had never worked.

She didn't know how much time had passed when the phone rang. She was surprised to see that it was after nine.

"O'Roarke," she said.

"It's Sara. Is Mick at your place?" Her friend's voice had an edge of panic to it. She'd never heard Sara sound like that before.

"No. When did you see him last?" Andi asked, reaching for her watch and putting it on.

"When he walked away from you. What am I going to do? I didn't want to call the cops because they all know him and—"

"Calm down. I'll be right there. We'll find him." Andi took a deep breath. Mick was a constant. The one guy she counted on to always be stable and steady. Sara's pregnancy and cancer must have rattled him more than Andi had noticed.

Dammit, this was what came from getting involved with a man like Tuck. She'd missed something important with Mick. Something that had cost him his concentration on the job and then caused him to walk out on Sara.

Andi hung up with Sara and dialed Mick's cell phone. Sara answered on the second ring. "He left his phone here."

"Sorry. Did you try the station house?" Andi asked. A lot of times guys who were off duty stopped by. It was just that the fire station was a second home. Many of the guys felt that the firehouse was their real home.

"Yes, Ari said he wasn't there."

"When did you call?" Andi asked. Ari came on shift in the evening. So Mick might have come in before Ari was there.

"Just after midnight."

Well, then Ari would have been there. She'd call Ari next. Have him do a quick bunk check before they all started searching for him. "Why didn't you call me?"

"I didn't want anyone to know that he walked out on me."

Those words echoed around in her head, and for a minute Andi heard in Sara's voice all that she'd felt in her heart since she'd realized that having Tuck stay with her wasn't going to work out. "Mick's not that kind of guy."

"I know. So once I figured that out, I started panicking. Where is he, Andi? I'm really worried."

"What have you done?" she asked, wanting to know where Sara had been and to whom she'd talked. Mick was an orphan and had no family. His friends were all firefighters.

"Drove down the street but he isn't close by. I have no idea where else to go. I called the ER, and he hasn't been brought in."

"Okay, I'm going to call the guys. They might have seen him. I'll be there as quick as I can be."

"Thanks, Andi."

"No problem." If she hadn't been so distracted by her fight with Tuck, maybe she would have handled Mick better. Rationally she knew she wasn't responsible for Mick's decisions, but it hurt that she'd been the last one to talk to him. What if he never came back? What if she had to face Sara, knowing she'd been the one accountable for making her husband leave?

Andi pulled on a pair of jeans and the first shirt she touched. She tugged it over her head, and it fell to her hips. She realized it was Tuck's shirt and started to take it off, but she felt closer to him with it on. She knew it was silly since the reason he'd left had been because she couldn't give him what he wanted, but she hadn't wanted him to go.

She swallowed hard and forced herself to concentrate on finding Mick. One problem at a time. A firehouse family problem. Something she could handle. Not a six-foot-three burly man who saw straight to her soul.

She talked to Ari, who ran upstairs and did a head count. No sign of Lieutenant Palmer at the station. She thanked him and started calling her crew.

Andi tried McMillan first. "Yo."

Loud music blared in the background. She could barely hear him over it.

"Pete, it's Captain O'Roarke, have you seen Lieutenant Palmer?"

The music immediately shut off, and she was grateful. Nothing like a little authority to get some silence. "No sir, Cap. Is he missing?"

Andi took a deep breath. The last thing Mick would want was for his business to be known to everyone, but she and Sara couldn't search everywhere for him. For one thing the crew frequented three different bars. "He didn't come home last night."

"Where should I look?" McMillan said.

And Andi felt a sense of pride that he didn't even hesitate. Her crew was first-rate. It was heartening to see it off duty as well.

"I'm going over to the Palmer residence. Want to meet me there?"

"Yeah, I'll round up as many of the crew as I can. We'll meet there."

"Uh, Pete?"

"Yes?"

She hesitated, unsure how to word this so that he would

get her message and not think she was treating him like a kid. "Palmer would want this kept quiet."

"Understood."

Andi hung up the phone and put on her boots. She looked at the pillow Tuck had slept on all night and quickly hugged it to her. She hoped she was the tough woman he thought she was because she had a feeling it was going to be a trying day.

Chapter 21

Tuck didn't wait for the phone to ring. Andi wouldn't call. He drove back to Tallahassee, which took almost six hours. His home on the wooded live oak lot was his sanctuary. His place to escape and regroup after he'd figured out why someone had set a fire and how they'd done it.

But the fire Andi had started in his soul still burned, and this time no amount of analysis of burn patterns or acceleration was going to help.

He had two messages on his machine from his boss. They needed him in Miami as quickly as he could get there.

He checked his watch and decided to fly. It would take him twelve hours to drive, and he was sick of spending time in his truck.

He booked an evening flight and checked his e-mail, reading the report on the arsonist who was definitely targeting wealthy home owners on West Palm Beach.

When he reached Miami he'd check in at the fire station. They had a guest house for him to stay in on West Palm Beach. The island was accessible only by boat or ferry and had once been the private retreat of the Vanderbilts.

Tallahassee was on central standard time, so he added an hour to the clock on the wall and determined it still wasn't too late to call Andi.

And do what? She was done talking. And frankly, he had

more pride than to keep after someone who clearly didn't want him. Their paths had crossed, he thought. It was time for their lives to move on. For his life to move on.

He called Station Forty-two to check in with the fire chief . . . another O'Roarke.

"This is Tucker Fields from the fire marshal's office."

"Good to hear from you, Fields. I'm Ian O'Roarke. When can I expect you?"

Ian, Andi's older brother. The protective one. He experienced an uncomfortable moment, talking to Ian after having spent the night in his sister's bed. After having left her when he'd really wanted to stay. He rubbed the back of his neck and focused instead on his business.

"I get in after nine tonight. I can be at your station in the morning." Tuck knew fires and fire starters. This was the life he'd chosen, and this was what he was going to focus on. No more thinking about having a home away from this place.

"Good. Did you get the reports I e-mailed you?"

"Yes. I've skimmed them. I'll review them on my flight down so I can hit the ground running." He paced to the window and looked out at the land surrounding his home. He was isolated and away from everyone. This was how he was meant to live.

"Heard good things about you from Auburndale," Ian said.

Andi wouldn't have talked about him. He knew that. Ian must have heard other rumblings from the crew members he'd spoken to or the fire marshal's office. "Thanks. Took a while to get a handle on the fires, but in the end it was straightforward. What did the insurance investigator say about your fires?"

Tuck reached in his pocket for a pen and encountered a condom. He wouldn't be needing that for a while. He tossed it on the desk and grabbed a pen from the drawer. His notebook was in his bag on the end of the couch, and he retrieved it.

"That the fires were set by gas . . . but we all knew that. The cans were left on site."

Tuck wrote down what Ian said. When he got to West Palm Beach he'd interview O'Roarke again, but he liked to have some preliminary information before he got to the site.

"What's your gut say?" Tuck asked. He tossed some clean clothes in his suitcase and loaded his laptop in his briefcase and headed out the door.

"That it's an amateur. Someone who accidentally lit the first one and then liked it and tried it again."

"Why do you say that?" he asked, but he heard the same methodical analysis that he'd come to expect from Andi. There was something about the O'Roarkes that was solid and smart. They knew fires and the way they started. Tuck had the feeling that this case wasn't going to prove the distraction he needed. But Miami would.

Nothing like hot nights and a fire starter to take his mind off his love life and the problems in it. Plus he had to make time for a trip to Chicago.

"The other two were almost identical to the first, but the buildings weren't."

"So the burns weren't as quick."

"Yes. I'm thinking our guy—or gal, my sister gets on my case when I act like there's only men in the world capable of committing or solving crimes—anyway, I'm thinking this person is frustrated because the latter fires haven't matched the first one."

"Your sister doesn't take kindly to stereotyping," Tuck said. He didn't either; there'd been a number of times when he'd been taken off guard by Andi or another woman because they'd reacted in a way he hadn't anticipated.

"Makes a man uncomfortable sometimes, doesn't it?" O'Roarke asked.

"Yes. Your theory sounds good," he said, changing the subject. He wasn't about to talk to Ian O'Roarke about anything other than the arson in his district. "I think I've got a meeting with the other investigators. We'll figure out who your fire starter is."

"I know you will."

Tuck hung up the phone, thinking that after this assignment he was going to need a vacation from arsonists and O'Roarkes. A nice long vacation where he could lie on a beach somewhere and figure out how to keep moving on when he wanted so badly to go back to Auburndale and put down roots.

Three days later Andi was back at work. Mick had been at an EMS station in Auburndale. Had witnessed an accident and ridden back with the EMTs because they'd been short staffed. It had never occurred to him that Sara would be worried. So when he showed up the next morning about the same time Andi, McMillan, and Johnson had, he'd been speechless. Sara had started crying and yelling at him, and they'd all decided to leave the husband and wife alone.

Mick was still avoiding her. And that suited her just fine. She wasn't herself, and so far no one had noticed. In fact, the only one she worried would see through her was Mick, but since he was ticked off at her, he hadn't noticed a thing. Marilee had tried to start a conversation about Tuck, but Andi had cut her off and retreated to her office.

She was caught up on paperwork and filing, two things she was never caught up on. She'd also done the schedule for the next eight months and factored in things like leave for Mick when Sara gave birth.

The fire station was quiet because there wasn't much going on in the county. It was rainier than usual this year, and that meant more calls for accidents but no fires. And that meant too much time to think.

"Got a spare minute?" Mick asked.

"Sure, come in."

He closed the door before coming into her office and sinking into the guest chair. Before Tuck had come here no one ever shut the door. Now Mick was.

"What's up?"

"That's what I want to know."

"What?"

"You know exactly what I'm talking about. God knows I was ticked off for a while and not noticing anything, but now that's worn off and you're different."

"That doesn't mean something's up. I just . . . I don't know. Something changed."

How could she explain what she still didn't understand. It was as if by accepting her the way he had, the entire woman, Tuck had changed her. He'd made her more comfortable with herself, and she couldn't go back. Couldn't push aside her own personality any longer.

"Was it Tucker Fields that changed you?"

She shrugged. "If we get personal, I'm going to be talking about you and Sara and her pregnancy."

He put his hands up. "I'll back off, but I know you, Andi. You keep everything inside, and while Tuck was here there was a new you. I like the way you smiled more and let your guard down with the crew, but now . . . you're quiet again. And I don't like it."

"Me, too, Mick. So how's Sara?"

"Good, we talked to her oncologist yesterday, and he said determination was the difference between life and death. Well, you know Sara. No one can change her mind once she makes it up."

Andi smiled at Mick. He seemed a lot less angry than he had the last time they were on shift. "Something's changed for you, too."

"God damn, we're turning into a freakin' Oprah cry

fest," Mick said, propping his feet on her desk. He was settling in for a long bullshit session. It had been too long since they'd just chatted.

"We all know you'd prefer Jerry Springer," Andi said with a laugh.

"Damn right."

There was a rap on the door, and Mick leaned back in his chair to open it. Marilee stood there. Face pale, hands shaking. Her cordless headset still active.

Andi's heart sped up, and she was on her feet before she realized what she was doing. "What's wrong?"

Marilee glanced at Mick, then turned back to Andi. "Sara's boss called, Mick. She collapsed at work."

Mick pushed past Marilee and out into the main station house.

"He needs to get there quick. Want me to call for a police escort?"

"I'll let you know. Thanks for delivering the message, Marilee."

Johnson, McMillan, and O'Neill, one of the men who rotated on and off their shift, were standing outside. She noticed Powell in the kitchen making coffee.

"Marilee, call Lieutenant Adams and ask him to come in. Who is familiar with Lakeland?"

"I am, Cap," Powell said, stepping out of the kitchen and wiping his hands on a towel.

"Lieutenant Palmer needs to get to Lakeland Regional ASAP."

"I'm on it. I am the best driver in this bunch."

"Yeah, right. Just get him there in one piece."

Mick stalked out of the house without saying a word, but she felt better that Powell was behind the wheel. She called for backup since they were two men down.

The other guys looked at her, and for a minute she almost

retreated to her office without explaining. "Sara is sick at work."

"Did the cancer come back?" McMillan asked.

"Yes." But she couldn't say more than that. Andi turned away, ready to retreat, but for some reason the men followed her. It was as if they needed to be around her.

And she realized that they were upset and worried, too, though they'd never admit it. Sara was part of their family because they'd spent so much time together. The firehouse was the family that really mattered. They'd all bonded, and if something happened to Lieutenant Palmer's wife, they'd all mourn.

She knew that if they had a call right now, it would be dangerous to them all, but she wished one would come through. They needed to be active, not hanging around here.

"Anyone up to the chin-up challenge?"

"I've been working out, Cap. I think I can take you. Maybe even one-handed," O'Neill said.

"Careful, O'Neill, women don't like show-offs."

"That's not what they tell me."

"To your face maybe," Johnson said.

They took turns doing chin-ups and playing basketball until the sun went down. Then they retreated to the den area to watch TV but no one slept all night. Marilee stayed when her shift ended, and finally close to dawn Mick called to say that Sara was in intensive care.

Andi left the station house and drove to her place. Tuck's scent was still on the pillow, and she put on his shirt and wrapped her arms around the pillow. She was scared for her friends and needed to talk to Tuck, but was afraid to reach out for him. Afraid that after the way she'd sent him away, he would have already moved on.

Tuck took one look at the setup on West Palm Beach and knew he wouldn't mind staying there. Ocean breezes, tanned fit women and great sunrises and sunsets every day. The only problem was when he pictured living in this paradise in his mind, he pictured Andi sitting next to him.

The investigation was the kind Tuck hated. He had brass from every division even remotely connected with the fires breathing down his neck. They wanted answers and wanted them quickly, and Tuck just needed room to think.

He crashed in Ian O'Roarke's guest house. There were pictures of Andi on the wall with her nephews and with Ian's deceased wife. It was sad to see a family torn apart the way they had been. In the pictures everything looked so perfect.

That was one thing Tuck didn't have of his own family. His dad had never smiled in any pictures. Their family photos were mainly him and Jayne. Sometimes one of them with their mom. There was one picture that stood out in Tuck's mind of Jayne, Mom, and him that he remembered his father taking. They had been at the park overlooking Lake Michigan, it had been a rare warm late spring day and they'd been picnicking.

Mom had been laughing, and for once Tuck's dad had almost joined in. The picture wasn't perfect, but in Tuck's mind everything that had led up to the moment made it so.

He was booked on a flight to Chicago on Friday. He was staying only through Sunday because he was lucky to get approved for those few days off. But he knew his mom would sleep better once he'd met Jayne's new guy.

Looking at Andi's family pictures now, he wondered if they had really been as happy as they seemed or if this was just a moment captured in time when everything gave the impression of being so.

There was a knock on the door, and Tuck opened it. Ian stood there in his cutoffs and a faded fire department T-shirt.

"Want to join me for a beer? My dad and two of my brothers are coming over."

Tuck leaned one arm on the doorjamb. He liked Ian, but he wasn't interested in talking about his investigation with anyone else. "Am I going to be grilled about my progress on the investigation?"

Ian laughed. "Nah, the old man's retired, and Liam and Pat don't care about politics."

Tuck stepped out onto the porch, closing the door behind him. He didn't want Ian to notice that he'd been staring at a picture of Andi. "Then yes. It's been too long since I had beer with the guys."

"What about Andi? She didn't take you out with her crew?" Ian asked as they started walking toward the main house. Ian's home sat on three acres of land. The house itself was a 1930s beach cottage that had seven bedrooms, a huge pool with cabanas around it and a path leading to the beach in one direction and the guest house in the other.

"Andi's not a guy," Tuck pointed out as they walked. It bothered him that her own family hadn't ever realized that. He thought that maybe if her father and brothers had just once shown her it was okay to be a woman, maybe she would have . . . What? Asked him to stay when he'd offered her nothing but sex? Tuck cursed himself for a fool. Barely aware that Ian had stopped walking.

"You're not supposed to notice," Ian said.

Tuck glanced at the other man. What could he say? The fact that Ian didn't think someone would be conscious of Andi's sex was too crazy for words. "I'm kind of a details guy."

"I'll give you that, Fields," Ian said.

Tuck harbored a brief hope that the subject would change. In fact, he'd be happy to talk to his boss and his boss's boss about the investigation at this moment. He'd talk to anyone about the investigation if it meant he didn't have to have this conversation now.

"How much did you notice about my sister?" Ian asked.

He took a step closer. Ian was a tall man but not taller than Tuck, and for a minute Tuck feared he was going to end up in a fistfight over Andi. Not that he wouldn't fight for her.

"I think this conversation ends here, O'Roarke," Tuck said.

"I'll decide when it ends, Fields."

Tuck rubbed the back of his neck. "You've known Andi longer than I have, but I think she'd be pissed that we're talking. Whatever happened between she and I isn't your business."

"I'm her big brother; that makes it my business."

Hell, he wasn't ready to go three rounds with a guy he really liked. "I've got a sister, too. Trust me."

"Dad, Grandpa and Uncle Pat are here," Josh yelled from the pool deck.

Ian backed away, still staring at Tuck. "We'll talk later."

Tuck nodded. "Am I still invited for a beer?"

"Yes."

Ian pushed past him, walking up the path. Tuck heard the sounds of the men talking and the kids greeting their uncle with a surprise blast from a SuperSoaker. And he realized he wanted to be a part of this family. Not because he'd never had brothers, but because they were Andi's family and they cared about her. They protected her and nurtured her, and he wanted his turn at it. For the first time since he walked out of her house, he realized he should have stayed.

That he should have fought for the woman he loved. And he did love her. She filled that empty part of him that had always been roaming. He knew that, and now he had to convince her.

Chapter 22

Andi almost didn't get out of Auburndale on Tuesday afternoon. Sara was out of intensive care and resting at home. Mick was fine to work. Both he and Sara said he needed to get out of the house. Sara's collapse had stemmed from hyperemesis gravidum, which Sara explained was normal in the first three months of pregnancy.

Sara said if Andi missed her father's birthday bash because she'd been stupid and neglected to eat and sleep, she'd never forgive herself. But Andi had wanted to miss her dad's bash because she knew that Tuck was down there and she didn't want to see him.

Not yet. Maybe in a few more months when she'd had the time to forget about him. To forget how much she still missed him. To stop sleeping in his T-shirt, she thought. *You can't face a man and pretend you don't want him when you've been sleeping in his shirt.* But she didn't say that to Sara. She wasn't about to admit to her friend that she thought she might have made a mistake. She really needed advice but felt as though her love-life problems—wait a minute— was it love? Was that why she felt the way she did? Was she in love with Tuck?

A horn sounded out front, and she peeked out the window, expecting to see Rory's truck. Though they lived two hours apart, he always insisted on coming to pick her up when they were both going home. Something about them both going the same way, which was totally lame. She knew he was doing it because he was her big brother and didn't want her on the road for a five-hour drive alone.

Instead of his old Chevy truck, Rory pulled up in his brand-new BMW 645Ci convertible. Andi knew she was driving with Rory because he was going to be taking a lot of heat once they reached Miami.

"What is that?" she asked as she stepped outside.

"My new car. Like it?" Rory asked, getting out of the car and patting the hood. He wore a pair of black pants and an open-neck, button-down shirt. He looked as if he'd stepped out of *GQ*—not like her easygoing firefighter brother.

"Of course, but O'Roarkes drive trucks. Didn't you tell me that when I wanted to buy the Miata?" She was still trying to come to terms with this. Dad was going to freak out. Rory seemed different than he had on his last visit. There was an edge to her brother that had never been there before. To be honest, she wasn't sure she liked it.

"Yes, well . . ." He cleared his throat. "Successful investment counselors drive flashy cars."

She totally ignored the investment thing for now. When he'd said he was thinking about a change she'd had no idea he'd meant to make one quickly. But to be fair, they were both in their late thirties, so changes couldn't wait forever.

But change was hard. She wished she could be like Rory and just reach out and take what she wanted. But what did she want? The answer came to her in a flash; she wanted Tuck.

"It's flashy, alright. What's it got under the hood?" she asked because their family had always driven big vehicles with powerful engines.

"Do I look like I'd drive anything but a V–8?" he asked with a half smile.

"No, you look like someone who wants to rock the boat," she said.

He came around the car and leaned back against it. "This isn't what the old man is going to focus on."

"What, then?"

"I quit the department."

"You what?" Honestly, she had no idea he was going in that direction. He was a good firefighter. A good man to have on a crew. She knew because she'd met his chief a few times and he always spoke highly of Rory.

"I told you I wasn't happy," Rory said in that belligerent way that told her he was expecting a hard time.

She wasn't the one he had to worry about. "Yeah, but that's a big change. What are you doing? The Fidelity thing?"

He took off his sunglasses and put them in his shirt pocket. "Yes. Natalie moved back in, and I'm going to ask her to marry me once I buy a house."

Andi wondered about that. Rory had always been the free spirit in their family. The guy who rented and never owned. Now he was going for the whole shebang, house, wife, nine-to-five job. "Is that what you want?"

He looked away from her for a minute, and when he looked back she saw determination on his face. "Yes."

Andi wanted her brother to be happy, so she wasn't trying to hassle him. But some things didn't seem right to her. "She moved out to pressure you to change jobs."

He put his sunglasses back on. "Are you riding with me or not?"

"You know I am," she said.

"Then let's get going."

She walked away from him, hoping that Tuck didn't think she wanted him to change his entire life for her. She wouldn't want a man to do that. How could they be happy in the long run if he pretended to be someone he wasn't?

And Rory wasn't a financial guy, no matter how much he wanted to be one. And Tuck . . . Well, she didn't know about Tuck. She realized then that maybe she hadn't given him a real chance.

He'd wanted her to change, and she'd been afraid to. But she'd changed anyway. He'd made her view life differently, and the woman she'd once been she was no longer.

She went into her house and looked around her small place. Tuck had filled it with life. He'd made her come out of her shell and stop living in her fantasies and start living with a real man. The kind she'd always wanted but had never had the guts to go after.

She grabbed her suitcase. She locked the door and found Rory waiting for her on the porch. He took her bag and put it in the trunk.

Andi got in on the passenger side of the car and watched her brother as he drove. He was trying a new lifestyle not because Natalie wanted him to, she thought; he was doing it to save a relationship, and maybe it was time she did, too.

Tuck had worked day and night with two other investigators, and finally they'd unraveled the mystery. The arsonist was Conner Barman, a sixteen-year-old boy who'd started the first fire in his own house so he could move in with his girlfriend's family. But as Ian had suggested and they'd all agreed, the kid had liked the feeling of setting the fire and had struck again.

It had taken almost two weeks once Tuck got there, but all the signs pointed to Conner, and when they'd gone to his house, he'd confessed.

There was really no reason for him to stay on at Ian O'Roarke's guest house, except that Andi was coming to town for her father's birthday and Tuck knew he had to see her again. He'd noticed that everything with Andi's family was a competition. The other night he'd gotten into a beer-drinking contest with Pat and Liam. Ian had declined, saying his boys were watching.

But when Pat and Liam had left, Ian had cornered him and started asking questions about Andi again. And Tuck hadn't had to feign being drunk. He'd steered the conversation off of that topic and escaped.

Having Ian grill him had made him realize how much he'd missed her. He'd flown to Chicago and checked out Jayne's new man, Stuart Markem. He was a nice guy, good job and seemed to genuinely care for his sister. While he'd been at dinner with his family, he realized how gun-shy they all were when it came to commitment. Jayne had confronted him when Stuart was out of earshot. And Tuck had wrapped his arm around his thirty-five-year-old sister and told her to go for it.

It was time they all stopped hiding in the past. She'd been startled, but had laughed and hugged him back. He'd flown back to Florida thinking that trying to force Andi into asking him to stay had been his insurance. His reason not to leave because he hadn't trusted himself enough.

There was a rap on his door, and he opened it to find Josh standing there. The teenager wore a pair of board shorts and a classic Rolling Stones T-shirt.

"Are you old enough to even know who the Stones are?"

"My mom was a huge fan. This was her shirt," Josh said.

Tuck had one of those moments when he felt like an idiot.

"It's cool. I think Mom would want her shirts to be worn and not stuffed in a box somewhere. Dad agreed. The food is on, and everyone's here."

"Who's everyone? Are your uncles here? I don't think I'm ready for another drinking competition."

"Yes, they are here and my Aunt Andi. Have you met her?"

"Yes, I worked on a case in her jurisdiction."

"She's cool for a girl."

"Don't let her hear you saying that."

"I know it. She hates when you say 'for a girl.' But girls are different. Even Aunt Andi has to admit that."

"Josh, I bet you make her crazy."

The teenager grinned. "I try. Dad says she's too serious."

Tuck left his place and walked up to the main house with the sixteen-year-old boy. He knew he had better change the topic to something safer. Something not about Andi since he wasn't sure what kind of reception he was going to get from her.

"Do you know Conner?" Tuck asked.

"Yeah, I do. That was weird him being the arsonist."

"Did he have any problems at school?" Tuck had concluded his investigation, but the psychiatrist thought something was off with Conner.

"Not that I noticed. We didn't hang in the same crowd."

"What crowd do you hang with?" Tuck asked. He knew Josh was an athlete and a math whiz.

"The cool crowd," he said with a grin that reminded Tuck of Andi. It was part cocky, part self-mocking.

"What was I thinking?" he asked himself.

"I don't know, man."

Music blared from speakers set around the pool, and tiki torches had been set in the perimeter. The huge built-in grill was fired up and loaded with more meat than Tuck had seen on one before. Josh left him to jump in the pool and join a water volleyball game already in progress.

Andi and the brother he hadn't met—Rory, he thought his name was—were arguing loudly with Liam. Ian manned the grill, his father beside him. Pat and a bunch of guys Tuck had met at the firehouse were divided into two teams in the water.

"Want to play, Fields?"

Tuck shook his head. Not yet. He wanted to find a quiet place and watch Andi. He'd missed her too much. Seeing her again brought that all back. He knew in an instant that no matter what happened, he wasn't letting her leave here without him. He had two weeks' vacation starting tomorrow, and spending it in Auburndale convincing her that they could make their relationship work sounded like the perfect trip.

Andi looked up, and their gazes met. He thought he saw all those emotions she'd always hidden away when they were in public. He knew she wouldn't acknowledge him here. Wouldn't want her family to know that they'd been lovers.

For a minute the craziness of the pool area dropped away. She sat up straighter, stopped talking to her brother.

Tuck started for her, but Ian stepped in front of him. "Where are you going, Fields?"

"Wherever I want to, O'Roarke." Tuck was sick of Ian's attitude. Andi was almost forty. It was time for Ian to back off. When Ian didn't move out of the way, Tuck pushed past him, bumping Ian into the pool.

Ian grabbed Tuck's arm, pulling him into the water with him. A free-for-all ensued. Tuck found himself in the middle of an intense water battle that left no one the victor. Tuck swam for the side of the pool, got out and sat on the edge. He tossed his wet T-shirt over the back of a chair.

Ian lifted himself up beside Tuck.

"Sorry about that," Tuck said.

"Nah, it was me. I've been kind of wanting to test you, see what kind of man you are."

Tuck didn't want to know if he passed or not. A shadow fell over them, and he glanced up at Andi. "Can I speak to you alone, Tucker?"

He nodded and got to his feet, following her out of the pool area and down the path to the beach.

Andi had always loved the ocean. The only thing she didn't like about living in Auburndale was that it took almost two hours to get to either coast. She heard Tuck behind her, but she didn't turn around.

Instead she watched the waves cycling in and out on the shore. Saw how the sand was left pristine without marks each time the waves retreated and wished for a moment that a wave could wash over her and wipe away all the mistakes she'd made.

"Want to walk?" she asked, gesturing toward the south. The sun was dipping lower in the sky on the west, but there was still a lot of daylight left. The beach wasn't too crowded here since this section was mainly private homes.

"You're the lady in charge," he said, falling into step behind her.

But she'd never really felt in charge unless she was barking orders or giving him a hard time, and right now, she had no idea what to talk about.

Then she remembered him and Ian in the pool. "What was going on with you and Ian?"

Tuck stopped walking. "Your brother and I were having an ongoing discussion."

"About?" she asked, turning to face him.

"You."

She shouldn't ask. *Don't ask*, she thought. *Just start walking again.* "Me?"

"Yes, he didn't like it that I noticed you were a woman." Tuck reached toward her but let his hand drop before he touched her.

"Oh. But I am a woman," she said. She was his woman, she realized. And she wanted his touch. Wanted to feel his big hand in hers again. Wanted that more than she'd ever expected to.

He smiled at her. "We both agree on that."

She took a deep breath. It didn't matter if her family was

all gathered nearby or that this was the worst time to talk when she'd soon have to deal with them and the ensuing argument between her father and Rory. She needed to make Tuck understand that firefighting wasn't her entire life anymore.

"I'm sorry," she said, knowing the best place to start was right there.

"For?" he asked, giving her an opening to hedge her bets and protect her fragile emotions.

And they were fragile. It wasn't as though she knew how he'd react. She had no way of predicting if he'd be there when she jumped off that emotional precipice and told him how she felt. But with each breath she took she knew it with greater certainty. She was in love with Tucker Fields.

"Being stubborn, making you leave like that. I think . . ." Andi felt that tingling on the back of her neck, the same sensation she experienced right before she entered a burning building. It was part fear, part excitement and part confidence that she could handle whatever the flames threw at her.

"What?" he asked.

She took another deep breath and then determined breathing wasn't going to help calm her nerves. Reaching out, she snagged his hand and pushed her fingers through his. He closed his fingers around hers, and she smiled up at him.

"I realized that I'm in the same pattern, and on one level I know that, but it's comfortable and safe, and I don't want to change.

"But you won't let me stay there. You pushed and made me feel things that I'm still not comfortable with," she said at last.

"I can't lie and say I don't want you to change, because I think we both have to make adjustments for a relationship to work between us. But I'm not going to push so hard. To be honest, you should know that I'm not a great prospect for the long run."

Tuck was always honest, and that made her care a little more. She liked that she wasn't the only one dealing with new feelings and not sure where they'd lead. "You are a little old to still be single."

"Hey, so are you."

"Well, I never met a man who could handle all of me."

He waggled his eyebrows. "I can. Handling you is a full-time job. Do you want it to be full-time; is that what you're saying?"

She almost didn't want to say the words out loud. The last time she'd tried a serious relationship it had backfired so horribly. She knew Tuck was different, but still. He just watched her with patience and a well of caring in his eyes. "Yes, I want a relationship, but I don't know how it will work."

"However we want it to. I'm sorry, too."

"Why?"

"For pushing you too hard. Something else was going on that night, and I should have just let things alone."

"Why didn't you?"

"You have this ability to completely disappear inside yourself. You made me feel like I wasn't needed."

"I can't say that's going to change. But I do know that I need you, Tuck. I've been sleeping on your pillow and wearing your old T-shirt, and I still wake up aching in the middle of the night."

He pulled her to him and crushed her in a bear hug. His mouth found hers. She opened her lips under the onslaught of his. Clutched him closer to her and held on as if she would never let go. And she wasn't going to let go for a long time.

Chapter 23

Tuck cupped Andi's face in his hands, afraid to let her go. Not that he really thought she'd leave. But he couldn't believe his good fortune in having this woman to call his own. His good fortune in having stumbled upon her in that small town of Auburndale and now having her in his arms. Back where she belonged.

He dropped biting kisses down the length of her neck. Suckling at the base to leave his mark. He wished he had a ring, that he wore something he could give to her so she could wear it out in public for the world to see that she belonged to him.

"Don't leave a love bite on me," she said, but she didn't try to push him away. Her fingers scraped against his back, tracing patterns on his skin. He wished he had a tattoo wrapping around his chest and back; he'd have her trace it with her smooth fingertips, then her warm mouth.

She tasted too good to stop, and it had been too long since the last time he'd had the flavor of her skin on his tongue. Slightly salty, a little sweet and a hundred percent Andi. He lifted his head. "Why not?"

She slid her fingers into his hair and rubbed her cheek over his. He tightened his arms around her and prayed that this wasn't some kind of bizarre dream. That he wasn't going to wake up to Josh knocking on his door.

"My dad has eagle eyes, and I'm not about to bring his attention to us." She dropped a sweet, soft kiss on his mouth. He assumed she thought he'd be distracted, and he was. He wanted her. He wasn't going to believe she was his again until he was buried hilt deep in her body with her long legs wrapped around his hips.

But right now he needed to make it very clear that the time for hiding was over. He shook his head. If he was going to make major changes, and he knew he'd be the one to make them, then she couldn't hide him away. He was going to have to quit his job and find another one. Move from his secluded house in Tallahassee to Auburndale. Life was definitely going to be interesting, and he hoped he'd find that he had staying power. But when he held Andi in his arms he had no doubts that he'd ever want to leave her side.

"I thought we were through with secrets."

She put her hand on her neck, her finger moving over her own skin, rubbing the spot where he'd kissed her. He saw the faint bluish mark and felt like throwing his head back and howling.

"We are. But my family is—"

"No buts, Andrea. Either we're together or we're not. We're too old to play clandestine games." He traced his finger around the lines of her bikini top. He followed the string to the tie at the back of her neck. Glancing up and down the beach, he saw that they were pretty isolated. He tugged on the ribbon and released the knot but held the string ties at the back of her neck.

"Tuck, what are you doing?"

Her hands snaked around his waist. He wanted to thank Ian for dragging him into the pool. The smooth skin of her stomach brushed against his chest. Her breath grazed his neck. He felt the delicate curl of her tongue against his shoulder.

"Whatever I want," he said, but he wondered who was really in charge here.

He let the strings slip through his fingers and then followed the fabric as it fell away until he was cupping her bare breasts in his hands.

"You are looking for trouble," she said, undulating against him.

He knew this wasn't the time and place but couldn't resist. "I think I found it the day I met you."

"Really? Am I worth it?" she asked, but the teasing note was gone from her voice.

He retied her top, cupping her face in his hands and tipping her head back so their eyes met. "I'm sorry I haven't told you how I feel. But you are definitely worth it. In fact, you are more than worth it, Andi. You gave me something I didn't even know I was searching for."

"Me, too. I love you, Tucker Fields."

He knew he was grinning but couldn't help it. He lifted her off her feet and spun her around. Joy bubbled up inside him. He'd never thought—never dreamed—he'd have a woman like Andrea. That she was a real woman who embodied everything he'd ever secretly wanted.

He kissed her because he couldn't wait another second to claim some part of her body as his own. He thrust his tongue deep in her mouth, rubbed his tongue over her teeth and tasted every crevice he could reach.

He lowered her to the ground again but didn't let her go. "Well?" she asked.

"What?" Did she want to make love here? He glanced around. Having sex on the beach sounded romantic, but he knew that sand got into places that it shouldn't be and was very uncomfortable later. But taking her back to a house filled with all her family didn't sound like a good idea either.

"Do you love me?" she asked, her voice low-pitched and soft.

He shook his head. He loved her so much, sometimes he almost stopped breathing. "Do you really have to ask?"

"Yes."

"Sweetheart, of course I do."

"That's not good enough."

"What's not?" he asked, but he thought he knew where she was going. She'd bared her soul and made her confession; now she wanted him to do the same. Andi liked to keep the scales even.

"I'm not taking any stupid 'ditto' for a response," she said. "I want the words."

"What words?" he asked, just to yank her chain.

She hooked her leg around his calf and leaned up to whisper in his ear. "You know the ones I want."

Then she tugged him off balance and fell on top of him. "I'm not moving until you give them to me."

"You better be giving Fields CPR, Andi, or else we're going to need an explanation."

Andi jumped to her feet. She felt as if she was thirteen again. Embarrassed and afraid of what her brothers and father would say. Tucker lazily got to his feet and stood next to her as though he had no worries.

"I can explain," she said, then realized how that sounded and crossed her arms over her chest. "Not that I'm going to."

"Yes, you are. I can't wait to hear this," Ian said.

"I knew I should have pounded you when I had the chance, Fields." Her brothers had formed a circle around her and Tuck, and Andi didn't like it. She knew the way they could be. In a second she'd find herself outside a circle of flying fists and masculine tempers.

"Don't start, Ian," she said. Her oldest brother could sometimes be counted on to be the rational one. She didn't like the way Pat and Liam were bunching their fists and moving closer to both of them. And Rory, she glanced at him, hopeful he would be on her side, but despite his new urbane look he seemed ready to fight as well as he rolled up the sleeves on his dress shirt.

"I'll start if I want to," Ian said. "I don't take orders from my little sister."

"You just like a good fight, and Tucker isn't going to give you another one. Didn't you settle it in the pool?"

"He might have, but I didn't." Rory pushed past Ian and reached for Tucker. Andi put her arms out and blocked Tuck's body with her own. Her brothers were ruthless in a fight, and they fought all the time. Even now when they were supposedly grown.

Tuck wrapped his hands around her waist and lifted her off her feet. He set her next to him.

"I don't need you to defend me, sweetheart." He had a tender smile on his face as he looked down at her. She wished her brothers would just go away. She wanted to be alone with Tucker. To be allowed to finally enjoy this man that she'd never dreamed she could have.

She smiled up at him. "I know that, but they are all bull-headed."

He gave her that sardonic look of his. Then flexed his biceps. "I think I can handle them."

Tuck had enough ego for four men, and he was more than a little like her brothers when it came to the way he worked out and kept himself in top shape. She didn't doubt that he could defend himself.

She curved her hand around his face, trying to make him understand some important facts. "There are four of them, Tuck. And they are all your size."

"Hey, I'm bigger," Pat said, pushing past Rory. And glowering at them both. He grabbed the back pocket of Andi's jean shorts and pulled her back. "Take your hands off him, Andi."

She reached out and slugged Pat on the shoulder. He was

such an ass sometimes. He thumped her back. Not too hard, but hard enough to knock her away from Tuck.

Tuck steadied her and then turned and punched Pat, catching him on the jaw. Tuck's blow wasn't like hers had been; it was a full-out punch that sent her brother to the ground.

Rory grabbed Tuck's arm and started to twist, but Andi got between them again. Rory wouldn't hurt her. None of her brothers would really hurt her, but they always fought together. She pushed them out of the circle and a few feet away from her brothers.

"Tuck, what are you doing?" she asked, wondering how this entire situation had gotten so out of control.

"Defending you. I was raised not to hit women."

"I don't need you to defend me," she said. She hurried to her brother's side, but he was already on his feet and approaching Tuck. A trickle of blood was at the corner of Pat's mouth, and she had the feeling this wasn't going to end well.

"Do you really want to have a knock-down, drag-out fight with your brother? What does that prove, Andi?"

"He didn't really hurt me. He wouldn't," she said. Knowing that the same couldn't be said for Tucker, she once again placed herself firmly in front of him.

"Patrick Henry, stop right now," Andi said with a sinking stomach. She'd been hoping somehow that she and Tuck could just sneak back into the house and away from this place without ever facing this. But she remembered what Tuck had said. Hiding their relationship wasn't what he wanted . . . She hoped he was ready for the consequences.

Pat took two steps closer and said, "Not even if the old man were standing right here."

"I am standing right here, Pat. Stand down."

"Dad, he had his hands on Andi."

"I know. I saw it, too. Want to tell us what's going on here, Fields?"

"No."

Tuck was as mule-headed as her family. She elbowed him, but he just gave her a good hard glare. "I'm not going to explain myself to them."

"Fine. I'll take care of this."

"How? Going to fight all your brothers?"

"If I have to."

"Why am I not surprised? Fighting is one of the things you do best. That and competing. Always have to be a winner, right?"

Andi swallowed hard. She was always competing, especially with him. She didn't want to be . . . weaker. It didn't matter that she was female and nature had made her weaker than men. She'd never backed away from anything.

Her dad reached around Tucker and pulled Andi up against his side. He was looking down at her as if he'd never really seen her before. Never really noticed who she was. And Andi, who'd never felt as though she measured up in her old man's eyes, felt a part of her die inside.

Tucker walked away from them, moved down the beach, and Andi felt a part of her die inside. She didn't know how to fix this.

Pat and Rory started after him. But her father said, "Go home, boys."

Her brothers grumbled but left. Pat was still mumbling threats under his breath. Once they were all gone her dad let go of her. She stood there, arms wrapped around her waist, feeling . . . as if she wished she were anywhere but here.

"Andi, you don't have to fight anymore," Dad said.

"With the boys you always have to fight. I never shied away from holding my own, Dad."

"I know that. I made damned sure you could do more than hold your own."

That was the truth. He was always harder on her than he'd ever been on the boys.

"Why, Dad?"

"I wanted to make sure you were tough enough to survive on your own."

"Well, I am," she said.

"I know. I'm very proud of the woman you are. You're a good firefighter, an excellent fire chief, and I think with that man you might even find you can be happy. The way your mother and I were."

Her dad wrapped his arm around her shoulder, and she squeezed his waist. Feeling for the first time that she measured up in her father's eyes.

"Fields?"

Tuck glanced over his shoulder at the two of them.

"Can I have a word with you?"

Tuck came back to them. "Yes, sir."

"Fighting's not the only thing we O'Roarkes are good at. We're also very good at loving, and once we find the person who owns our hearts, we never let them go.

"You take care of my daughter, young man, or—"

"I know, you'll sic your sons on me."

"Hell, no. I'll take care of you, and if there's anything left, the boys will finish you off."

"Understood, sir."

Her dad walked away, and Andi was left alone with Tuck. She had no idea what to do or say.

Tuck watched Andi, knowing that they'd settled things before and this was just a little hiccup. His family was nothing like hers. He knew his mom and Jayne would love Andi and be happy to have her in their family. Andi's dad had made a point of warning him not to hurt her.

Tuck would never hurt Andi or allow anyone else to ever

again. What he felt about her scared him, it was so intense. And he thought maybe that was why he'd left her in Auburndale.

Maybe it was easier to walk away than have to deal with his feelings for her. But now that she was back, he knew he'd never leave her again. Whatever the deal had been with his own father, Tuck did know that it would take death to pry him from Andi's side.

"Sorry about my dad," she said, moving closer to him. There was something very tentative in her body language, almost as if she wasn't sure how to proceed now that they were alone again.

"Don't be. He loves you." Tuck knew that she'd bared her soul to him and he hadn't reciprocated. He'd been teasing her and himself, enjoying the feel of her in his arms, and planned to tell her he loved her. But he wanted the moment to be right.

"I know. But I've always felt it was kind of like, well, she's mine so I have to care for her," she said, coming closer to him. They both faced the waves, the sunset toward their backs.

"I always felt like he was disappointed not to have one more boy," she said at last.

Tuck's own experiences had shown him that the thing with parents was you never really left behind the feelings that you had in childhood. For Tuck, he'd always be the boy whose father abandoned him. No matter what he accomplished or how successful his relationships were, inside he'd always remember and wonder why his father had left.

But Andi didn't need to worry anymore. He could set her straight on a few things. "Your dad is really proud of you. We had drinks a few nights ago, and all he talked about was how hard you'd worked to become chief. How proud he was that you were one of only a few women in the U.S. to achieve that rank."

"Really?" Andi glanced over her shoulder at the path down which her father had just disappeared. "He never said anything to me."

Tuck couldn't wait another second to touch her. He pulled her to his side, tucked her up under his shoulder. She wrapped her arm around his waist, and the tension that had been riding him since her brothers had arrived on the beach evaporated.

"Talking is not really the strong suit for a lot of men, especially about things like pride and love."

"You, too?" she asked, tipping her head back.

He leaned down and kissed her. He needed to make love to her. To hold her in his arms and let all the other stuff drop away. He took his time, trying to put into his embrace everything that he felt.

He wanted to cherish her. To make it so Andi would never feel she had to compete to be loved. Never feel she couldn't relax her guard around him to be accepted. Never feel that she didn't have his love at all times.

"Sometimes a hug just works better than trying to come up with the words. I'd rather not express my emotions out loud. I'm better at showing people how I feel."

"Is that what you're doing now?"

"Maybe. I can do a much better job of showing you how I feel when we're alone."

"Want to go to the boathouse?"

"No. I want to go to the guest house where my bed is. Think we can get by your brothers?"

"No. Pat is going to want some revenge."

"I'm not too pleased with him either. I can't believe he hit you."

"He didn't hurt me," she said.

"Still, no one hits you anymore." He didn't like it. It may have seemed harmless to Pat, but Andi had been knocked off balance. He knew she was tough and could take whatever they dished out, but from now on she wasn't proving she was as tough as the other kids in her family. She was going to be the cherished princess if he had anything to say about it.

"Wow, I'm beginning to think you really do care," she said. In her eyes was the question that she wouldn't ask again.

He knew he owed her the words. "You know I do."

"I know you haven't said the words I've been waiting for."

Still he hedged, waiting for the right moment. Waiting until he had her exactly where he wanted her. He pulled her around in front of him. Held her loosely in his arms once more.

"Do I really need to? I was willing to take on all four of your brothers."

She wrapped her arms around his shoulders and scraped her nails down the back of his neck. His blood flowed heavier in his veins. His erection pushed against her stomach.

"That was sweet. I think you would have been in a world of hurt, though."

"Nice impression you have of me."

"It has nothing to do with you. There are four of them."

He leaned down, resting his chin on her shoulder, and she stilled in his arms, holding him close.

"I love you, Andrea."

Her arms tightened around him, and he felt her smile against his chest before she kissed him. "About time you admitted it."

Author's Note

Auburndale is really a small town in central Florida; in fact, I graduated from Auburndale Senior High not so long ago (well, longer than I'd rather admit!). But there is only one fire station in the city. I made up a second one and made it a little larger than it would realistically be. I also added a first station to West Palm Beach.

Two lovers. And an unforgettable passion
that transcends time . . . in
AGAIN
by Sharon Cullars.
Coming in May 2006 from Brava . . .

Inner resolve is a true possibility when temptation isn't within sight. Like the last piece of chocolate cheesecake with chocolate shavings; that last cigarette; that half-filled glass of Chianti . . . or the well-defined abs of a man who's had to take his shirt off because he spilled marinara sauce on it. Not deliberately. Accidents happen. At the sight of hard muscles, resolve flies right out of the window and throws a smirk over its wing.

Part of it was her fault. Tyne had offered him a shoulder rub, because during the meal he had seemed tense, and she'd suspected that his mind was still on the occurrences of the day. After dessert, he sat in one of the chairs in the living room while she stood over him. Even though he had put on a clean shirt, she could feel every tendon through the material, the image of his naked torso playing in her mind as her fingers kneaded the taut muscles.

As David started to relax, he leaned back to rest his head on her stomach. The lights were at half-dim. Neither of them was playing fair. Especially when a hand reached up to caress her cheek.

"Stop it," she whispered.

He seemed to realize he was breaking a promise, because the hand went down, and he said, "I'm sorry." But his head remained on her stomach, his eyes shut. From her vantage, she could see the shadow of hair on his chest. She remembered how soft it felt, feathery, like down. Instinctively, and against her conscious will, her hand moved to touch the bare flesh below his throat. She heard the intake of breath, felt the pulse at his throat speed up.

She told herself to stop, but there was the throbbing between her legs that was calling attention to itself. It made her realize she had lied. When she told him she wanted to take it slow, she had meant it. Then. But the declaration seemed a million moments ago, before her fingers touched him again, felt the heat of his flesh melding with her own.

He bent to kiss her wrist, and the touch of his lips was the catalyst she needed. The permission to betray herself again.

She pulled her hands away, and he looked up like a child whose treat had been cruelly snatched away. She smiled and circled him. Then slowly she lowered herself to her knees, reached over, unbelted and unbuttoned his pants. Slowly, pulled down the zipper.

"But I thought you wanted . . ." he started.

"That's what I thought I wanted." She released him from his constraints. "But right now, this is what I want." She took him into her mouth.

She heard an intake of breath, then a moan that seemed to reverberate through the rafters of the room. She felt the muscles of his thighs tighten beneath her hands, relax, tighten again. Her tongue circled the furrowed flesh, running rings around the natural grooves. She tasted him, realized that she liked him. Liked the tang of the moisture leaking from him. And the strangled animal groans her ministrations elicited.

There were pauses in her breathing, followed by strained exhalations. Then a sudden weight of a hand on the back of her head, guiding her. She took his cue, began sucking with a pressure that drew him further inside her mouth. Yet there was more of him than she could hold.

He was moments from coming. She could feel the trembling in his limbs. But suddenly he pushed her away, disgorging his member from her mouth with the motion.

He shook his head. "No, not yet," he said breathlessly. "Why don't you join me?" Before she could answer, he stood up, pulling her up with him, and began unbuttoning her blouse, almost tearing the seed pearls in the process. The silk slid from her skin and fell to the ground in a languid pool of golden-brown. He hooked eager fingers beneath her bra straps, wrenched them down. Within seconds, she was naked from the waist up, and the current in the room, as well as the excitement of the moment teased her nipples into hard pebbles. His fingers gently grazed them, then he grazed each with his tongue. Her knees buckled.

"How far do you want to go?" he breathed. "Because I don't want you to do this just for me."

Her answer was to reach for the button of his shirt, then stare into those green, almost hazel eyes. "I'm not doing this for you. I'm being totally selfish. I want you . . . your body . . ." She pushed the shirt over his shoulders, yanked it down his arms.

"Hey, what about my mind?" he grinned.

She smiled. "Some other time."

They undressed each other quickly, and as they stood naked, his eyes roamed the landscape of her body with undeniable appreciation. Then without ceremony, he pulled her to the floor on top of him so abruptly that she let out an "oomph." His hands gripped the plump cheeks of her ass, began kneading the soft flesh. She felt his hardened penis against her stomach and began moving against it, causing him to inhale sharply. His hands soon stopped their kneading and replaced the touch with soft, whispery caresses that caused her crotch to contract with spasms. One of his fingers played along her crevice as his lips grabbed hers and began licking them. His finger moved to the delicate wall dividing both entryways, moved past the moist canal, up to her clitoris, started teasing her orb just as his tongue began playing along hers. She grounded her pelvis against him, desperately claiming her own pleasure, listening to the symphony of quickly pumping blood, and intertwined breaths playing in her ears.

He guided her onto his shaft. Holding her hips, he moved her up, down, in an achingly slow and steady pace that was thrilling and killing, for right now she thought she could die with the pleasure of it, the way he filled her, sated her. She felt her eyes go back into her head (she had heard about the phenomenon from other bragging women, and had thought they were doing just that—bragging. But now she knew how it could happen.)

"Ooooh, fuck," she moaned.

"My thoughts exactly," he whispered back and with a deft motion, changed their positions until he was on top of her. Straddled on his elbows, he quickened his thrusting, causing a friction that drove her to a climax she couldn't stop. Her inner walls throbbed against the invading hardness, and she drew in shallow breaths as her lungs seemed to shatter with the rest of her body.

She put her arms around his waist and wrapped her legs around his firm thighs. His body had the first sheen of perspiration. She stroked along the dampness of his skin, then reciprocated the ass attention with gentle strokes along his cheeks.

"I want . . . I want . . . " he exerted but couldn't seem to finish the sentence. Instead, he placed his mouth over hers until she was able to pull his ragged breaths into her needy lungs. The wave that washed over her once had hardly ebbed away before it began building again. Now his pace was frantic, his hips pounding her body into the carpeting, almost through the floor. Not one for passivity, she pounded back just as hard and eagerly met each thrust. The wave was gathering force, this one threatening a cyclonic power that would rip her apart, render her in pieces. She didn't care. His desperation was borne of sex, but also she knew, of anger and frustration. He was expelling his demons inside her, and she was his willing exorcist . . .

Blood was everywhere. On the walls, which were already stained with vile human secretions; on the wooden floor, where the viscous fluid slowly seeped into the fibers of the wood and pooled between the crevices of the boards. Soon, the hue would be an indelible telltale witness of what had happened, long after every other evidence had been disposed of. Long after her voice stopped haunting his dreams. Long after he was laid cold in his grave.

He bent to run a finger through one of the corkscrew curls. Its end was soaked with blood. The knife felt warm in his hands still. Actually, it was the warmth of her life staining it.

He turned her over and peered into dulled brown eyes that accused him in their lifelessness. Gone was the sparkle—sometimes mischievous, sometime amorous, sometimes fearful—that used to meet him. Now, the deadness of her eyes convicted him where he stood, even if a jury would never do so. The guilt of this night, this black, merciless night, would hound his waking hours, haunt his dreams, submerge his peace, indict his soul. There would now always be blood on his hands. For that reason alone, he would never allow himself another moment of happiness. Not that he would ever find it again. What joy he would have had, might have had, lay now at his feet in her perfect form. Strangely, in death, she had managed to escape its pall. Her skin was still luminescent, still smooth. If it weren't for the vacuous eyes, the blood soaking her throat, the collar of her green dress, the dark auburn of her hair . . . he might hold to the illusion that somewhere inside, she still lived.

He reached a shaky hand to touch her cheek. It was warm, soft, defying death even as it stiffened her body.

He bent further, let his lips graze hers one last time. Their warmth was a mockery. Her lips were never this still beneath his. They always answered his touch, willingly or not.

He saw a tear fall on her face, and for a second was confused. It rolled down her cheek and mixed with the puddle of blood. He realized then that he was crying. It scared him. He hadn't cried since he was a child. But now, another tear fell, and another.

Through his grief, he knew what he would have to do. She was gone. There was no way to bring her back. Her brother would be searching for her soon. She wasn't an ordinary Negress. She was the daughter of a prominent Negro publisher, now deceased, and the widow of a prominent Negro lawyer. She had a place in their society. So, yes, she would be missed. There would be a hue and cry for vengeance if it were ever discovered that she had been murdered.

Which was why he could not let her be found.

He knew what he had to do. It wasn't her anymore. It was just a body now. Yet, he couldn't resist calling her name one last time.

"Rachel."

Then he began to cry in earnest.

Tyne pushed through the sleep-cloud that fogged her mind. The dream-world still tugged at her, reached out cold fingers to pull her back. But her feet ran as fast as they could, ran toward the name hailing her, pleading with her to hurry. The name reverberated around . . . *Rachel . . . Rachel . . . Rachel . . .*

"Rachel . . . Rachel . . . "

The sound woke her. She slowly opened her eyes, lay there for a moment, not remembering. Gradually, disorientation gave way to familiarity. Shaking off sleep, she became aware of her surroundings. Recognized the curtains that hung at the moon-bathed window, saw the wingback chair that was a silhouette in front of it. Sometime during the night or early morning, he had retrieved her clothes and laid them neatly on the chair's back.

He was shifting in his sleep, murmuring. Then she heard the name again, just as she had heard it in her dream. "Rachel." He strangled on the syllables, his voice choked with emotion—with . . . grief, she realized. She sat up, turned. His back was to her, shuddering. He was crying . . . in his sleep. Was calling to a woman—a woman named Rachel. Someone he'd never mentioned before. And obviously a woman who meant a lot to him, and whose loss he freely felt in his unconscious state. So he'd lied about never having been in love. But why?

A pang of jealousy moved through her, pushed away affection, gratification. She didn't want to be solace for some lost love he was still pining for. Didn't want to be a second-hand replacement to someone else's warmth in his bed. She looked over at the clock. It was almost four anyway. She might as well get home to get ready for work.

She shifted off the mattress delicately, grabbed her clothes from the chair and started for the door. She would dress downstairs to make sure she didn't wake him. She turned at the door to look at him. The shuddering had stopped. There was only the peaceful up and down motion of deep breathing. She opened the door, shut it lightly and made her escape.

Don't miss Donna Kauffman's,
"Bottoms Up,"
in her sexy new anthology
BAD BOYS IN KILTS.
Available now from Brava!

Honestly, she really did need her head examined. One minute she'd been giving Daisy MacDonnell the evil eye, and not ten minutes after her rival had extended the olive branch of friendship, Kat was pouring out her frustrations and desire for Brodie, carrying on about how she wanted him to look at her the way he looked at Daisy. Or any other woman.

To her credit, Daisy had laughed and taken the news a whole lot better than Kat might have if the opposite had happened. It helped that the only part of Brodie she wanted to get her hands on, or any other man in Glenbuie for that matter, was his publicity business. She'd come to town ostensibly to take over Maude's shop, but in fact, she was hoping to bring her skills and talent as a marketer to the local shopkeepers.

After listening to Kat bemoan her lack of feminine wiles—she still couldn't believe she'd done that and had decided to blame it on the aftereffects of a very long day, far too much of which had been spent brooding over Brodie—Daisy had confessed that back in the States, she'd been known as something of a matchmaker amongst her friends. And though she didn't claim to know Kat or Brodie all that well, it had appeared clear to her that there was definite chemistry between the two, and that maybe all Kat had to do was get him to open his eyes and notice her in a different way. She said that most men didn't appreciate subtlety and suggested that perhaps it was time to take a more direct, more blatant path to getting his attention. It was all about marketing, really, according to Daisy.

Hence one of the more embarrassing moments of Kat's life. My God, she'd never be able to show her face in Hagg's, or anywhere else in town, for months after her little stunt last night. What the bloody hell had she been thinking? A dress, makeup, her hair hanging all over the place? Could she have looked any more ridiculous? They were probably still laughing it up at her expense.

Sure, sure, there had been that wee moment when Brodie's look of shock had worn off and he'd actually given her a once-over that at any other time in her life she'd have swooned over. But she'd immediately realized that if the only reason he was noticing her like that was because she'd had to tart herself up, then she didn't want him. Marketing be damned. But it was the truth. She knew right then that the only way she'd have him was if he wanted her for who she was.

And the only thing he wanted from the Kat Henderson he knew was a hot game of take-no-prisoners darts and a shoulder to occasionally lean on when times were tough. A friend. That's what he wanted. A friend.

She wanted him as a friend, too. She also wanted him naked, sweating, and hot for her.

Here's a look at Amy J. Fetzer's
PERFECT WEAPON.
Available now from Brava. . . .

He smiled slightly as his gaze traveled over her face, the fall of her dark hair, just noticing the gold flecks in her brown eyes. Her expression was at once innocent, and sexy. A hell of a combination. Jack wasn't much on centerfold types, pretty was good but most times, after a couple months, he didn't like what he found beneath. With Syd, he already knew what lay beneath, aside a wicked sense of humor.

"Well, don't just jump to answer. Take your time."

"I'm thinking, a kiss will never be enough," he murmured, lowering his head.

"I'm so wide open to suggestions it's pathetic."

His dark chuckle rumbled in the hallway an instant before he laid his mouth over hers. Something unfamiliar crackled through him. It wasn't instant, it'd been there, waiting—in that place he'd packed away most of his emotions, the need to link himself with her when he'd been solitary for so long. He kissed her and kissed her and somewhere in between, the barrier broke, poured like water from a shattered dam.

Sydney felt it, a difference in him. Patience turned possessive, as if he was staking claim, that he knew she'd deny him nothing of herself. She wouldn't. His hands splayed her back, driving up her spine as his warm mouth rolled back and forth over hers. She felt his restraint, his need to crush and take. Her brain went fuzzy, her thoughts centered on only one thing. *More. I want more with this man.*

Jack gave. "You know where we're going." It wasn't a question.

Yet her answer spoke when her tongue slid into his mouth, in her hips rising to mesh with his. Jack nearly roared, letting go a little more. His hands mapped her contours and she moaned, a delicious little sound that nearly tore through his restraint.

Impatiently, he backed her up against the nearest wall, devouring her mouth as his hands plowed over her body.

She winced and jerked back. "Ow, sorry, oh, that stings."

He looked down at her leg. It was bleeding again. "Oh, hell. Sorry, baby. Let's have a look now. Have a seat in the kitchen, the light's better."

Almost robotic, he turned away, and went deeper into the house. She stared at his back for a second, too turned on to move.

Then he called out, "And take those pants off, too."

She smiled. "You're always telling me to do that." She went into the kitchen and slipped her jeans off.

He came back with a large plastic toolbox. "And you keep doing it. What's that say?"

She sat at the kitchen table in panties and a T-shirt, peeling the layers of gauze. Her breath hissed.

"Stop that before you tear the skin," he said and she looked up. He tugged her to her feet, gripped her at the waist, and lifted her to the counter. She gasped at the cold stone under her bare skin.

"Do you always just do what you want without asking?"

He looked chagrined. "By your leave, ma'am, I'm not used to waiting to take action."

"That just excites me all over. Bossy men, who'da thunk it?"

He snapped on latex gloves. "Wiseass." He carefully cut

the bandage away and started cleaning the wound. It was bleeding at the point of impact, but the rest was dried and sticky.

He wasn't all that gentle and Syd smacked him on the shoulder when it hurt too much. "Ease up. I'm not a Marine, ya know."

"Oh, I know." He winked, then rummaged in the large kit. He snapped the cap of a small plastic tube with a needle on the end. "This will help."

"Is that necessary?" Though it felt on fire right now.

"Unless you have an amazing pain threshold, this is really gonna hurt. Too much blood is caked on the wound. There could be fibers from the jeans in it, glass. It did pass through the window. And who was telling me about how fast germs multiply?"

She gestured for him to keep working. "You could have stopped at fibers."

"I have to open it back up."

"Gee, no stick to bite? No whiskey?"

"I have morphine."

She shook her head. "Go ahead." He injected the topical anesthetic, then while he waited for it to take effect, he laid out his bandages.

Syd grabbed a stack and with some antiseptic, cleaned the couple of cuts on his jaw and neck. "They aren't bad. But you have flakes of glass only a shower will clean."

"We can try that later."

"We?"

He slid her a dark sexy look that liquefied her muscles. "Nothing gets past you, huh, Einstein?"

"Not unless I want it to. And I could jump on you right now, boo-boo and all, like an undersexed teenager."

"Undersexed?"

She lifted a bottle from the kit, read the label. "Antibiotics? Prescription?"

He got the message. She didn't want to discuss her sex life. Fine with him. His mind was already on that lacy bra he'd bought and how it looked on her—because the transparent panties were just about driving him nuts as it was.

"Rick's a corpsman, Navy."

"I thought he was a Marine."

He soaked a cloth in the sink. "Might as well be." He hesitated for a second, in voice and moves, then said, "He found me in the mountains."

Sydney felt oddly privileged. The tiny piece of him made her feel closer to him. Rick had saved his life. "I should thank him for that. But I swore an oath."

He glanced, flashed a smile, then applied a wet cloth to the wound, softening the dried blood. He blotted and rubbed, taking tweezers to pluck out debris. "This will burn," he warned and drizzled hydrogen peroxide on it. He blew and blotted again, but when she didn't utter a sound, Jack looked up.

She sat perfectly still, gripping the counter ledge, her lips tight. Yet tears cascaded down her face.

"Aw, honey I—"

"Keep going, please."

He felt helpless, a first in about a dozen years. Silent tears were a powerful thing to see, and he hated causing her more pain. She'd had enough for someone who didn't wear Kevlar to the office. She bit her lip, swallowed hard, trying so hard not to sob, and Jack leaned in and kissed her, focusing everything into it, a slow molten roll of lips and tongue. She responded instantly, and he felt a tender ache in his chest when she cradled his jaw and took control. It was an eating kiss, as if her pain flowed through it, almost dark and ravenous, and when he pulled back, she looked more exotic than before.

"It still hurts like hell." She sniffled.

"I was trying to take your mind off it."

"And that's all you came up with?" Her fingers dribbled down his chest to his jeans.

Christ, the woman was going to make him an idiot. "Give me a minute, I'll think of something else." Jack went back to cleaning the wound down to the tissue. It bled again.

Syd wanted to cry like a baby, but what good would it do? She stared at the long, narrow gouge, seeing exactly how close they came to dying today. She'd have a permanent reminder of how precious life had become.

"I know it looks bad," he said, "but it has to heal from the inside out. It's broad enough that stitches would just make the scar worse."

"The scar's the least of my problems."

He covered it with antibacterial ointment, then bandaged it. He sat, and propped her leg on his shoulder to wrap the ace bandage around her thigh. "Bad fashion statement in a bikini?" He secured it, then pulled off the surgical gloves.

"As if. You do not want to see this body in a bikini." She was glad to think of anything but the pain right now.

His gaze lingered over her. "You underestimate yourself, Einstein." He kissed her bandaged leg.

"I rarely do, Jack. I know my weaknesses." She slid her leg off his shoulder, and for a moment she just stared. "Algorithms, English Lit, loading iPods . . ." Suddenly, she gripped handfuls of his bloody shirt, yanked. "And right now—you."

Her mouth covered his in a swoop of heat and put every seductive nuance into it. There wasn't much information in her past to gather. She'd spent her adult life getting her doctorate or using it. But she tried.

And she was winning.

Jack felt like a puppet being played and he let her. Her life was in shambles and she wanted control, wanted to command something and he let it be him. She teased, drawing back and making him chase her, then erotically licked the line of his lips before she pushed her tongue between. A hot, desperate need riddled him down to his heels as she kissed him. He wanted her, right now, on the counter, and the image made his dick like lead in his jeans. When she broke the kiss, it was to peel off his shirt. Her hands scraped over his skin, and she dragged her tongue across his nipple, then suckled.

It left him trembling, his head thrown back, and he gripped her hips, wedging closer. His hand slid upward, under her shirt, shaping her ribs, teasing the underside of her breasts cupped in a lacy bra. Her kiss intensified.

"Keep that up, Marine. Please."

He drew off her shirt, his lip quirking at the pink lace bra. A quick flick and it was falling. Jack swept it away. His gaze rolled down her body, and everything between them seemed to go still for a moment. By increments she leaned closer, her nipples grazing his chest. That first press of flesh to flesh held a sort of euphoria, crossing the line of intimacy. Jack had helped a lot of people, rescued many, killed to save them, but nothing compared to the single moment when you invited someone this close. He fought for patience when he was craving her like air, his body flexing with need. Although Syd might have a mouth on her, he sensed this was a brave thing to do.

She was still, waiting for his touch, watching his hands come toward her and when they did, Syd experienced something close to nirvana. She covered his big hands and arched and Jack kissed her and kissed her, loving her moans, her eagerness.

He wouldn't last long.